P9-APY-933

A
SURVEY
OF THE
ATLANTIC
BEACHES

For Arden & Nathan

A SURVEY OF THE ATLANTIC BEACHES

A novel by

DON HENDRIE JR.

CROWN PUBLISHERS, INC.
NEW YORK

Fic
HEN

Copyright © 1987 by Don Hendrie Jr.
All rights reserved. No part of this book may be reproduced
or transmitted in any form or by any means,
electronic or mechanical, including photocopying, recording,
or by any information storage and retrieval system,
without permission in writing from the publisher.
Published by Crown Publishers, Inc.
225 Park Avenue South, New York, New York 10003,
and represented in Canada by the Canadian MANDA Group
CROWN is a trademark of Crown Publishers, Inc.
Manufactured in the United States of America
Library of Congress Cataloging-in-Publication Data
Hendrie, Don.
A survey of the Atlantic beaches.
I. Title.
PS3558.E4952S8 1988   813'.54   87-8874
ISBN 0-517-56691-5
Book design by Dana Sloan
10 9 8 7 6 5 4 3 2 1
First Edition

ALSO BY DON HENDRIE JR.

Boomkitchwatt

Blount's Anvil

Limited edition:
Scribble, Scribble, Scribble

PLUM ISLAND

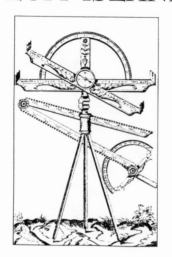

S OME INSIST it is best to live within sight of salt water. On the northeastern seaboard men and women can be found who love a domestic perspective that includes blocks of pious houses separated by streets giving onto harbor or beach, boardwalk or salt marsh; much is promised by a glimpse of water, whether that water is protected or unfettered. Life may be better if a body can stroll to a watery threshold and there partake of a refracted light and a better scale of being than perhaps might exist a block or two inland.

It's appropriate to begin in Massachusetts where the Merrimack River collides with the Atlantic in the extreme northeast corner of the state; at Newburyport—a fashionable town whose harbor is protected from the sea by the thumb and forefinger of the northern end of Plum Island.

One day in late May of a recent year, the graduating seniors of the town's high school failed to notice a gray Japanese sedan with creased bumpers travel past the school on High Street, although one set of 100-percent-cotton parents may have taken dry note of the car's Alabama plates—as rare, say, as a black teenager on Plum Island—and if so, the father was quick enough with his eyes to catch the driver's unclipped beard, but not quick enough to understand that the driver had nothing more in mind than a survey of the Atlantic beaches from Massachusetts to North Carolina.

The sedan continued along a high street overseen by the mansions built by sperm oil, rum, and slavery; it passed a granite jail, a park with a slate-colored pond, a town center nifty with restoration, and dozens upon dozens of lesser houses from which most traces of involuted Puritan gloom had been removed by free-flowing money. Once the sedan turned left into Federal Street, the down-slope made it simple for the car to fall through the perspective until the driver could glimpse a steel blue portion of the harbor at the distant foot of the street—his first saltwater sighting of any significance. Now a right into Milk Street—the way narrow with box houses pressing forward to crowd the cars parked in front of them; the way well shaded by maple, sycamore, elm; the way leading to the canary yellow, two-story box where the driver would pass the night.

A blonde girl-child in front of the house watched the arrival and parking with eyes of understanding. She did not think, My uncle Devereux, but she did remember the smell of coconut-oil soap and a slow, deep voice that said her name funny. Her name was Laura, but he wanted it *Lawr* because he was from far away. Her babysitter came to the screen door and said, "Is that him? Look, he has a beard like Captain Nemo."

Laura *looked both ways* and crossed the street. "Hello, Nemo," she said. He had a big nose, looked gruff, but was not. He said "Hey" and touched her where her T-shirt was torn at the neck. Then he said "Laura Begora," rhyming it right. His corduroys had a round black stain on one pocket. Ink, she decided, and put her face up for the kiss. The beard was black with white hairs and felt like a bird's nest. Old mint blew in her face from his mouth before he went back up. She knew he had a big son named Carl in prep school nearby . . . but no Carl was to be seen.

"Here's a note for ya," called the babysitter, sticking her arm out the door and tapping some fingers on a square of white tacked to the yellow clapboards.

Man and girl crossed back over the street, and Laura watched while he read the note. "My dad wrote that," she said. Nemo nodded and put the note away in his pants. "What's it say?" she asked. The babysitter had gone off to the television. He told Laura it said how to get to her mother, Jessica, in the gallery where she worked.

"Jessica's at the gallery," said Laura, thinking of her mother standing in the gallery door with her arms crossed over her chest and smiling at Captain Nemo in a way that popped out her wrinkles.

Nemo, a.k.a. the Surveyor, whose true name was Devereux Hoopes, touched the child again and walked off in the direction of Federal. He went downhill in the compelling direction of the water, his face as stern as a prophet's. Ignored by the gray, tan, and white houses he passed, he moved his legs in the deliberate way of someone used to walking long distances without any particular notion but to go a ways out, then return by the same path. On the other hand, his former wife, Tracy, sister to Jessica, once said, "Dev is the only person I know who can walk down the street and look like he's sitting on a couch at the same time."

Ahead of him, at water's edge, a brick warehouse curved in the sunlight; beyond it a light green fishing boat passed over the water. At the end of the last block before the warehouse stood a two-story frame building with double-wide glass doors thrown open to the breeze. A flag on a pole blazoned "Antiques/Art." He stepped through the doorway and into a room full of clocks.

Upstairs with the American and British art of the last century sat his ex-sister-in-law, Jessica, in her red skirt, long slender legs crossed, then intertwined so that the top of one bare foot pressed against the other foot's Achilles tendon. She held a flat rectangle of telephone and gazed beyond her desk top at her domain—four walls of nautical oils interrupted from time to time by lush gardenscapes. Jessica was entirely handsome in a frowning, New Englander way; thirty-five years old last time around. White, luminous skin.

As she spoke, Jessica could not know Devereux Hoopes was among the timepieces below, but she did sense the moment had come to cut off the voice in her ear, the voice of a local contractor named Walsh who carried a burden of persistence some women might have found endearing. "Hey, Tom," she said, interrupting his pleas, "I've got to close up." He permitted this with some graciousness, and as soon as she put down the phone in its doohickey, she thought of the way his blonde hairs licked over his ears. Stop that. Her brow furrowed. Wrinkles popped.

"I like your feet," said an easy voice from the stairway behind her. She turned and looked down at Devereux's head and torso. When she tried to leap out of her chair, uttering a small girl's nonsense cry of welcome and pleasure, her feet refused to untangle properly, and she nearly fell to her knees there in the presence of her new job and ex-brother-in-law. She managed to find her red shoes.

Their embrace took place in front of a $7,000 rendering of Horatio Nelson's flagship, the surrounding sea in perfect, emerald equilibrium. Jessica's way of kissing Devereux was abrupt; she struck first the cheek, then darted at his lips. He might bite? She could not help it; she said, "Oh, you're so handsome," and pushed him away.

He looked and was incredulous. The part of his beard surrounding his mouth twitched in what those close to him had learned to recognize as a smile; others might see it as a grimace of pain. Call it a surveyor's professional tic. All Jessica knew was that since she'd been a twelve-year-old ugly duckling, this man had existed for her as a forceful, enigmatic mountain . . . although they were exactly the same height, and in a tussle she could probably pin him to the floor with a quick scissoring of her powerful legs.

Devereux's appraisal moved from the bound breasts beneath her white blouse to a curl of brown hair next to her reddened cheek. He touched both cheek and curl. It seemed to be an objective examination of those qualities his memory might be doubting. Into her deep brown eyes he said, "I saw Laura. Your husband left me one of his laconic notes."

Jessica improved her posture in preparation for a slow turn around the room. She would give him a lesson in seascape quality. Later she intended to cook him chicken and fill him up with wine until one of them offered the other revelation. It best not be she.

"He left this afternoon for a seminar in Maine," she said.

Devereux, who was peering in a museum manner at the descriptive tag beside one of the paintings, shrugged his "That's too bad—you can't connect with everyone in this fragmented life." A door at the far end of the room opened, and from his apartment emerged the proprietor of the gallery. While Jessica retired to her desk and locked it, he took over the tour and failed to sell Devereux one of the works displayed. Downstairs, Julio Jiminez crooned over the sound system, and the current mistress of a local leftist philosopher put into her kleptomaniac's shopping bag the smallest Seth Thomas clock she could find and went into the tangy afternoon air.

Sundown found the yellow house on Milk Street full of children. While Jessica skinned and boned the chicken breasts, Laura in the living room directed that Rhett, Thomas, and Caitlin stop bugging her and go to their own homes, so she could watch "Sesame Street" and listen to her uncle talk to Jessica. When Rhett flung a hard thing and hit Caitlin in the ear, a crying hit, Jessica screamed "Everyone home!" from the kitchen, and suddenly Laura was alone with the bright people on the television. Upstairs, under the low ceiling of the bathroom, Devereux stood in the shower and rubbed shampoo into his beard until it came all suds the color of his sunless flesh. He heard Jessica's shout, which he found remarkably shrill.

Jessica made Laura a dinner of McNuggets (frozen) and tartar sauce. While Laura dealt with the nuggets and ignored the side order of tomatoes, Jessica finished dealing with the chicken. She had substituted for her red skirt and blouse a pair of jeans and a light flannel shirt; she looked lithe and capable making her kitchen rounds, and it is doubtful anyone would have understood that the sole occupant of her mind was the fierce man who stood like a wet otter in the bathtub a few feet above her head. She remembered telling her husband, long before she married him, "Leave me alone, I have to check out my feelings for my brother-in-law." And now she was still at it. Was this guy—who squinted a lot, she'd noticed—still taboo? Still a rough mountain looming over her?

She sighed and said "Oh dear." Laura looked up from the table and mimicked her exactly.

"Sunday's the beach day, Mommy," said her daughter. "Tomorrow."

"If it doesn't rain." Jessica brushed her hair away from her eyes. "Devereux could use a beach."

"So could you." Laura burped. "More nuggets, please."

In the guest room, also a playroom, also a room where Jessica made small, precise drawings with pen and ink, Devereux Hoopes searched through his few clothes. When he descended the stairs sometime later he wore a crimson sweatshirt with the word "Bama" in white letters over his left nipple.

Jessica took one look at the sweatshirt and pinched its lettering between thumb and forefinger; in doing so, she managed an awful tweak of the nipple below. He flinched. "I'm sorry," she said. "I never knew you to advertise on your body." He said it was time to admit what he was—a worker in the mind fields of Alabama. Skull-crushing work for a man of forty-one, born and bred in Camden, New Jersey. She smiled and sat him down with his round of chicken breast, a tomato, and a large glass of white table wine. Laura lay on the floor in the living room and watched her very own Muppet tape on the VCR. From time to time she turned her head and saw Jessica eating with Nemo in flickery candlelight. By the time Laura went upstairs to her bed, she had heard Nemo on two trips up there to make water, and she had heard her mother laugh too much.

"So," Jessica said into her wineglass, "we both have places in us no one can reach. Not your timid Alabama girlfriend . . . not my gentle husband."

Although Jessica didn't know it, Devereux's squint was

8

only a parody of concentration. With his thumb he rubbed at the two vertical lines between his eyebrows. "So far," he said, knowing-not. "But Tessa isn't timid, not really. She resented my coming on this trip alone. Probably resents my being with Carl, with you, with anyone. It's simple."

"The only simple thing is you'd rather travel alone," she said.

"For now."

She nodded. The wine had brought color to his nose, and when he kissed Jessica good night, the organ lay alongside her cheek like a rose on a satin sheet. They undressed in their separate rooms. He removed everything and enveloped himself in the coverings of the daybed. She entered her double bed wearing a cotton T-shirt and briefs. Their dreams were neither erotic nor worrisome, but before Jessica fell into the abyss, she said aloud to the darkness, "He's no mountain." In her own room, Laura twitched and continued pressing her left thumb into her palate. She dreamed of humongous horseshoe crabs wearing spectacles and droopy, bird-nest beards. Outside, along Milk Street, the leftist philosopher strolled with his mistress and made plans to replace her; time had caught her short.

Dawn entered Jessica's room and nudged her out of bed and along the hallway to the bathroom, her legs beneath the T-shirt as shapely as her age would allow. In the shower she brushed her teeth and soaped her breasts, checking the tiny surgical scars on each for signs of disappearance—no such luck. But then the luck had lain entirely with benignity. Dry, she put back on her night clothes and went into Devereux's room where she stood over his shape like a serious maiden just come slick-haired from the sea. In sleep his face seemed more prayerful than angry, although the truth is he had been fully conscious since halfway through her shower. When he opened his eyes to her, his mouth reached for and gained his version of a smile.

Jessica slipped under the bedclothes, and they lay together in fitful harmony—he hiding his wine-foul mouth in the valley of her shoulder; she with one leg over his back thighs, thighs he had turned into the mattress for the protection of his groin. She held him and frowned at the ceiling. "It's still taboo," she said presently. He hummed agreement and kissed her shoulder with platonic fervor.

"So the body says," Devereux said to her star-bright skin.

"What a relief," she said. "We're exactly the same size. We're equal beings."

In the adjoining room Laura sat straight up in bed and looked out the window. Above the knobby treetops the sky gave her back a brightening blue glare. She whooped at the same moment her mother readjusted her conception of the universe.

Beach Report. Devereux Hoopes's Japanese sedan crossed the bridge over the estuary and turned right into a road that ran south on Plum Island between the salt marshes and the low, rounded dunes. At first the sedan passed by a hodge-podge of beach shacks and vacation cabins scattered along the dunes. Spaced regularly in the salt marshes were black boxes on stilts—machines designed to lure the vicious green-head flies to a hot death. Once the sedan breached the toll-gate in the public sanctuary and pulled into A lot, nothing could be seen but sand, sea oats, and the duckboard walkway leading up from the lot and over the dunes to the Surveyor's first sighting of the actual Atlantic.

Over the duckboards went first Laura, then Jessica, then Devereux. A pink tank suit, a green tank suit, a pair of faded blue shorts with deep side pockets in which Devereux's hands were buried. Jessica carried a man's colorless shirt, towels, a Thermos, and a tattered beach blanket. They dipped into the lee of the final set of dunes, went up again, and at the crest beheld the unfettered, gun blue water—on this day a gentleness of minor waves against the easy swell of the background's vast blueness. Few people roamed the visible beach or sprawled on the khaki sand. Later, the space would be impossible with radios, Frisbees, and lotioned thousands, but now, peace.

Jessica's leggy, translucent flesh dominated the space, dwarfing the squinting, trout-fleshed man who aspired—like any traveler willfully oblivious to past or future—to be her simple companion. They made camp. Laura approached the water and performed the usual ritual of stomping spindrift until an unseen wave caught her by the shins and began her morning's connection with the bone-chilling water she considered more perfect than a bath.

Jessica lay on her side on the blanket, her torso facing Devereux who, perched on his butt with his hands clasped around upraised knees, was looking out to sea with an expression that suggested both tranquillity and his preference for the sweet curve of the horizon over the erogenous details evident beneath the nylon of Jessica's tank suit.

"I wish I could curl around you," she said, still drawn to his flesh as to her own.

He nodded, enigmatic—sure—but they both knew the wish was sufficient. Perhaps it would be so for a lifetime. Below them the surge of the Atlantic was quelled by the shore, and Laura wondered why.

WELLFLEET

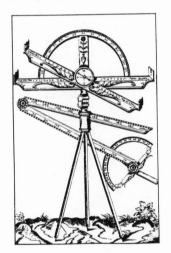

THE BOY sitting next to Devereux in the sedan bore little resemblance to his father. At sixteen, he was on his way out of a galumphish look, and for this he was grateful. His thick, brown hair had been carefully trained to cantilever over his forehead like a curly cap bill. A person observing Carl Hoopes strolling down the street—say the mistress of Newburyport's leftist philosopher—would think "Now there is one good-looker; two more years and I'd swoon for *him*."

Carl's ears were the size of cream pitchers. Through the left lobe had been driven a silver post, affixed to its blunt end a bit of bright green malachite. He was as proud of the earring as he was of the fact that he'd just successfully completed a year (his first) at a New Hampshire prep school usually referred to in the news magazines as "tony" or "exclusive." Carl thought a better appellation would be "not too fucking easy," but, for now, the joint was behind him, and he could bask in this trek with his father back to Alabama, although at the moment they were driving to Wellfleet on a narrow spit of land about as far out into the Atlantic as America got—Cape Cod: an up-yours fist raised at Europe.

Carl was hungry, more or less his permanent condition, but he feared that fish would be the sole fare on this stage of their journey—boring fish served by boring historians on a boring beach. Or so his dad had promised. You had to be wary of old Devereux, though; he was a heavyweight in the irony department where he kept a secretary, Ms. Sardonica.

Carl smiled to himself at the neatness of the conceit. But, as was his habit, he kept his own counsel.

They pushed through the pines that crowded Route 6, the sedan nosing quietly through the Cape's transparent air. A disagreement over music and musical taste had caused Devereux to shut off the deck, and miles of easy silence between father and son were not broken until Devereux grunted at the traffic light in the middle distance, one he had been told to mark well. He turned them left, then right, and the sedan drifted down into a woodsy glen in which gray-shingled houses lay as if in random ambush. Devereux swore, braked, reversed, and turned into a steep hidden drive where a navy Swedish sedan greeted them with its long snout. Beyond it, in a natural bowl of green grass encircled by the trees, squatted a two-story wooden house, white, which reminded Carl of a country cottage David Copperfield might have been forced to occupy with a mean-spirited aunt. Or something. It's certain the walls were raised prior to Dickens's death.

"Eighteen fifty-seven," according to Kit McGuffy, who came swift-footed from the house in bespattered cutoffs, his tanned, medicine-ball belly the color of dried apple skin. The balding, spectacled man had a scratchy and wet kiss for each of his guests, and a staccato "Hey baby, how are ya?"

Devereux brandished a pink plastic bag in Kit's face. "These are Carl's *sneakers*," he said with a solemnity Carl recognized as the beginning of a project of exaggerated proportion. "These sneakers are in wretched shape, they're infected with fungus and dormitory life." From his back pocket he pulled a rectangular packet, and this too he brandished. "New innersoles!" he cried. "Do you have a bucket, McGuffy? Do you have disinfectant, stain remover, duct tape? What about water? Do the rich and notorious of Wellfleet have such a thing as water?"

Without a doubt: Carl's dad could be a nut, of the first water.

Kit McGuffy took it all quite seriously; he fetched out the requested items, and Devereux set to work. Soon, Carl's only pair of shoes was soaking in an evil-looking substance, the bucket standing in front of the door like a galvanized promise of perfection-to-come.

Inside, Ellen McGuffy heard the commotion and stopped tapping at the keyboard of her no-nonsense word processor. She noticed an error and could not ignore it—she ran the cursor over the word "humplace" and changed it to "home-place," then she rose to her guests with a sigh. She would have to explain Kit's recent tragedy, his obsession of the day—Kit certainly would not . . . the tantrum-prone stoic. A woman of an age equal to her husband's, forty-eight, Ellen had short blonde hair, a fit body thickened by childbirth, and a commonsense face many people considered perfect in its humanness. Good Yankee stock. She had the staying power of cut lilies.

She came upon the three males in the kitchen. Carl's lower lip was thrust out in response to the temporary drowning of his sneakers. Using a paper napkin, Kit cleaned his thick eyeglasses and peered blindly at Devereux, who now used his own good eyes to smile at Ellen like the prophetic wise-man she believed him not to be. He came along to her and offered up a minty kiss, a remarkably strong embrace. Then she went on to Carl, kissed his satiny cheek, and offered the usual comments on his size—he oversaw everyone in the room by a couple of adolescent inches.

"Kit's processor is broken," she said to Devereux.

"Oh, darling," Kit wailed, as she knew he would.

"Down? The flow of history interrupted?" said Devereux, alight with glee. (Truth: He believed only in cars, not in faggy, green-screened word-movers, but Ellen didn't know this.) Kit McGuffy moaned and replaced his still-spumy glasses on his nose as Devereux prattled on. "Disks gone blank . . . his profession come to nothing but *terminal rasa*—"

Kit rallied. "Shut up, Hoopes."

Devereux raised his hands as in prayer and touched finger-tips to his brow. It was all in good fellowship, was it not?

Kit's wide mouth formed itself to indicate splendid,

Hibernian mirth; his love for Devereux Hoopes ran all the way from his peeling skull to his horny feet . . . like a nonexistent nerve that could easily be activated by his current desire to yank the other man's teasing beard and cry out "Hosanna!"

Instead he commanded, "We'll take a spin to the beach," noting Ellen's blown-lipped resignation. "Then back here for hamburgers and my phone call from the goddamn processor lady in Wellesley."

"All right!" Carl exclaimed, his first words in this low-set McGuffy house. "Meat."

Beach Report. After a curving drive of two tree-lined miles in the austere comfort of the McGuffy sedan, the four entered the environs of the Cape Cod National Seashore. Kit parked them in a sandy lot, and they went barefoot through a gap in the reddish, anti-dune-drift fencing. None was dressed in swimming costume; all carried a garment to cheat the wind Kit had promised this outer beach would deliver.

The parking lot rested on the flattened summit of dunes so grand they had better be called ramparts of sand; even the sand grains themselves were coarse, enlarged, in keeping with the scale of things here. Devereux stopped in the fence gap and looked down down on the great expanse of fawn-colored beach and on to the gun-dark sea—its surf an oncoming turmoil of what seemed from his superior advantage man-high waves.

Carl went away down the slope as fast as his legs would carry him, and he somersaulted and rolled the last ten feet and onto the flat. That would show the ambling fogies behind him. He leapt up and began to run north into the wind.

The adults clambered down the slopes, Kit in the lead, a bandy-legged man with an old jacket knotted about his waist and falling over his flat posterior like a skirt. When they reached the flat, the threesome veered north toward Truro, Carl so far ahead of them by now that he looked in the distance like a small ostrich hastening to a convention of its own kind.

During the next half-hour, Devereux's Alabama-soft feet were sorely tested by the gritty sand through which they wallowed. He was able to herd his companions to the firmer wet sand at surf's edge, but soon found the downward slope too awkward, too unbalancing for such serious walking as Kit, the pacesetter, seemed to intend. Also, the noise of the insistent waves—not so tall as Devereux had thought—made conversation with loquacious Ellen and mum Kit impossible. So they settled on the middle ground, a four-wheel-drive track, and went forward beneath the loom of the rampart dunes, past a once massively contemporary house whose deck and seaward rooms had been broken off by storm, and which was now an abandoned hulk on the cloven crest of its section of the northern run of dunes.

Walking with her arms folded beneath her breasts and resting on her paunch, Ellen spoke of much, but never did the words "word processor" pass her lips. She could tell from Kit's sandpiper walk ahead of them how close he was to an eruption of self-pity and remorse over a dumb, but nonetheless accusatory, machine. Kit probably *had* willed the notes for his current project to disappear into the deep, mocking caves of the machine's "memory"; at one point this morning he had wailed, "Oh Ellen, I can SEE them in there . . . but they won't come out to me."

But solicitous Devereux need not know any of this. She spoke to him of the nude beach in Truro, of its besiegement by local bluenosed authorities. She had heard one young, peach-fuzzed officer, not much older than Carl, say to a nymph with breasts like butternut squashes, "Ma'am, do you have some identification on you?" Then Ellen ticked off for Devereux her own children's recent particulars. She asked about the nature of Devereux's own trip. "On Plum Island," he said with profundity, "I made friends with Tracy's sister Jessica . . . finally." Ellen smelled a rat but prodded Devereux no further. She told him that the Wellfleet section of the National Seashore, now so deliciously deserted, had come to be her true home, and she offered silent thanks that Kit's prizes and the resulting monies had been able to secure their foothold near this stretching of sand and wild water. Ellen did not tell Devereux that an academic dean had recently called her a "dogmatic, flea-brained bitch," and she didn't even conceive of mentioning what they were saying Kit had done to a young male scholar in San Francisco only a month before. In Devereux's hubris-bright eyes, she could see that he believed he knew the "truth" of all he looked upon . . . but boy, was he wrong. He knew nothing of the wilderness of male love.

Ahead of them Kit unknotted his jacket and slung it around his shoulders. From far above, hidden in the saw grasses that gave tenuous stability to the dune tops, Carl looked down upon the oldies and contemplated tactics. His feet, like his father's, were raw, and his arms were scratched from the stealthy bounds he had been making along the dunes' ridge line. He watched the three turn about and begin the trudge toward the car, toward the hamburgers. Abandoning idle thoughts of a surprise attack with a driftwood bat—Devereux would have gone down like a hundred-pound wrestling dummy—Carl leapt into space.

Kit, now behind Ellen and her charming friend, was the first to see Carl begin the series of arcing leaps that would bring him onto the flat in seconds—having covered a distance of at least 150 feet. Kit winced each time the boy's feet struck sand and left visible craters as evidence of his unlawful descent. My God, where had he gone up? Carl's final landing—a perfect two-point—brought him within feet of Kit. Carl bowed with the sort of pride you'd expect from a pretty boy with but one fruity earring, with but one pair of sneakers in this world (and those soaking, fetidly).

"It's against the law, kid," Kit growled. "We should call you Erosion Carl." The boy erased his smile and replaced it with a feigned bewilderment. "Don't give us that 'who me?' malarkey," Kit went on, conscious that Ellen had turned to look back at him. Uh-oh, his beloved schoolmarm; she shouldn't look at him like that. He stepped toward Carl and knuckled his hair and scalp in a way meant to be jokey.

Carl said, "Don't," in a rather imperious way, but made up for it by putting his long arm around Kit's jacketed shoulders and leading him to where the others were waiting like tattered judges on a desert track.

Kit prayed that the bitch from Wellesley would call . . . or he'd be a dead man, dead son, dying bastard of the failed disk-drive. Oh, woe and putrefaction. Carl's skin on the back of Kit's neck felt like heavenly chamois.

Eventually they all donned their wind-cheating garments and in this fashion made their way back to the lofty parking area. Behind and below them the Atlantic beat against the outer edge of the Cape with no intention of ever ceasing. No one had entered the water. Had they? Carl could not allow this.

At the gap in the fence Erosion Carl snatched his sweater over his head, tossed it to Devereux, and before anyone could say "No . . . you'll freeze your gonads to ice pellets" . . . such as that . . . the boy was off down the slope, across the flat, and—as soon as he'd upped a fist at distant Gibraltar—buried in a crash and froth so cold he thought his brainpan had become the Iron Mask.

It was fucking glorious!

Here is the essence of what transpired in the McGuffy house between five P.M. on Monday and five A.M. on Tuesday:

The "bitch" from Wellesley called promptly at five; after quizzing Kit for several minutes—Kit's voice a gem of modulated hysteria undercut by ignorance and enraged helplessness—she crooned the simple statement that she had to be in Hyannis on Tuesday morning. Would he meet her there with his defunct machine? Does the sun rise! Does the sea kill! Ellen from the kitchen heard the shrill pipings of his gratefulness, smiled in fond relief, and reached into the cupboard for the king-size bottle of scotch. Once more, tantrum had been expelled from the homeplace.

Outside, while Carl unloaded a few items from the Japanese sedan, Devereux knelt reverently beside the bucket and sluiced the sanitizing agents from his son's sneakers with a hose. They were a sad assemblage of canvas and rubber, but in the world of disinfectant, tape, and replaceable innersole . . . there was hope. Carl came along in his salt-damp clothes, and when Devereux saw his blue lips, he told his boy to take a shower, to use the beach shower on the side of the house. Carl, true to form, said that had been his plan all along—why did he have his shampoo and rinse in hand? Why was he going to ask Ellen for a towel? Huh, Pop?

Devereux stood up and clapped the soggy sneakers together until all excess water had flown. His face seemed compressed, the features drawn together to a point just in front of his nose—the point of pure and absolute concentration. Now, if he could only prevail upon Ellen to tolerate the sound of heavy footwear tumbling in her kitchen dryer.

Carl stepped from the house wrapped in a towel and carrying his hair equipment. He went over the grass, past his father, and around to the tree-shaded side of the house where, out of sight, he found and employed the rudimentary shower that—contrary to his fear—did have plenty of hot water to offer. A hummingbird sped through his vision, headed for the front yard. Carl hoped the mite of vibrating bird might pause beneath Devereux's nose, seek the weird sweetness there.

No such luck. Devereux stood, a sneaker dependent from each hand, and watched the bird seek out a glass device hung from one windowsill—a beaker of McGuffy glucose for the iridescent creature. From inside, Devereux heard Kit exclaim "Oh, darling!" Curious about what sort of outdoor shower McGuffy might have purchased or invented, Devereux ambled to the clapboard's edge and peeked. Before he pulled back—guiltily—he had seen the boy's finely curved and porcelain-white posterior; and he had seen that which did

22

not seem to belong, not at all: a down-curving but blood-swollen adult penis. Startling, even painful, to confront a son's emergent sexuality beneath the heart-shaped leaves of a catalpa tree on Cape Cod . . . sixteen years after the first sighting of the then innocent, retiring organ. Old Devereux went into the house like the walking definition of bemused. If Jessica or Tracy or even lovely, tentative Tessa in Alabama could see him now . . .

Kit's hamburgers, nothing muddled about them—they were as crusty and pink and juicy as the mood that had come upon the chef with the phone call and the subsequent infusion of scotch. The four of them crowded around the makeshift plank table and—while the sneakers clunked and thrummed in the background—they made their American meal. Carl drank a bottle of pale India ale and pronounced it superior. (Truth: Many pronouncements were made, some pompous, some wise, some silly; but in the main it was a pleasant dinner among friends bathed in the non-illusory electric light of a New England kitchen.) Outside, in a darkness of impeccable quiet, no philosopher or bimbo walked the curving lanes of Wellfleet, no dog barked, no nautical ghosts stalked the thin Cape-scape. Everyone went to bed at a healthy hour—a sober bunch.

Or so Carl concluded as he climbed a narrow and dark set of stairs as steep as a ladder leaned against a wall. Behind him, Devereux said, "Not so boring, eh Carl?" and Carl agreed by reaching down and knuckling his father's rising skull. By flashlight they clambered into a low-ceilinged room that contained a double bed and an old print of whaling New Bedford. This room adjoined one other—where Carl would sleep—a room that could be reached either by going through a hallway or by opening both doors of a closet that served both rooms. After Devereux switched on a lamp, Carl went on through the empty closet, leaving both doors ajar in order to take some of the light from his dad's room. He figured that Devereux's extreme sobriety (unusual on such semi-vacation jaunts) would make for only minor snoring, and thus it would be all right, this open closet connection between the two of them while they slept.

And soon enough they did sleep, as did Ellen and Kit below, although that married couple—their bed surrounded by cartons of as-yet-unpacked books—made a quiet, successful love that went undisturbed by the shuffling and disrobing going on above them. In the kitchen the dryer had long since cured the sneakers to a shrunken, hygienic perfection, and now the pair lay tongue to tongue in the metal drum awaiting tomorrow and Devereux's efforts with tape and glue, awaiting their new innersoles.

Carl, a young man fond of his sleep—prep school murdered sleep—found his brain invaded at the eyeholes by a Cape dawn so bright it stung. Low in its bowl as it was, McGuffy house could not escape the sunrise that hurtled the bay and the salt marshes around the Wellfleet harbor. He groaned, said "Yo-mama," and rolled away from the offending window, but sleep would not return to him, and he opened his eyes. Through the closet space he could see Devereux in his own bed, asleep on his side with his face pointing more or less at Carl. He thought the older man looked like Poseidon floating in the seaweed of his own tangled hair and beard, a peacefully drowned Poseidon who would never again cause storm or earthquake. Carl closed his eyes, but his ears remained alert to the muffled sounds of someone—it had to be Kit McGuffy—mounting the ladder staircase. Carl slitted his eyes and imagined that the man was entering the other room on all fours; only when he stood up on the far side of Devereux's bed could Carl see the complete Kit in his raggy cut-offs. His side hairs stood out from his head in Mister Micawber tufts, and Carl thought his face was genial in this scheme to wake his buddy.

Kit stood for several moments with his hands in his back pockets, his belly thrust forward. Never once did he look in Carl's direction. But eventually he reached down with both hands and lifted the sheet and covers from Devereux's sleeping body. Carl opened his eyes fully; what he saw was a man caught up in admiration of a pure sort. Nothing sniggery about it, Carl decided. Still . . . Kit's head seemed to tremble with a momentary but infernal ague.

"I love ya, baby," Kit whispered, then more loudly after he dropped the bedclothes, "Hey, Devereux, it's time for a dip in your wine-dark sea."

Carl saw Devereux's eyes snap open, and father and son stared at each other in a way that Carl forever after would think of as "The Look." Both of them knew what had occurred; both of them knew that the act—the act of the Ass-Gazing Oldie, as Carl would term it—was as innocent as cheesecake or hummingbirds or refurbished sneakers.

SAGAPONACK

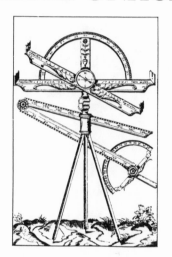

S OME SAY that the eastern reaches of Long Island facing the Atlantic are fraught with those who suffer a sloe-eyed, edgy fame. Certainly the area's potato fields are overseen by a potlatch of architectures meant to inspire respect, awe, or envy in the casual surveyor. There is little visible humor in the region, although vegetable stands sell cold pasta salads and crocks of Dijon mustard. In June, here, when the jitney traffic from Manhattan quickens, all the things of life are as fresh and whitely glistening as a leek just pulled, just washed. Pheasants stutter beneath the potato plants; Japanese gardeners perform wonders with hand and hoe; and in the houses, folk come and go with fervid intensity, for many of them are on the island for the duration of this fresh, perfect summer. There will be infrequent rain and an abundance of the *light* so justly famous. No hurricane or plague will stalk this opulent bit of land; all will be well.

To reach Potato Land from the north of New England, a man would be wise to move himself toward Providence and then southwestward to New London where—with reservation previously arranged—he and his boy and his car can be safely stowed aboard one of the large and efficient ferries yo-yoing between New London and Orient Point, Long Island, New York. On the ferry you may stroll about or, as Carl did, sit on a bench on the upper deck with your shirt off, eating the sunshine and wondering why your father had shaken his fist at a behemoth Trident submarine under construction in a drydock belonging to the oddly named Electric

Boat Company. In any event, the ferry's exit from the harbor and entrance into the Sound is marked by a lighthouse that is, on the face of it, a perfect, miniaturized replica of a Georgian mansion—inhabited, Carl was told, by a keeper who sleeps on a cot in a bare room behind the elegant façade.

This Tuesday's ferry took an hour and a half to reach Orient Point over water like thick, royal blue ink. The first landfall happened to be Plum Island, a geographic fact duly noted by Devereux, though Carl had reason only to note the existence at one end of the island of a compound of windowless, Coast-Guard-white buildings—peculiar in that braced metal smokestacks and dishy antennae stuck up from each roof, and the entire functional caboodle was cordoned off with a high and barb-topped chain-link fence.

"I've been told," Devereux said to Carl in ponderous tones, "that that's a federal animal disease center."

"No shit," said Carl.

"Genetic research. Manticores."

Carl goggled. "Manticores?"

"Frightening hybrids," Devereux said, jutting forward his chin like Ahab. "Think of a combination of man, lion, dragon, maybe a little scorpion thrown in. Government-sponsored beasts."

Carl eyed the slipping-by compound. "Godzilla City," he said, his lower jaw falling loose in the old galumphish gee-whiz. Didn't the swelling, supermonster head of Caliban rise at that moment from behind one of the chimneys? Whoah! The two of them shared a laugh, there in the peach light of the approach to the slip at Orient Point.

A flat, grassy expanse provided *firma* for the sedan to sail across in the only direction available, toward Greenport and yet another ferry to Shelter Island—an island cradled in the yawning mandibles of the mother island. Shelter crossed, the third and final ferry awaited them. A man pays fifty dollars for such a miles-saving episode of ferries; fifty dollars meant a lot to Devereux Hoopes at this stage of his life, but the clarity, the freshness of the landscape through which he and Carl passed, enabled him to transcend such mundane matters as checkbook, prep school tuition (although Carl's scholarship was a whopper), and the fact that his tax bite helped to construct death-dealing Nautiluses . . . and even to maintain Godzilla cities.

"Now, where are we going?" Carl asked as they pulled away from the last ferry and headed for Sag Harbor.

"Sagaponack . . . it's somewhere near Bridgehampton."

Attached to the steering wheel's center with tape were a set of typed directions sent to Devereux weeks back by Barry Kessler, a friend of such long standing that both men had begun to forget how the union came about, or at least each had begun to change the true story beyond recognition. In Kessler's case it had become his business to transmogrify "truth" into great and small yarns for the silver screen; he was also a rabid, middle-aged athlete given to the long run and the heavy weight. His move to Sagaponack in April had been noted in the news magazines, and for this reason, Carl—a movie buff from the fifth dimension—was prepared for all the celebrity glitter he could absorb during their sojourn on the island.

Neither Carl nor Devereux, however, was prepared for the potato field to which the directions eventually led them. It is one thing to encounter in such a place structures so contemporarily glassy, triangulated, and aluminum-quilted as to move the surveyor to arson; it is another matter to flank a sizable field of potato plants on a survey-straight road and come upon a capacious New Hampshire farmhouse in pristine condition.

"It's the color of moonlight," said Carl, now certain his fantasies of wealth (and virgin starlets) were justified.

The house had been moved from New Hampshire, in pieces, and lovingly reconstructed by a Japanese builder upon this chomp of land taken out of one corner of the field. The only addition to the original structure was a two-level barn/garage, cold red, attached to the single-story portion

31

of the house, which in turn joined with the two-storied, federal-style principality that anchored and dominated the whole affair. A gravel driveway fronted the barn, and sod so new the joints showed formed side and front yards. The potato expanses and the roads would eventually be concealed by newly planted trees and shrubs, exotic and quick-to-grow varieties. Neighbors? Nary a one in any decent proximity unless you could count an aging but still contemporary chunk of upthrusting barn board perched across the way from Barry Kessler's. In the distance behind the farmhouse, also in Potato Land, could be seen a mansion of Newportian dimension under construction; it seemed to lack only a scaling of raw cedar shingles. Kessler's place was complete down to the activated sprinkler system whose driveway picket fired a warning stream at the Japanese sedan when its radials crunkled the gravel and pulled in between a black German touring car and a beat-up Camaro Carl figured belonged either to the maid or the gardener, or both.

"Where's the beach?" Carl said.

Devereux stared at the greening potato fields beyond the row of fledgling poplars. "I dunno," he said. "I'm disoriented."

Inside the farmhouse—really a manse of seven-bathroom capacity—standing at the top of the stairs leading to his concrete-slab basement, Barry Kessler parsed the electronic control board for his sprinkler system and state-of-the-art interior burglar alarm. He didn't particularly mind soaking Hoopes and his son with water intended for his own damned vegetation, but how nice it would be to be able to *control* the patterns of soaking. He had been promised this, but here these lighted red dots and throw switches and timer dials puzzled the bejesus out of him; and the so-called instructions decaled to the inside of the control box door . . . they had been written by a mad cryptographer. Screw it. He dashed from the stairway into the hall and to the front door, which he flung open and yelled to the advancing, luggage-bearing Hoopeses, "Sorry, Dee-Vo, it's out of my hands!" With darts, leaps, and some decent broken-field running on Carl's part, the two of them managed to reach the stoop, bedraggled but undrowned.

Barry Kessler posed in the doorway with his hands on his hips. He wore running shoes, fresh white socks to his knees, filmy green shorts, and an immaculate T-shirt with the words "Oscar Wilde Sucks" in diminutive letters over the breast pocket. A short man, narrow of waist, large of chest, he had the gone-craggy face of a former (and successful) child actor who had kept his confidence and improved upon it with a great deal of strenuous effort. He clearly *owned* the house, loved occupying its doorway like a stocky spud baron with expanded horizons. Beside him on the wall, the digital console of the alarm system beeped its vigilance.

There were *abrazos* and a kiss under the ear for each guest. Carl wondered if he would roam the entire Atlantic coast being kissed by middle-aged men—a barren fate for a youth. He was sent upstairs, first door on the right, pick a bed, towels in the bathroom. Barry and Devereux went through the hardwood spaces of the first floor and came eventually to a room whose decor was heavily weighted toward white. The room belonged to an absent son. White wicker furniture, white coverlet on the double bed, white curtains on the windows and on the doors leading to the considerable decking and the swimming pool behind the house. In the bathroom—white tile, brass faucets, Jacuzzi—Barry whispered to Devereux, "This is my nest, Dee-Vo, I'm finally home," and in normal tones, "I'm going to take a twenty-minute run, all my knee can stand. The house is yours—kitchen, pool, sauna upstairs, weight room in the barn. Somewhere you'll find Natalie, my girlfriend Jer's daughter; Jer will be out from the city tonight, I think. And there's Mr. Ya wandering around outside." He patted Devereux's gut—always checking, every time they met; gone soft yet, my boy?—and began to leave, already stretching himself for the run. "And Betsy will be in and out in that Camaro, in the way of laundry and food and liquor."

Upstairs, Carl changed out of his wet britches and enjoyed the attic-like slope of the raw wood walls, the dormer alcoves, the beds heavy with European down quilts—encased in sheeting. A first for him. And, son-of-a-gun, a bathroom he would share with no other man or child. Buttoning up his oversize fatigue pants, he turned toward the open door and in it discovered a beautiful girl with the gray, smoky eyes of Victorian photographs. She wore a loose green smock or sundress that exposed her flesh from armpit to waist, and her straight blonde hair fell over one side of her face in a single sheet she whipped back over her shoulder as soon as she had gained his full notice. "H'lo there, sodjer," she said in a voice he reckoned she'd trained to huskiness.

He finished buttoning (whoops), his ears gone red as pomegranates, before offering up his own "How d'you do, my name is Carl"—and his voice had to go and crack on the fucking "Hoopes." She beckoned to him and—naturally—like a good soldier he followed Natalie into the mysterious byways of this second-floor maze.

Below, Devereux found himself on a walking tour dressed in his old blue shorts and the Bama sweatshirt. He checked books, tapes, overstuffed couches, oaken tables, prints of remarkable fishes, prints of erotic eels, butcher-block counters, a refrigerator with oak-paneled doors . . . from which he removed a Dutch lite beer and a piece of blue-pocked Stilton before continuing to the VCR space, the house-maintenance space (closets closets closets), a door to a garage containing one vintage Mustang, and then the stairway to the weight room, where Devereux found the tools of the trade carefully arrayed around a plastic mat. On the walls were color photographs of the Kessler family—father and two sons—at sport, at victory. The room was as peaceful and fresh-smelling as the outdoors, as a meditation room, as the rest of this spread, this nest, this house that the movies built or, better said, this house that the film industry transported beam-by-numbered-beam from Campton, New Hampshire, to Sagaponack, Long Island, Suffolk County, New York. Devereux approved. He felt at home himself; he felt freewheeling possibility lurked here.

On the deck he was greeted by the oddity of a black swimming pool set into the blonde decking like a blank, elliptical eye of rippling disinvitation. Although it hadn't turned five o'clock, and the sun continued to provide a fine light, a steady warmth, the pool made him shiver. He walked way beyond it, past the spanking new red and white deck furniture, in what he hoped was the direction of the ocean—a beach man in flight from the menace of a man-made water vessel. He heard sounds of distant construction, hammering, a voice crying, "Eat me, Robinson!"

On a rise of raw earth beyond a boggy area off the deck's edge, a small, brown man sat on the earth with his legs crossed and stared across at what Devereux at first thought were his feet, but then realized was a large, veined boulder between the deck and the bog.

After a while, after Devereux had time for the beer and the remainder of the randy cheese, the man ceased staring, got up, circled the bog and stood by the boulder, not looking at Devereux, not looking at anything. He had a full head of silvery hair and wore work clothes much the same color as his wrinkled skin. "I'm Ya," he said. "This rock is *not* in the right place." Devereux had no response. "I am thinking two inches to the east," Ya adjudged. Then he shook his head and the silver hair billowed and spangled in the sunlight. "But Mr. Kessler, he is two inches further from perfection than I am. Good day, sir." With that, Mr. Ya returned to the rise—a future tree line and windbreak—went between the saplings and onward in the direction of the construction noises, treading carefully the furrows beside the perfectly lined hillocks of potato plants.

"Pop!"

Carl's voice came from one of the upstairs dormers. His

35

face hung behind the window screen like a pale, excited moon, and was finally located by a Devereux somewhat dazzled by the waning sunburst coming over the second story's shingled roof peak. He squinted fiercely and waited for some revelation from his mooning boy, who only said, "There's something neat up here. Come see."

Easy compliance. Rid of the beer bottle, he found the back stairway off the VCR room and ascended to an area of heavy ceiling beams, shadowed rooms, a hallway leading to the master bedroom into which he strolled freely ("your house").

In the bathroom off this large but plainly furnished room he discovered Carl peering through a porthole set into a narrow redwood door, a clear sign of sauna within. Carl was in the midst of a rapid and uncharacteristic ha-ha-ha version of a laugh. Devereux asked if the device were lighted. Carl shook his head and told him to open the safe-like door. There, of course, sat Natalie . . . laughing behind one groomed hand. "This *is* neat," Devereux said, appreciating his son's obvious appreciation of a striking young girl whom he, Devereux, found disturbingly old around the eyeballs; even in full, unmotivated laugh she looked like she was studying him for defects.

At that moment Barry Kessler came into his bedroom, proofed by a full lather of sweat and breathing with robust puffs. Joining the crowd in his bathroom, he took one look at Natalie and growled, "Nat, your mother's decided to stay in the city tonight, so we're only seven for dinner. Please go find Betsy and let her know . . . and stop laughing in my sauna like a brainless child—I haven't even used it yet."

To Carl's shock he received from the cook Betsy a plate of marinated swordfish, asparagus spears, and new potatoes. The glass of white wine might protect him from the soy-brown dangers of the fish marinade, but the asparagus must be made to disappear. By way of consolation, Barry told him that he and Natalie could eat by themselves in the VCR room . . . instead of in the fish print room where Devereux—on his fourth beer, now switching to wine—had roosted with the famous couple and their protégé, whose names Carl had already forgotten, so gripped was he by Natalie's habit of leading him about with her smoky grays. He followed her out of the kitchen, sipping wine as he walked—fascinated by the way her sundress played games with concealment and revealment. He understood the phrase "fair flesh" for the first time in his life and prayed Barry Kessler's videotape library might include, say, *Romeo and Juliet* or, at the very stupidest, *Blue Lagoon*.

Betsy—a woman handsomely long of tooth—looked at the retreating young people and thought that Kessler would be smart to put the little minx back in her cage before the Hoopes kid got his pug nose bit off; but then Betsy was not inclined to charity or toleration or rose glasses when it came to teenage love, or what passed for it these days: getting laid in the shade with an already jaded (and stoned) maid. She served Barry Kessler some of his fancy swordfish and wished his impossibly brown eyes would rest on any part of her, instead of checking the goddamn wine cases she'd hauled in that afternoon.

In the fish print room, a flushed Devereux sat with his hands folded in his lap like a man overaware of manners and of his companions, who were: a sad-eyed man of sixty; a beady-eyed woman of forty-some; and a doe-eyed sycophant of a few notches less than thirty. The conversation that ping-ponged over the waiting dinner plates as Barry Kessler entered the room and took his place at table's head might be characterized as an amalgam of The Show Business . . . if generic torque can be put upon the phrase so that it includes dog shows, writers' lobbies, rodeos, congressional hearings, film screenings, genetic research victims such as poor Godzilla, and all monies advanced against future earnings. When Barry took his seat, forks rose and fell, and the amalgam went into a full-tilt and wine-rich blur—which

Devereux enjoyed as much for its inherent politeness as for its low-keyed frenzy. Within half an hour it was simple enough to conclude that the sad-eyed man was a depressed saint, that the woman had bones made of burning ambition, that the sycophant would sing any tune whatsoever for his supper, and that sloe-eyed Barry Kessler was not his usual monologist self in the presence of old sad-eyes. Easy, then, to sip and sip the tart wine and ponder nothing more than the smell of the marinade's ginger and the superior quality of the saint's sorrowful blue eyes. Devereux Hoopes's present-tense contentment could be seen in the way he lofted a piece of swordfish, regarded it in the candlelight, and then bore it to his mouth as if its cold flakes said more of the world and its seas than could any saint.

Meanwhile, in the VCR room the teenagers sprawled themselves over a crackling new sofa (roses emblazoned on a field of white) and cast speculative eyes at the video version of an early Barry Kessler flick called *Mystery Train*. Natalie had eaten both portions of asparagus, neither had touched the swordfish, and Carl had made a good job of all the available potatoes. His trip to the kitchen for a second glass of wine—Natalie drank nothing—had been marked by a glower from Betsy that he tried to fend off with a smile. The woman appeared to think he was up to no good. It always puzzled Carl, this way adults had of eyeing you as if crimes were hatching, when in fact all he had in mind was vino, the weird movie (a solemn fairy tale of railway life in eastern Europe), and the incredible heat that came from Natalie, even though she mostly acted like Carl was another harmless rose on the upholstery. When he returned to the flaring colors of the VCR, Natalie said, "Lookit," and on the big screen Carl determined that the fey young stationmaster was having his way with the daughter of the local goose-stuffer . . . right there on the black sofa in his office. It looked like a very painful process. "In Europe," Natalie observed, "fucking is quite grim. I think it's a metaphor." Carl had no idea what to reply. He sipped; he wondered at the truth of things beyond tube images and magazine porn; he waited for the stationmaster to finish his maybe ill-fated grunting.

Outside, the sprinkler sentries continued to send water cannonades into the unknowing darkness; inside, beneath the fish prints, the adults moved inevitably toward coffee and cognac; in Sag Harbor, Mr. Ya sat with his wife and determined to mount a vigorous campaign to persuade Barry Kessler to fund the relocation of his boulder; and in Manhattan, Jer told a producer that Barry's next project would feature a death by hacky-sack. Up north and much farther east the McGuffys made notations in book margins before a modest fire; and in Newburyport Jessica's phone went unanswered. As the Atlantic settled down for the night, good weather prevailed from Calais to Key West.

But wait. Natalie plucked the VCR's zapper gizmo from her lap and hit the fast-forward button; the stationmaster's fate gained such momentum that the arrival of the sealed train became all mixed up in Carl's mind with the manufacture of pâté and the stationmaster's betrayal of the goose girl. The end. *Fin.* Natalie tossed the zapper into his lap—uhhh—then she stood up and untied the sash that kept her sundress (a kind of airy poncho) in the neighborhood of modesty. "I'm for the pool," she said, flicking at him with one end of the sash. He saw the clean curve of flesh from her armpit to her knee, broken only by the green thigh-string of her bikini underpants.

Carl looked at her unreadable face, at his own fatigue pants, and said, "Me too," without quite knowing he'd said it. Certainly she'd disappeared before he could swallow down the remaining wine and decide not to go upstairs for his suit, which in many parts of the world, including ass-gazing Wellfleet, would be unnecessary. Rising decisively, he found Betsy suspended and glowering in the light from the kitchen doorway. You are a servant, he thought (immediately struck by guilt), and walked away from her, removing his T-shirt as he went, away from her censure and the babble of adult laughter that rose up just then from the fish print room.

Moonlight and house glow could not defeat the blackness of the deck and the pool itself. A blackness that made Carl's skin bump up, although it wasn't particularly cold, not even when he and his jockey shorts eased into the water and began the search for Natalie.

"Carl Hoopes," she said from nowhere and everywhere. "Have you ever baptized a sauna? Have you?"

"I'm not baptized." He grinned, breast-stroked—such invisible embarrassment.

"Maybe you'd prefer the weight room . . . the mat . . . the pec machine?" She gurgled from somewhere in front of him.

He deepened his voice. "I don't get your drift."

"Aren't your parents divorced?"

"Sure." No movie star elocution there; he sounded like a castrato in a Viennese choir. His expensive education was being washed away by this black water, this dumb girl. At that point a hand softer than the water rendered pleasure from his collarbone to his belly button.

Then she was out of the pool, a faint sylph in his grateful night vision. "Divorce brats," she said from above, "have a special responsibility. A mission."

Carl found the pool edge and hung on with his elbows. Did she think they were genetic experiments? Perhaps so. More to the point: what did people *do* with unrequited erections in real life? He wished she would go away. Dessert would be an improvement. Would Betsy bring him a piece of cheesecake if she knew what an innocent little bugger he really was?

"I prefer the sauna," Natalie went on, doing something with the shadow of the sundress. "You hafta shower first. Barry promised to gut the first kid who dripped chlorine on his precious redwood. I'll meet you there."

So matter-of-fact, this love in Potato Land.

Steady, fair Carl, life is parting before you.

In the fish print room, amid the melee of table clearing prior to coffee, Devereux found himself standing up from his place and gazing down at the saint's great aureole of what seemed a younger person's blonde curls. Beneath the curls, the saint's voice said, "My blood-sugar level has just flip-flopped. We must go."

Barry Kessler passed behind him, equally fascinated by the curls. "So predictable," Barry said to no one in particular. Devereux wheeled from the table and walked with studied deliberation in the direction of his furiously white room, there perchance to pee away the wine's devilish sugars, there perchance to dream away the dinner's conflicted and confusing and sometimes lovely smatterings. Along the gleaming hardwood path he met Carl, shirtless and glum, and for some reason wet about the hair. He touched his son on the back and found his skin to be hot. These curiosities he didn't remark, and Carl passed into a hallway with the words, "Vino, Pop, love's fool." Food? Fool? But by the time Devereux had groped himself into the bathroom and had his pee, he could think of nothing more than a sweet rest on the bed before returning to coffee and the visitors three.

Carl's private shower—actually a half-tub, a phonelike head attached to a metallic hose, and clear plastic curtains at waist level to protect the raw wood walls—offered him a respite from wondering about Natalie's world, Devereux's world, all the worlds he lately slipped in and out of like a loony wielding his VCR zapper. He pleasured himself by running the shower head over his soaped body, changing with a finger flick the speed of the water, its heady pulsation finally producing in him a thoughtless rapture that prevented him from noticing how much water bypassed both his body and the protective curtains and dribbled and streamed down to where wall joined the tub's edge. Because Mr. Ya was not completely perfect, this water was dammed by no expertly beaded grouting; the rivulets continued downward, along the studs, over the lining of the fiberglass insulation, along the backs of the exterior clapboards, and finally pooled atop the digital console that controlled Barry Kessler's state-of-the-art alarm system.

When water enters an electrical system of such sophistication, all logic goes by the boards.

The "noise," once it began, turned the Federal farmhouse into a Trident-like organism that would have instantly crash-dived with all aboard had not such a phenomenon been prevented by the concrete, soil, and rock of Long Island. The artificial whoop and howl broadcast within a decibel range calculated to pierce and prevent both thought and idle conversation, calculated to turn Carl into a soapy pillar of salt, calculated to notify most of Potato Land that within Barry Kessler's home great mischief was afoot.

Within the staunch structure itself, several actions occurred at once: Barry K sprinted for the front door and punched hopelessly at the console keys—6-7-2-4-0!—and only when his fingers came away wet did he make the connection with the showering above; he leapt the stairs and barely heard himself shout, "Turn off the fucking shower!" at stricken Carl; in the kitchen, Betsy huddled on the floor beneath the counter, her hands pressed to her ears, and made herself think of quitting her employment in this degenerating hell; three sets of feet passed within a foot of Betsy's head on their way to the side door—the saint, the ambitionist, and the sycophant, all determined to take their after-dinner coffee in some quieter realm, though the saint would have preferred to remain as a deaf observer of the transcendent comedy of Barry Kessler dealing with this late-twentieth-century symphony; Barry himself appeared in the kitchen during their exit, and grimaces of thanks were exchanged before Barry seized the telephone and dialed the number of the security company; his shouts finally got through to the numskull on the other end of the line, and his desperation turned to rage when she said—a stern dwarf's voice at the bottom of a mine shaft—"Sir, you're only supposed to give me your number . . . I don't want to know *who* you are . . . only your number, sir . . ."

In the white bedroom, in complete darkness, Devereux Hoopes knew the levitation of Death by Wine; once fallen back to the bed, and convinced that Doom had arrived, he prepared himself for it by cocooning his head in the bed's three pillows. It did not help. No one would come to his celibate's bed on this night—no size-chopping Jessica, no loving McGuffy—not here. Not thirteen feet above Devereux's sodden head, Carl crept through the master bedroom, a cool, now-sober youth in bedlam. A towel encircled his center, and when he reached the door of the sauna, he entered with all the confidence of a man seeking shelter in a luxurious crypt.

As he had half expected, the sauna's superior insulation made it the one available refuge from the wailing wall of clamor he now believed he had caused. When the door closed him into the reddish dimness, the alarm receded to the level of a neighborhood problem and was replaced by a dry vat of heat in which Natalie floated like an unadorned babe. Shazam! he thought, feigning interest in the powerful heater with its topping of rocks. From her perch on the higher and narrower slat shelf, Natalie made a giddy sound that Carl interpreted as enjoyment of their isolation from the oldie fuck-up. He explained to her kneecaps that his shower must have leaked into the guts of the alarm; she said Barry enjoyed a good crisis—maybe he'd split the alarm's electric cable with an axe. She reached for his earlobe and twirled the silver post in the lobe's pierced hole. She told him to get rid of his silly towel; Carl breathed a chestful of heat, turned toward her knees—my Godzilla, his eyes were level with her breasts—and blindly dropped the towel onto the lower shelf. He located her smoky grays (calmly lurid in this light) and held them with his own in hopes she would not be distracted by his damned drawbridge of a penis. Her knees moved apart to form a natural V into which he might insert his chest if he cared to take one step forward; but the choice was not his, for she took hold of his shoulders and pulled him into the mythical V with such amused, careful purpose that Carl in the weird months to come would be more and more certain that love was nothing more, nothing less than this glorious intersecting of their two bodies. For him, in America, fucking would never be grim.

Meanwhile, down basement, Barry Kessler managed to destroy both sound and light by swatting circuit-breaker switches until the box hung askew from the concrete wall. In the peculiar, lifeless silence that came over the entire farmhouse could be heard his call for candles, flashlights, matches!—a call heard by no one. Not Betsy, who had long since fled in the beat-up Camaro, leaving behind—her special way of giving notice—an "I QUIT" written in soy marinade across the kitchen counter's butcher blocking. Certainly not Carl and Natalie, entombed and entwined in their redwood bower. And not Devereux Hoopes—dead to the world in his head-dressing of feather pillows. In Bridgehampton the saint chuckled over his cognac; his blood sugar was back on track.

Beach Report. Pity the hungover, the vinous unfortunate who must beg solace from the late morning's painful salt air, from the accusatory shrieks of gulls, from the infernal endlessness of waves—their pump and hiss—from the unwillingness of his bare feet to slog through a sand gone thick and drifty with his own pulsing weakness, and from his own son . . . who positively *capered* in front of him in his eagerness to extract from Devereux's foul mouth permission to remain here in Sagaponack as replacement for the flown Betsy, as factotum to the one and only Barry Kessler, as lover (Devereux could not admit this possibility, quite) to the Natalie gamine, who only this morning had been threatened by Kessler with forty whacks for leaving his precious sauna running full blast the night long.

The skin of Devereux's face not bushed over by the beard had the look of rice paper, and he was dimly aware that Carl was taking excessive pleasure from Pop's obvious pain. They had driven the short distance from the farmhouse to the beach parking lot and were now walking past architectural bewilderments and among occasional clumps of beach denizens, who looked far too perfect for Devereux's stained taste. Everyone seemed weighted down by body jewelry, makeup, or parachute jumper's clothing in colors too bright for the squinting eye of the Surveyor.

Devereux repeated his question of minutes before: "How will you get home? I'm too broke to fly you."

Carl put an arm around his father's slumped shoulders. "Aw, Dee-Vo, who wants to be in Alabama in the summah? You and Tessa need to sweat in private." True true true. "With what Barry's gonna pay me I can buy my own plane ticket down after Labor Day . . . and even fly back to school. Not one penny out of your pocket . . . or Mom's. Say yes, or I'll break your neck. Barry even has a car for me."

Devereux glanced into the glowing face of his threatener—his son, changing before his very own rheumy eyes—and felt (a not unwelcome surge of self-pity) like the lonely keeper of the mock-Georgian lighthouse at the mouth of the New London harbor: a raggedy man on a rickety cot behind the elegant façade . . . visited from time to time by Jessica, by the good McGuffy, by confidence-bearing Kessler, even by wonderful, puzzling Tessa.

Bosh and cold pasta salad!

He had to get on with his avoider's journey.

"Sure, stay," he said to Carl. "But be careful."

Carl punched his old man in the shoulder and darted for the bluey water—his first dip off a beach he believed he would own by summer's end.

Love!

That same day, not an hour after the security expert permanently disarmed the potent alarm, Mr. Ya and his crew began the massive task of shifting by two inches Barry Kessler's boulder.

OCEAN GROVE

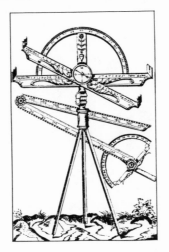

ROOM NUMBER twenty-three of the Wesley Inn: an off-white box for the celibate Surveyor; a clean American space designed in 1919 to receive generations of Methodist resolutes; a chamber of retreat and prayer and rectitude; a cheap refuge from the suspect Jersey sun. Two slim beds, an exposed sink, a lavatory shared with number twenty-four, chintz curtains over a door opening onto a balcony with a second-story view of Main Street—similar verandaed hotels, chock-a-block. Awnings of every conservative stripe. Rocking chairs. Scalloped shingles. Gables. Turrets—from which the interested might gaze upon a slice of the inky sea, cream sand, and the impertinent interruption of the boardwalk running north to the blight called Asbury Park.

Devereux Hoopes languished on a bed in room number twenty-three like an unanxious and weather-bitten duffel sack; thus do Sagaponack hangovers evolve. Through the open door to the balcony came a gentle afternoon light and the mutter of slow traffic. For a change, he had no obligation, no appointment, no social embroilment, no traveling companion. He missed Carl, an emotion that sprawled over his chest like a sleepy gerbil, but Devereux knew full well that the precious guy had lucked into one wet dream of a summer. Only now did the lazing parent begin to wonder what might *be* in Alabama, in Tuscaloosa, where Tessa Dixon surely wandered among her things, her fingers echoing the constant motions of her fugitive thoughts. Stop it! He would call, later, would connect his brain to hers. Meanwhile, it was sufficient to enjoy the dregs of hangover and to anticipate the remainder of the Jersey day . . . the noisy evening to come.

Devereux had been given this room by Miriam Shore, heavenly sister of the absent owner of the inn; at the moment, dark-haired Miriam was rolling off-white paint onto the walls of number thirty-one, silently worried that her lover Willy Liebling would fail to find his absentminded way from Newark Airport to Ocean Grove, where—should he make it—he would be rendered catatonic by the presence of the man she believed to be sleeping a floor below her in number twenty-three. Just a joke, the catatonia: Willy Liebling could be stilled by no one but her—and then only in bed, briefly.

On the inn's veranda, well shaded by a green-and-white-striped awning, two widows sat side by side in black wicker rockers, gossip their mission. "Miriam," one said, "is not herself this summer."

"The inn neither," the other observed after a pause. "It reeks of paint . . . and sex."

"Not only is Miriam's man-friend married . . . he's a coarse old goat. Did you hear—"

"I've heard. They do it right on the floor . . . with a fan."

"A fan?"

"Don't be stupid. People like them sweat like pigs when they rut."

"And this new one? With the face hairs?"

The widows seemed to join together at the ear. "A thug from Alabama, a bigot . . . Miriam's ruint. It's the mid-life sex craze, I'm telling you."

Well.

In the lobby off the veranda, behind a pulpitlike reception desk, a telephone rang. The phone sat in a pass-through slot that connected the reception area with Miriam Shore's miniature and spartan apartment; above the pass-through was a large picture window, curtained, which could well allow a late-night, passing widow a glimpse, however gauzy, of any nefarious floor activities in Miriam's living room. The phone rang six times; the widows ignored the sounds; and Miriam above was out of earshot. Most of the inn's other occupants were either beached or hymning at the huge Methodist tabernacle a couple of blocks away.

The caller—Willy Liebling—crashed the receiver of the Greyhound station's pay phone into its abused cradle with all the force a coarse old goat could muster. Jesus Nattering Christ! . . . his beloved off painting tacky hotel rooms when he need a frigging *ride* the seven blocks to the inn. Muttering, he humped into the heat, a short potbellied man of sixty-two with a brilliantly sunburned dome surrounded by wisps and licks of graying fringe-hair. He lugged a vinyl kit bag and, strapped over one shoulder, a woolen Greek pouch stuffed with papers, notebooks, and unanswered letters. A peripatetic Literary Man: he wore baggy-assed dungarees, scuffed brogans, and a yellow polyester shirt, untucked. Rimless glasses emphasized his stubbled scowl, and as he marched his way to his most beautiful of beloveds, he worked his mouth so that at times it appeared near to coupling with his broad nose. On the whole a powerful, snuffling figure who would say anything to anybody at any time.

A block from the inn, near Kimball's, his favorite ice-cream parlor in all of New Jersey, he put down his burden and took out a handkerchief with which he wiped away the sweat of his brow and scalp; then he knotted each corner of the white rag and placed it upon his head where it comfortably tented his dome for the duration of the journey.

He limped up on the veranda of the Wesley and greeted the widows. "Hello darlings!"—western Pennsylvania in every syllable—"Did you miss me?" The ladies inclined their torsos in his direction but made no audible response.

Willy's croaky, challenging voice did, however, reach up to the balconies of the second and third floors . . . pleasing the ears of both languorous Devereux and laboring Miriam. Both of them smiled as if given a whiff of risible gas, although Miriam, as she put away her painting things, took the even deeper breath of someone preparing for a long and unquittable roller-coaster ride. She was a solid, well-proportioned woman of forty-two with tawny skin unharmed by five children and two rip-off marriages. Her face was dominated by brown eyes quick to display emotion. Spattered black toreador pants covered what she privately considered "chicken-skin legs," and up top a blue work-shirt—shirttails hitched together under her breasts to expose belly and navel: yes, a nifty woman with as firm a hold on herself as on the inn she managed and maintained every summer from May through Labor Day.

She met Devereux in the stairwell on the way down to her apartment, and they exchanged the awry looks meant to signal awareness of the big fellow's invasion of the inn; that their conspiracy of surprise was intact.

They found Willy on the floor, on his back with his head toward them. He lay next to the chrome legs of a Formica-topped table, under the table a floor fan, a rolled foam mattress, and the strewn contents of Willy's Greek bag. The handkerchief chapeau now covered Willy's face, making of it a relief map of a small but rugged country. Devereux stood in the doorway while Miriam strode to her lover and placed a bare foot on either side of his head.

"Is that you, love?" Willy groaned with fake pitifulness, then delivered himself of a long, loud sigh that trembled his risen belly and caused the handkerchief to flutter over his mouth-hole. "I had to *walk,* my darling . . . and now I fear my back—"

"Willy." Miriam's sharp voice.

One of his hands curved up and fondled her paint-dotted thigh. "Ahh," he sang, "the femur of my fair sea-maid." She slapped the hand away and snatched his cloth mask. His unspectacled eyes squinched at the sight of Miriam's crotch overhead. "Oh . . . the pudenda that murdered my former life."

She boxed his ears with the soles of her feet. Discipline the jerk.

"Mr. Liebling," Devereux said with an extravagant Alabama drawl.

"Who-zat?!" Willy dug his glowing pate into the carpeting in a failed attempt to identify the person in the doorway behind him.

"I bring you greetings from Tuscaloosa."

Miriam moved away from Willy, whose head was now stretched back so far, his neck so tendoned, it appeared rigor mortis had set to work.

"Sweet Shelley, is that Devereux Hoopes from Camden? Is that you there in your body electric? Goddammit, Miriam, give me my glasses." But his groping hand had already found them at the edge of the table's surface. He fumbled them onto his face by the time Devereux had walked from the doorway to Willy's side, and from that height he offered the downed man his hand.

After a dinner of pesto, beer, and spinach salad, the three took themselves out of the hot apartment and made a triangle of wicker rockers on the veranda. Because the only light came from the lamps of Main Street, both Willy and Devereux were unaware of the widows plunked down like living sculptures in the shadows at the opposite end of the veranda; but Miriam—who could see them beyond the heads of her two men—knew very well that ancient ears were flapping, especially when Willy's resonant exuberance filled the entire space and sometimes spilled out into the street where it might easily stop traffic.

In fact, not long after Willy gingerly accomplished the occupation of his rocker, two punked-out girls in old-fashioned, ankle-length dusters passed along the sidewalk eating ice-cream cones.

"My beauties!" Willy called out. "Yes, you two." The girls stopped with alacrity—braces flashed from both sweetened mouths.

Miriam rolled her eyes heavenward; the widows curled their toes.

"What kind of ice cream?" Willy demanded.

"Kimball's. What's it to ya?"

"Don't be fresh, dear." Willy raised his hands prophetically. "Do you know the big guy, do you know John Wesley?" Huh-uh, no way. "You poor schmuckas. You wouldn't catch the big guy eating ice cream on a Wednesday's Youth Fellowship night." Now he thundered: "Methodist goyim, abstain!"

"But we're from Asbury Park," said one set of braces.

Willy slapped his palms against his temples. "That's it! Devereux and I will go to Asbury Park and recruit a bargeload of Rastafarians. . . . We'll float them across the moat that isolates this sissy, bluenosed Ocean Grove. . . . We'll march them down the boardwalk in their chalky dreadlocks . . . and we'll rent us a building right next to the tabernacle. The Blue-Balled Reform Rasta Who Gonna Git You!"

Willy slumped back in his rocker.

Miriam smiled at the perplexed girls on the sidewalk. "Don't worry," she said, "he's a famous lunatic."

"I'm sublime Homer, kids. You wanna hear the tale of mighty, penis-bearing Achilles?"

Alarm on the street. The space on the sidewalk was quickly vacated. The widows silently agreed with each other that the better part of valor would be to remain seated in the shadows; if they tried to make it to number twenty-four, *he* might swat them with his goatish hoof.

Devereux attempted to restore the integrity of the triangle: "So, Willy, when are you going to stop running around like a candidate for high literary office?"

Miriam winced. How would her beloved embellish his latest illusions this time around?

Willy said to her, "My back is melted suet. Put me to bed, my darling." But he immediately turned to Devereux, and so did not see the stubborn shaking of her head. "Dev-Roo," he said, "I remember our delicious days in Alabama."

Miriam inwardly choked; tears jumped; thanks be for the murk of night. For her, Alabama had been true exile . . . if only for six weeks.

Willy rolled on. "The night your sweetheart cooked the ultimate filé gumbo, and we talked of living cheek to cheek in Lesbos."

Devereux nodded.

The widows inclined themselves as if a breeze had sprung up—lesbians cheek to cheek!

"Willy—" Miriam began; she wanted to stop the tale-spinning.

"Wait," he barked. "I'm curious about old pie-face here. What about Teresa? Why isn't she with you? She has the sense of sin, that one. Such candid melancholy, such holy uncertainty about the world, about *life!*"

Miriam watched Devereux rear back with the force of Willy's exclamation; he looked, momentarily, lost, then curved his lips to cover himself. He said nothing.

"Well," Willy went on, "*my* intent is to earn bags of money on the circuit this summer; then Miriam and I will spend the fall teaching in Indiana. Come January—Paris. February—Florence. And by Blind Homer, Lesbos in March. Come with us, Dev-Roo. Bring Tessa, who told me she'd never left the blighted South. Bring her, you dope. We'll own the fucking *light* of Greece!"

"Why not?" said Devereux, apparently bending himself to the fantasy.

"And what about Joel?" Miriam asked, referring to her youngest son, now with his drunken papa.

Willy snuffled and sputtered as he levered himself out of the rocker. "Come to bed," he said.

"No."

Willy Liebling froze in the stoop he'd managed to attain. "I beg your pardon?"

"I want to talk with Devereux." Her voice rose. "You expect too—" The widows had to strain to catch the goat's interrupting syllables.

"You asshole."

Miriam believed that Ocean Grove had come to a sudden and complete halt. In forty-two years not a single human being had flung this word at her. She longed to laugh in disbelief. Instead, she leaned tearfully toward Devereux and whispered, "I've seen the best minds of his generation enter paradise bullshitting."

Devereux managed to achieve a neutral blankness.

Willy held on to the back of Miriam's rocker, his eyeglasses catching a bit of the brownish light from the lobby. "Forgive me," he whisper-croaked. "I need you with me."

Miriam stood up. "Oh Willy," she capitulated, putting off her small revenge, "let's put you back on the floor."

The widows took long, knowing breaths as the threesome split apart; the adulteress helped the goat into the lobby while the laconic, bush-faced thug sat alone in his rocker for several more minutes. Silence reigned on the veranda of the Wesley Inn.

An hour later, the bed light in number twenty-three snapped off, and Devereux Hoopes settled into the slim mattress with a certain weary appreciation for the cotton sheets Miriam had probably washed with her own hands (she had); the sheets smelled as though they had dried in the sun (they had, on the roof); and that smell combined comfortably with the saline zephyrs from the Atlantic which entered through the open door to the balcony.

Perhaps to dream of a blue-doored cottage on sunstruck Lesbos . . .

One of the widows entered the bathroom from number twenty-four and pointedly locked the door leading into Devereux's room.

Later, he thought someone said, "There's nothing sexual about this nocturnal emission, I am only in need."

But as soon as he opened his eyes, the words—like most dreams—fled from his brain and were replaced by the perception of a darkness shared. Ahh, the head of Miriam not a foot from his own; she must be on the floor between the two beds. He smelled the pesto's basil and knew a brief desire to touch the dark thickness of her hair where it seemed to fall loose across her cheek.

"Hey," he said, this groggy receiver of bedside visits. "Shall I turn on the light?" He didn't particularly want to see any more tears, or even her flesh.

"No, it's okay, I just wanted to tell you that I do plan to devote the rest of my life to William Liebling."

"I knew that the day I met you."

"But he's such a shithead," Miriam said, a dash of hopelessness diluting the confidence of her voice.

"Not really—just wild to live. . . . Oh lucky Liebling."

She laughed quietly. "Yeah, but I can't give over everything to him. I've raised five children, Devereux. I've loved some of it, but I can't stand the thought of another needful *pup*." She thumped the mattress in front of his chest. "And I won't go to nowhere Indiana to cook his macaroni and nurse his miserable back."

"Don't."

She patted his cheek, twice. Her hand smelled of paint, the skin as callused as a carpenter's. "You're sweet," she said. He thanked her with charming irony. "I want . . ." she went on after a moment, "no, strike that, I'm *going* to go to Mexico as soon as the season's over. I've got a place to live in Pátzcuaro, and I'm going to write something resembling a book if it kills me. Just me." His night vision gained, he could now make out that she shuddered and clasped her arms over her breasts. "Then, then I'll meet Willy in Lesbos, and we can love forever after, and a day."

"And your son?"

She shrugged. "He'll be with his rat-fuck of a father until I send for him. Willy won't like it, but Joel will be on Lesbos with us."

"Good."

"Yes, but Willy won't *believe* Mexico; he won't even discuss it."

"Look," Devereux said, raising up and propping his head on a bent arm, "isn't he going off tomorrow to a gig in Seattle?" She nodded, then impatiently whipped her hair away from her cheek. "So write him a letter," he went on, "and say, 'This is the way it is, my love. Accept me as a full-fledged working being . . . or I'll be a *real* asshole and leave you flat.'"

She laughed. "Jeez, I never thought of that. It's so simple it might work, might make him look at the moon over Puget Sound and write an ode to Miriam Shore's temporary emancipation."

"It might," Devereux said. "Only one way to find out."

Her shadow rose up from the floor. "Thanks, Mr. Hoopes, you are as always . . . a rock. Aren't you?"

His own laughter had room for far more meaning than she knew—exactly how emancipated was Tessa? exactly how much of an asshole was Mr. Hoopes?—but Miriam shushed his sounds with a solid, basil-rich kiss that startled him with its purposeful intensity.

"We love you, Devereux," she said from the open door to the corridor. "Me and Willy. Don't lose us . . . and look to your own in Tuscaloosa."

"I better. Thank *you*."

In number twenty-four the widows knew a justified and prolonged insomnia. All along the Atlantic coast a great sleeplessness prevailed, and even young Carl Hoopes— searching for Natalie at a private party in Sag Harbor— sensed a peculiar lull in the air, an electric adumbration caused by much more than Natalie's wicked eyes.

Beach Report. The stately decrepitude of the Jersey shore can be well seen from a boardwalk vantage point in Ocean Grove. Early the next morning, Devereux stood outside a picnic kiosk served by the boardwalk and surveyed the damage. True, the Victorian beach "cottages" lining the boulevard leading to the tabernacle had had their gingerbread fretting recently painted; but nearer to the tabernacle were wooden-roofed structures with siding made of canvas—a gray-white canvasing that bespoke camp meetings and the mannerly fervor of another age, bespoke massive spillings of the faithful out of Queens, Hoboken, and Philadelphia. In the kiosk itself the picnic tables had been gouged and gouged again by generations of bluenosed Kilroys. Beyond the kiosk lay the cream beach in all of its cream blandness, as if the moundy sand and the minor, careful surf had been designed at the behest of a council of dour vacationists. It is a fact that no one is permitted on this beach before noon on a Sunday.

Devereux looked north, followed the line of the boardwalk past a wharf restaurant with a capacity of one thousand souls, until his eye fell on the massive, now-deserted Asbury Park amusement pier, if that's the term for such an orange and monstrous arcade where horses once leapt into the sea for the edification of one and all. Beyond the arcade, he knew, a black population suffered.

Time to move on, Mr. Rock?

He put a quarter into the telephone bolted to the wall of the kiosk, dialed ten digits, received simultaneously his quarter and his signal, then dialed fourteen more digits, and while blind machinery did its swift work, he gazed out to sea and took some comfort in connecting his eyes with the distant vanishing point where the dark, unpeopled sea met the innocent, blue haze of the sky.

His sweetheart—Tessa Dixon of the ultimate Alabama filé gumbo—was not answering their home phone.

CAPE HATTERAS

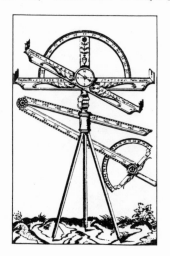

A FEW WORSHIP attenuated coastal islands. In thralldom to their flat vulnerability, in love with nature's perilous outposts, in connection with wind, sun, cloud, and tidal roil, these men and women might choose to raise their habitations on the lee side, the Sound side of these islands, these capes, these Outer Banks, but always they are drawn to the windward, to the outer edges where whatever rises or falls can be taken right in the face.

At four o'clock on this Thursday in June, Pamlico Sound, property of North Carolina, was in reddish brown chop as it lapped against and seemingly overloomed the western edges of the Cape Hatteras National Seashore, property of the United States Department of Interior's National Park Service ("Lock Your Valuables in Your Trunk"). Cape Hatteras itself, the farthest jut of the seashore's skimpy, 85-mile-long curve, is backed by the leeward settlements of Buxton and Frisco—convenience stores with gas pumps, box cottages on stilts, your seafood shacks, and the like.

To stand at the Frisco city limits sign, northeast of town, is to be less than a mile from the long rollers of the Atlantic surf, and not two hundred yards from the Sound's contained chop. In bright, turbulent heat, walk tender-footed alongside Route 12's pavement, swing a right into a sandy track leading soundward. Across the scrub flatness, beneath the sky's scudding cumulonimbus, the water's redcaps beckon like invitations to a safe-water harvest of salty manna.

Two pine cottages on stilts, both the old blood color of the

63

Sound, were served by the track: one boarded up with gone-gray plywood, the other clearly occupied by the owners of a blue four-wheel-drive Japanese station wagon parked on a concrete slab beneath the cottage and bearing two stubby surfboards on its roof carrier. A color chart of towels hung flapping from the railing of the stairs leading up to the cottage's deck and screened-in porch, which faced the Sound and the far-off East Dismal Swamp on the mainland.

At water's edge, attached to a rock breakwater, a wooden dock serving both cottages ran parallel to the shoreline. On this structure a man worked at harvesting blue crabs from the Sound. Tethered to the dock pilings were four wire-mesh traps blackened by years of exposure; he hauled each one out of the brine, extricated the crabs with fast, stealthy (but scarred) hands, and placed them one by one in a large, covered cook pot he kept beside him. Each trap he rebaited from a can of rank stew beef, and when all four were empty and armed, he jumped into the lapping, waist-deep water, waded with each one the length of its tether, and sunk them to the teeming floor of the Sound. Jack Vilna, possessor of a dozen or so clicky, soft-shelled creatures from the shallows.

He arm-lifted himself back up on the dock and stood dripping over his catch, his bait, his drink (rum and Coke), his crumpled pack of cigarettes. No Captain Nemo, no Poseidon; this man in the worn, crimson surfer shorts looked more a sleek, walnut-tanned assemblage of smoky hair and vague muscle—a chaotic shagginess of hair and beard formed his head into a rough triangle out of which his lens-magnified eyes fixed upon the watery world like wafers of passionate blueness. If anything marred his simian, other-worldly beauty, it was his busted chili pepper of a nose. Where his skin was not masked by fur or curly hair, it seemed to have the texture of fine, oiled leather. Six feet of Jack Vilna, age thirty-two, his rimless eyeglasses now smeary with random droplets of Sound water.

He bent over for his cigarettes and tucked them into the top of his shorts, where the pack bent only slightly from the pressure of a steady drinker's corselet of waist- and belly-flesh.

"Jackie!"

A woman's voice from the screened-in porch of the cottage; "his" woman as he might have put it two weeks ago when they came to this spot, but now . . . he was not so sure he wanted the possessive pronoun. "Yes, bread-brain," he said to himself, on the principle of refusing to raise his voice in the presence of the lively water and the doomed crabs.

From the vantage point of the porch, Ling Mullins pressed the narrow tip of her nose against the screening. From behind, in her short blue robe, she looked like a high-hipped and leggy pedestal for the heap of damp, dark blonde curls that clung to her scalp like a lovely new species of domestic pet. She watched her lover of six years with all the intensity of a woman who knew that he might at any minute dive into the Sound and make powerful strokes in the direction of the East Dismal Swamp, never to be seen again; the Buster Crabbe of this summer's Cape Hatteras. Jack Vilna picked up his cook pot, drink, and smelly can of bait, threw up to her one of his famous menacing looks—the flashy, madman smile was equally renowned—and started across the scraggly grass for the cottage.

Ling closed her wide mouth against the impulse to gig him with the fresh information (by post) that not only would Devereux Hoopes arrive within the hour (Jack knew this, welcomed this), but also that the questionable concatenation of summer visitors would continue tomorrow when Bob and Lily Wiggins pulled in with whatever burden Bob had lately designed for himself (Jack and Ling had yet to meet Lily). Well, Bart Maverick down there with his crabs and alcohol could damn well wait on discovering life's next surprise.

She withdrew to her favorite chaise longue near the sliding glass door. Mail lay strewn about on the porch's matting; she kicked the various envelopes under the chaise with a painted toe and then reclined herself—a woman who carried extra

flesh around her midsection with the grace of early pregnan-
cy; but there was no excess in the formation of her face—
large hazel eyes, the straight, narrow nose, and a generous
mouth that might persuade a celibate to sin. She allowed her
robe to fall loose of both her tanned upper thighs and her soft
breasts—perhaps Crabman would dig the invitation; more
likely he would turn away thinking of the last bitch he'd
planked in Miami or Granada or wherever his wandering,
journalist's cock took him. Still in all, Ling Mullins had
stubborn bones and a will to order that could not be shaken
by natural calamity or man-made infidelity. A session with
jealousy on the chaise longue was not really such a bad way
to make it through the afternoon.

After grimy urban rain in Norfolk and a flat tire in Kill Devil
Hills, Devereux Hoopes rolled into Frisco encased in air-
conditioning and the off-thump of Bob Marley and the
Wailers on the cassette deck. Before he had one foot out of
the sedan, before he could pop the tape or disconnect the
radar detector, Jack Vilna had reached in and seized him by
the scruff of the neck . . . had him out of the car and in the
back-thumping throes of embrace before Devereux had
quite absorbed where he was. In any event, he drew his last
truly sober breaths for thirty-six hours as the two of them
made their way past the station wagon and up the stairway
of towels in search of Ling and booze.

Before they entered into the empty, screened porch, Jack
again seized his friend's neck and brought their heads
together in a pungent wallow of sweat, rum, salt rime, and
an edge of meat gone slightly high. "So glad to see you,
man," Jack said. "Ling's a little peculiar these days, pay no
mind, unless you feel like stroking her your own self." When
Devereux recoiled at this, Jack delivered a disturbing heh-
heh-heh laugh. "Just kidding you, Hoopereux . . . this
old surfer's in sea heaven these days. Come on in. Here's
Ling's private porch where she sips her coffee, monitors

the surf reports on the radio there, and tries to track my ass from dawn to midnight. And now, slide that cheap-shit door, right . . . check out your contemporary motel decor."

They stood in a large, window-breezy space that included, in a paroxysm of efficiency, the living-dining room and kitchen functions. The linoleum floor was islanded with straw mats and a rationing of flimsy furniture, including tall lamps and a double-knit couch. A hallway led to three bedrooms, two baths, as Jack explained from the kitchen area where he cracked Devereux a can of beer and concocted himself another rum and Coke.

The men toasted each other, their faces firelit by the westering sun, which now centered itself in the square cre-ated by the sliding glass door and the porch screen beyond; the flaming canvas of the Sound had gone still as an inland lake. Devereux, his bearings now intact, watched the re-fracted sunspray in Jack's glasses and thought, not for the first time, that the younger man was like some extraordinary beast who couldn't possibly have been born, as claimed, in a suburb of Baltimore; more likely Vilna had sprung full-grown from the plains of eastern Europe—a fanatic Byelo-russian, say, exhorting his countrymen to slay the Bolshe-viks, one of those men who never refer to a *mother* . . . could not possibly have one.

". . . what dark things have you seen in your travels?" Jack was saying.

Devereux drained half the beer down his throat. "Beaches," he said.

"Beaches? . . . Beaches!"

On Plum Island, Laura stamped her feet in the spume and thought of Nemo's ink-stained corduroys, the same that now drooped from his hips, pants unwashed these past seven days.

Devereux said, "Yours is the last. Then home. To what, I don't know."

Jack's glasses flashed orange. "I'll show you beach," he

said, gesturing at the cook pot on the floor beside a portable hibachi and a cooler like a miniature playhouse. "You eat succ-ulent blue crab on any of those beaches?"

In the master bedroom Ling applied the last of the eyeliner and heard the word "succ-ulent" rise from the murmur of their conversation like an eroticism—Jackie playing a mean sybarite to Devereux's laid-back austerity. Men were dorks, blowhards, testicular gunslingers. She smiled at the notion. But then, they were so sweet if you brought in the morning coffee and served up a blow-job without having to be asked. But she'd served him *nada* these two weeks past. She tossed the empty tube in the trash, dropped her robe, and walked in her ample flesh to the bed where underwear, blouse, and wheat-colored slacks awaited her like neatly arranged tools. Devereux Hoopes. Curious man. Would-be dork? All she knew was that he kept his sexuality suspended behind a reef of stern charm, but it *had* to be there.

"Ling! Get your butt in gear, we're going to the beach."

Gurrr. She slowly buttoned the white linen of the blouse over her stomach and breasts; her nipples puckered in response to the kiss of the material. Which dork would notice? She shook the tight curls of her hair into an ideal of disorder and walked out of the room determined to be determined, a woman who feared only rats, scorpions, and the eyes of her lover.

Beach Report. A hundred yards off the pavement of Route 12, headed southeast on a furrowed track snaking through opalescent sand, the station wagon (Ling's) began to slip and wallow. Jack cursed, forced the vehicle into four-wheel, and they went on over the blank, rounding terrain; he slewed them left and left again until the wheels gained the firmer sand of the beach itself, and now they sped east, pursued by wind and grit. The surf paid the invading car no mind—it swelled, crested, curled, the sea's effort to provide millions of long, free rides for those humans who might wish this method of slipping over the vicious undertow of the last hundred yards to the visible sand edge of the American continent. Above the still-azure sea, above the grand emptiness of the beach with its single blue speeding automobile, sky-filling clouds played their fateful games with shadow and light, even now sucking evaporate from the Atlantic below.

An instinct for how long it would take to get *off* the beach told Jack the proper cook spot. While Ling and Devereux took a turn at the water's edge where the blowing sand was less troublesome, Jack made his fire on the leeward side of the station wagon after sealing off the windward space between sand and rocker panels with a fencing of folded beach furniture. Once the charcoal caught, he placed the covered cook pot—now half full of fresh water—on top of the grill. The crabs themselves were bundled in newspaper soaked with salt water in the back of the car. Then he freshened his drink from a Thermos, drank it down, and reached for the bungee cords that held the surfboards to the roof carrier. He freed the smaller one, the yellow fiberglass, and within seconds had sprinted past Devereux and Ling and was paddling into the surf's steady, roaring come-on.

Ling saw him running from the car like a breech-clouted warrior, bearing the narrow sea-shield that would make him invulnerable to anything the deep could throw up. Before he made his initial plunge, their eyes met just long enough for his—blind, unlensed glitter-holes—to hurl the coded message she believed she already knew: "Put the crabs to boil. . . . Stop flirting with the old fuck. . . . I don't need you. . . . The ocean! . . . I don't even need to SEE the mother to hump it, Ling!"

She knew her man.

She walked with Devereux to the lee of the car where he squatted to the cooler for another beer, his face slightly burnished by the alcohol already consumed, as well as from the sun of his recent travels. "How's Tessa?" she said, close to his ear for the sake of the noise of the water and the gusting winds—sandblasting the paint off her car layer by layer, sand in her clean hair.

Devereux turned his head in minor alarm. "Jessica? You know Jessica?"

"Tessa, Teresa! Your honey."

He looked away, shrugged, swigged the beer. "I really don't know. She didn't appreciate not being on this trip. Or at least she doesn't favor being alone." His face hardened. "I do . . . sometimes."

Beside them, in the darkness of the cook pot, the fresh water began to roil.

"Well then," she said, realizing that out of embarrassment or guilt or some male notion of discretion, he would say no more, "how's Barry Kessler? I read about him in some magazine."

That set him off. They shimmied their butts in the fine sand, their backs against the car, and Devereux told a story or two: the farmhouse, Mr. Ya, what he knew of Carl and Natalie, the water-queered alarm, the blood sugar of the saint—all of this rendered to her in a voice transported from its usual measured authority to the glib edge of excitement and humor. Did money and success do this? she wondered. Or was he using the glitter of travel to cover some mundane shit at home? No matter. Ling poured a measure of rum and Coke into the Thermos top and offered a toast to Carl—whom she loved from childhood days, before divorce, before his eye might be caught and held by the Natalies of this world. When the top of the cook pot began to teeter and froth, she sent Devereux for the newspaper wad of crabs and had him dump the whole mess of bluish pincers and dark green bodies into the boiling water, a task he performed with an energy she felt she had kindled.

On the glassy slopes of the surf, Jack Vilna rode and fell, rode and fell, but neither Devereux nor Ling glanced in his direction. Blind Jack knew it.

*　　*　　*

At the stilt cottage on the Sound the three of them watched the sun plummet into the East Dismal Swamp. They had not remained at the beach long enough to devour the crabs because Jack had come from the water to declare the wind a villain he would not allow to spoil his supper by lacing it with flung sand grit. Now, at table in front of the sliding glass door, they went at the crabs like intent laborers at slippery piecework. The movements of the two men were booze deliberate, and each time Devereux set upon a fresh crab, Jack had to show him the technique of zippering open the belly shell to gain access to the succulence beneath. Jack did this with a patience Ling found remarkable. Had it been she so stupidly forgetful, so slow to learn, he would have left her to her own devices. Men in their stuporous care for one another.

As twilight quickened its purple way to night, she sucked one claw after another and did not notice that drops of freed brine dotted the white of the shirt material risen over her breasts. Her decision to put a kink in the feast came when Jack suggested that tomorrow they should take the ferry to Ocracoke Island and—

"Jackie," she said, then allowed her dark pink tongue to work the crab juice before she went on blithely, "Bob Wiggins is coming tomorrow." Pause while the information sank through the depths of Aquaman's rummy brain. "And he's bringing—"

Devereux crumpled his beer can, an act of apparent unconsciousness. (Truth: He was stagger drunk and could only hold on to his current world by sheer concentration on the act of eating.)

"Alice," Jack muttered, using Ling's given name for the first time in months and simultaneously breaking a claw with his teeth. The hair on his freshly showered chest seemed to hackle where it showed in the V of his shirt

"—his new wife . . . Lily."

The lensed eyes pinned her, the pupils like two black voids. "I suppose," he said slowly, "you've known this for a while, bread-brain."

Devereux's head lolled into a semblance of alertness—domestic terrorism in the purpling air. Ling looked at him steadily as she spoke to Jack: "Since the mail came."

"What kind of hair is up your ass, Miz Mullins?"

Ouch. She would not cry. Devereux's eyes rolled toward her in sympathy. She wanted to touch his cheek where it emerged from his beard. Too many beard masks in her present life. "You *told* Bob to come," she said to Jack.

"But later, later," he barked. "I want Hoopereux to myself. You fucking stay away from him."

She shivered, but inwardly felt a small pop of victory.

Devereux squinted against a bright light that was not there before he moved his head to face Jack.

"Go easy, Jack," he said thickly.

"Going easy is for shit."

Jack drained his cup, stood up, and went to the kitchen counter where he poured rum into the cup as if he were preparing himself a glass of fresh, life-giving water, which he drank down in one long draught, his shaggy head a mass of intimidation—for her—there in the darkest corner of the room. "Devereux," he said, wiping his mouth on the back of his hand.

Devereux raised his trembling hands in the air as if to ward off what would come next. "Jack," he said finally; then the hands collapsed to the table like stunned birds.

A plague on both of you, she thought. Dork-drunk, crab-stupid, but . . .

Jack lurched against the door of the refrigerator. "Surfers *surf*," he said. "Reporters re-*port* . . . lightning *lights*." He was coming toward Devereux and Ling like a—God help her—frenzied ape. He stood over them, his forehead glistening with sweat. "Bitches *bitch!*"

"Jackie, cut it out," she wailed, cursing the tears already diluting her eyeliner.

72

Click: the famous smile came at them like an overloaded flashcube. "Sure, Ling," he said calmly, "I'm just horny is all. Come on, Hoopes, let's go for a *spin*." He took out his pack of cigarettes from the shirt pocket.

Again, Devereux's eyes swiveled slowly to hers, held steady for a moment, then drifted up to Jack's now boy-eager face—the burning cigarette held in his teeth at a jaunty angle that maddened her more than anything he could possibly say.

"Go ahead, bug-face," she said, resisting the need to wipe her eyes.

"I intend to. Hoopes?"

"I'm sorry, Ja—" Devereux slurred, then seemed to discover some lost power within himself, "I'm too damn tired, I'm too damn drunk. I'd be poor company, my friend."

Jack stared for several glitter-eyed beats, then began to move out. In making his way around the table, his thigh walloped a sharp corner, and—while he swore—a paper plate of crab debris fell into Devereux's lap; but Jack did not see this—he was already limping into the blackness beyond the sliding glass door, and no doubt on his way to wrecking her car, or driving it into the sea.

Before the engine even caught below, she was out of her seat and cautiously helping Devereux tidy his lap, an activity that fortunately amused them both. The ink stain over his pants pocket now had several lighter companion stains that she knew would respond only to some strong cleaning product. When she offered to set the trousers to soak for the night, he said he would have himself a shower and then bring them in to her.

"You're stained yourself," he said, pointing up from his chair to her breasts.

She peered down and brushed vaguely at the small circles of transparency flecked over the white. "So I am." Their laughter cut off almost as soon as it began. She told him to use the shower between the two guest rooms, that his room would be the one across from hers. Hers. She felt like a most *temporary* person.

After Devereux wandered off to his shower, she cleaned the table, cleaned the floor around his chair, and slung all the leavings into a garbage bag, which she sealed tightly. After filling a bucket with hot water and cleanser, she removed her blouse and tumped it down into the liquid. It surprised her that her anger had flown with Jack into the night; and it surprised her even more that she then walked bare-breasted along the hallway, both welcoming and dreading any accidental meeting that might take place.

None did. She went into her own bathroom and removed her slacks and underwear, then stepped into the shower—its tub as always aswirl with dark strands of sand—and did her rough best to scrub the grit out of her scalp and hair. Done, she walked into the bedroom with a towel wrapped around her head and covered herself with the robe that waited for her on the bed. The door to the hallway stood ajar, and she left it that way while she plumped the pillows—tossing Jack's as far away from her side as it could get—then climbed under the covers.

Beside the bed light lay a book, a novel, a stay against these all-too-common sorts of nights. She looked at its arty cover and pulled the sheets and yellow coverlet over her chest. Devereux passed along the hallway from the bathroom to his own room without a glance at her, a towel wrapped loosely around his waist. His flesh, the flesh of his torso, was the color—she smiled—of sweet crabmeat.

Outside, the Sound lapped the breakwater, and the knowledge of how utterly alone they were on this inner edge of the Cape came to her like a sudden blush. Oh Jackie . . . love of my life.

Devereux walked back to the bathroom wearing some sort of blue robe; then he stood in her doorway clutching his stained trousers to his chest. She told him about the bucket of cleanser. Except for a puffiness around the nose and a reddened sheen in the eyeballs he looked sober.

"Who's Bob?" he asked.

She had to think. "I dunno." Dumb. "He's an apprentice printer." Devereux waited, sniffing the air for more. "He's been married before. Now it's this Lily. I—we've never met her."

"I see."

"Bob's an aggressive, well-built . . . boy. A funny contradiction, but he's okay, pretty okay."

Devereux leaned against the doorjamb, squinting again against an absent light. "Are you guys, you and Jack, are you—?"

Her heart filled with a weirdly peaceful terror. "I don't know, Devereux." She sobbed. "Sometimes he's such a fucking cowboy."

He was leaning over her, whispering something. She could smell the unsoured maltiness of the beer. What? "He's one cowboy who always comes home." He kissed her, kissed one corner of her gone-dry mouth, and he went away like an insufficient consolation. But consolation enough to ease her into sleep within minutes of his going.

So early-evening sleep reigned in the stilt house. Dreams skirred here and there, some to be remembered tomorrow. In Ocean Grove's Wesley Inn, Miriam Shore slept alone and soundly on her foam mattress, while farther north, in Sagaponack, Carl washed his last pasta-gummed pot and turned his mind's eye to the upstairs sauna. Surrounded by Wellfleet's guaranteed peacefulness, Kit McGuffy composed the most crucial letter of his and Ellen's life together. Bless marriage. To the northwest of the Cape, Jessica sat at her desk and drew, from her perfect memory, Devereux's hands —back-curving thumbs and all. And, fourteen hundred miles to the south, Tessa Dixon pensively hefted a pocket spray canister of CN gas, then replaced it on the wooden rack in the bathroom where Devereux had left it. In a motel on the south edge of Nags Head, Cape Hatteras, Bob Wiggins said to Lily Wiggins, "I do not understand you"; and on the windward side of the Outer Banks, Jack Vilna spun the tires of the four-wheel deeper and deeper into a sand slough of his own making.

Ling woke at six to the smell of grease, sweat, and metabolized alcohol. Jack lay under the sheet on the far side of the bed like an ungroomed corpse. The hands cupped over his chest were black with oil grime; one thumb was bloody. He seemed not to breathe. Terrific: a filthy, dead drunk on her clean sheets. But then he broke the hopeful illusion by farting. Breath held, towel still wrapped around her hair, she rose from the bed and went to the closet where she traded her rumpled robe for a white shift. She got rid of the damp towel by dropping it on Jack's face and left the room, closing the door behind her.

Through the open door to Devereux's room she saw the tossing ground of his bed, a single foot thrusting beyond the loosened sheet. His snores came to her in arrhythmic sputters and drew her into the room where she might see the slack-jawed fellow in all his hungover dignity. But she retreated when she discovered the tenting of the sheet over his groin. Damn, they're either half-dead or boner-dumb.

To be alone in her airy shift in the clear light of morning. That's all. She prepared the dark-roast coffee and carried the steaming mug to the porch. The Sound was a tan slab, interrupted only by an angular fishing boat that pushed across its surface with a functional purpose she could admire. She sat down on the chaise and tuned the radio to a male, North Carolina voice that offered up a surf report that would make Jack goggle should she choose to tell him the day promised extraordinary long rollers, number nine on a scale of ten. Later on would come clouds, stiff winds, perhaps a thunderstorm to drive the surf to three-foot waves. She wished that a marvelously violent thunderstorm would knock Jack upside the head and make his cowboyism a matter of amnesia. Did she want a docile lad with doe eyes and hands soft as butter? No. Just a ying-yang, passionate symmetry is all. And, of course, she had had such symmetry much more often than her memory currently permitted. She blew across the surface of her coffee and wondered what had caused the bloody thumb.

"... tropical storm Alvin is heating up down Miami way ..." When the radio went to country, she switched it off and thought of painting her nails a color instead of the transparent polish that now glossed them. As she held her fingers up for inspection, she heard a distinct scratching from behind her, from the wall next to the sliding glass door. The sound of nails—or talons—pulled across the papered surface of Sheetrock. Awful. Gooseflesh covered her entire body beneath the shift, and she gazed in horror at her mind's picture of a large, silvery rat caught between the pine siding of the cottage and the interior Sheetrock. Get up. Bang the wall. Scare the thing into flight. She did so. She banged her palm hard against the wood again and again, but the scratching continued without pause.

"Devereux!" she screamed, backing away from the wall and stumbling against the raised back of the chaise. "Devereux!" Foolish to call on either corpse; equally foolish to be bawling for help like a woman in a cartoon. She closed her eyes and put her hands over her ears, but the scratching could not be shut out . . . nor could Jack's words from the doorway.

"What's with the towel on my face?" he demanded. "Are you trying to *kill* me now?"

She remained blinded. "Jackie, there's a rat in the wall."

He mimicked her falsetto: "Jackie, there's a rat in the wall . . . but I want *Devereux* to come help me."

She opened her eyes, saw the naked, hairy grossness of him, and screamed. He stepped back inside with the force of her sound, his penis withdrawing into its halo of peppery hair as if he'd been blasted with a stream of ice-cold air.

"Ling," he said. "Come here." The fucker was smiling.

"Why?! Just please make it go away."

"I will if you'll come in here." The scratching became more desperate.

She tiptoed toward his wretched amusement, her hands fisted beneath her breasts. He was looking to his right, into a corner of the room, his own stained hands on his hips as if he'd solved a simple crime. She peeked around the edge of the door and saw on the floor attacking the baseboard a large blue crab, its stalked eyes fierce with entrapment. Her fear became an orderly disbelief.

"How—"

"I dunno," Jack said, advancing on the scrabbling creature. "Maybe he fought his way out of the bunch before we went to the beach. It sure as hell didn't walk up the stairs."

He bent over and expertly caught the crab by the butt end, holding the waving pincers aloft and away from his unprotected body with his bloodied hand. Then he turned on her and thrust the weapon within inches of her nose.

Heh-heh-heh.

The laugh was far worse than being nipped.

But she didn't flinch.

At noon Devereux Hoopes found himself witness to the arrival of the Wiggins couple. Twelve hours of sleep had made of him a more sober individual, but against all normal habit his luncheon consisted of a can of beer and some strips of smoked flounder Ling had given him from the refrigerator after she hung out his pants and her blouse, and before she left on a shopping expedition to Buxton. She had told him that Jack slept on in the oil and blood of his night's adventure on the beach where he had been mired in the sand until four A.M.—finally jacked out with driftwood and manic will, the thumb smashed by a wild jack handle. And now he continued to sleep while Devereux consumed the fish and alcohol in his own room where he had found a magazine article by Vilna on the dangers of rape and mayhem for American women living alone in macho Third World countries—a solid piece of reporting, written with passionate elegance by the same man whose kitchen credo could be reduced to "going easy is for shit."

At the two hard car-door slams Devereux lifted himself off the bed and went to the window that looked out on the grass below. In the brassy heat beside his own sedan sat a burgundy Chevy Impala, early seventies vintage. A small, towheaded woman wearing dark pants and a jeans jacket stood uncertainly between the cars, talking to someone out of Devereux's sight, surely the notorious Bob.

"But this car is from Alabama," she called in the vague tones of a shy adolescent. "Are you sure—"

"Lily, only Vilna would live in a shack on stilts in the middle of nothing." The male voice was plump with patience, the only edge a nasal, urban burr.

"You go up," she said, beginning to walk in a curiously stiff manner, her head held quite still, as if something in it might shatter. "I'm checking out the water."

"Do that."

Devereux debated closing the door and adopting sleep as a ruse to fend off these new beings, but in the end manners took hold, and he went along to the living room and into the life of Bob Wiggins.

A wiry man in his late twenties with the surly Middle-Eastern looks of a Libyan despot. Wiggins? Perhaps black Irish, or perhaps his mother was an Egyptian movie star. They exchanged grips, a few pleasantries, information about bathroom and bedroom assignments. For some reason, Bob, like his consort, wore a jacket—this one of burnished auburn leather—a pair of black corduroys, and (Jesus) chrome-colored cowboy boots with riding heels.

"So, you're Hoopes," said Bob as he stalked about the room, apparently checking it for bugs. Devereux acknowledged his identity a second time. "Vilna talks about you," the other man said. "Calls you one of the great accommodators of women in the Western world."

"Sure," Devereux said evenly, though his nostrils whitened in anger at Jack's loose tongue.

Bob raised his thumb and winked. "Just kidding. Where is everybody?"

Devereux explained the shopping trip and the sleeping Vilna. As soon as he had done so, Bob's arrogance leaked away, and now he looked nothing short of lost. For the first time, Devereux felt himself in the presence of a truly *young* man.

"Aren't you hot?" Devereux asked.

Bob fingered the lapels of his jacket. "I just—I wanted Jack to see this, Lily bought it in Mexico, Lily's my wife." He began to shuck the leather. "You're right . . . it's hot as hell." The T-shirt revealed the corded veins and knotty muscles of someone intimate with physical labor. He slung the jacket onto the couch and moved for the porch. "I have to find Lily," he said. "She spaces out."

Then he was gone, leaving Devereux free to amble out to the porch and observe Bob humping over the grass in his absurd boots, bound for the new wife, who stood on the dock like a lonely waif fascinated by the stillness of the Sound.

The tableau on the dock, as Devereux viewed it, seemed to be an exercise in which repose (Lily's) refused to acknowledge insistent animation (Bob's). His arm shot skyward, pointed this way and that, encircled her head, implored the four directions . . . but Lily looked only toward the East Dismal Swamp, as if Bob were no more than a gnat in her airspace. But the gnat possessed a tactic of last resort; with one hand square against her jacketed back he tumbled Lily into the Sound.

No scream or curse crossed the space between the dock and the cottage. Bob stood on the far edge of the dock; his turn for repose had arrived. Assuming the water's shallowness, the girl's safety, goodwill, nothing more harmful than wet clothing and pure surprise, Devereux retreated from this domestic dunking to his room, where he shut the door and resumed Vilna's tale of atrocities.

In Buxton, Ling Mullins finished up her shopping at a fish shack called Stumpy's. Once the counterman—Stumpy? she didn't know—tired of practicing his X-ray vision on her shift, he turned neighborly. "You in Frisco in one of Ravenel's cottages, ain't you?" She nodded, shifted the squishy brown bag of fish so that it covered her breasts, and smiled at his revealed gums. "Looks like we gonna get it tonight," he said.

"Really."

"Y'all button up good," he said, linking his scarred hands on top of the display cooler. "Get some candles in case the electrics go out."

"We're ready as we can be," she said, then thanked him.

Outside, even her sunglasses could not foil the glare. She looked up to the towering clouds and wondered how nature could be so frivolous as to display such lovely sky monuments one moment and then turn them black and savage the next. Still, blistering lightning would be a wonder to observe from the safety of her porch. She climbed into the station wagon and drove home.

There, on her chaise, she found a sullen, wet-headed girl in running shorts and a strappy T-shirt. She had the face of a cute but disturbed rabbit, the hips and thighs of an athletic thirteen-year-old boy, and the large, high breasts of a dirty joke. The gaze she offered Ling conveyed all the liveliness of the grocery sacks Ling held in her arms. Still, she gave the girl a full, hostess smile.

"Lily . . . welcome."

"My husband violated my person."

"What?"

"Are you *Ling?*"

"Of course. What's Bob done? You look fine to me." The groceries were too burdensome. "Come with me," she said to pretty, foolish Lily.

Behind Ling, the breathy voice asked, "Why would any-body be called Ling?"

Ling allowed the sacks to bash down on the counter. She turned and found Lily's face so close to her own she almost reared back into the refrigerator. "Because in California, when Jack Vilna first met me, he in all of his wisdom thought I was nothing more than some hippie ding-a-ling. Dig it? I'm really just old pudgy Alice."

The girl dug nothing—remained immobile. "Men are without perception. It's a genetic defect."

"You haven't met the men in this house, honey." Lily's dazed shrug infuriated Ling. "What did Bob do? Did he snatch at your tits on your honeymoon or something?"

That worked: her downy skin blushed crimson. "In-tercourse is very painful for me," she said, as if by sad rote.

Resisting a terrible impulse to say "good," Ling placed a companionable hand on Lily's shoulder and turned her gent-ly out of the kitchen space.

Beach Report. On an area of beach north of Buxton, the section of the seashore facing east to Bermuda and beyond, a scrubbed and bandaged Jack Vilna had made an afternoon's camp for the five residents of stilt cottage. The wind, as usual, sandblasted Ling's car, but by his calculations they could cook in the partial shelter of the easy dunes in front of the parked car, and as for the rest of it . . . let them all fend for themselves in making the stinging journey from the car to the incredible surf spread before them like the orderly surgings of a great battle. Now, he sat smoking in the front passenger seat, his feet hanging out of the open door. In the seat behind, Devereux suckled his beer. Borne north a ways by the undertow or the power of walking were Bob (body-surfing), Ling (shelling), and Lily (sulking).

"Why you so mean?" Devereux was saying to Jack.

"I'm not mean, Hoopereux, I'm free. Whose side are you on?"

"Nobody's. She's in pain."

"Everybody should be in pain," said Jack. "It's human. You yourself look like you might be tight with the subject. How's things at home?"

"You're a hard boy." Devereux breathed in the oven heat of the car.

"That damn Bob," Jack said after a while. "See what he did with one of my surfboards? Fucker laid it flat on the sand, wax gone all soft with the heat. Now it'll take me two hours' scraping to get it right again."

Gulls were suspended in the air above the car like war kites. Jack took his drink cup from the dash and slid a mouthful of ice into his mouth. Crushed it. "I like that Lily," he said.

Devereux whacked his friend on the head with a limp forefinger. "You like the way she stares at your crotch."

Heh-heh-heh.

And so the day continued its course.

When Jack seized his one good surfboard from the roof of the car and carried it balanced on his head to the water, Devereux walked north in his old blue shorts, exposed flesh covered with a number six sunscreen. He pushed on over the abrasive, mounding sand until he encountered Lily Wiggins. She stood like a sentinel bird where dry sand met wet, and he was struck by the way her pink and green spandex tank suit accentuated a boy's graceful body unfairly dealt a pair of breasts so out of proportion to the rest of her. After they exchanged barren howdy's, he inquired as to the where-abouts of young Bob. Lily stared over one of Devereux's shoulders and smirked, an expression distasteful enough to send him on his way toward the distant stick figure he knew to be Ling.

But still, Bob damn well ought to be in sight. At one point Devereux veered into the dregs of the surf, stopped, and shaded his eyes for a look-see. To his right, Jack was a hundred yards out and beginning his first long, free ride. To his left, nothing marred the white froth. Then, in front of him, he spotted a pair of hands made into a slicing prow, and the top of a human head—Bob on the final leg of his run to the beach. Relieved, Devereux walked on—the satisfied lifeguard.

Ling seemed to be moving away from him at a speed designed to keep them forever separated by all this alabaster and blue emptiness. But eventually—aided by a spate of off-center jogging on the wet slope above the surf—he came within conversing distance. She wore an aqua bikini, and when she went to poke among the shells her legs reminded him of Jessica, of the translucent flesh of Plum Island. Ling stood up straight and smiled at him beneath the mask of her dark glasses.

"Shelling's no good," she said, displaying empty hands. She looked at the easterly sky and pointed to a darkening over the horizon. "But there's going to be a dilly of a storm."

Devereux squinted in that direction. "My first," he said. "There's been entirely too much good weather."

She moved closer to him. "I appreciate what you did last night. A lot of men would have made a mercy pass."

He reached out and touched the oiled skin of her upper arm. "I don't know how to make passes, kiddo." What a stupid thing to say. Let's tell the truth. "I wanted to."

In her surprise she lifted the glasses away from her eyes and offered him their full power. "And now?" she said, out of breath. He dropped his hand away from her arm, put both hands safely away in the pockets of his shorts, pushing down into the pockets and stretching so that the shorts dipped low on his hips. She poked a forefinger into the center of his chest and pushed hard until he stumbled backward. "No games, Devereux," she said with a fierceness he had never before seen. "No dorky games. Just tell me your feelings."

"I dreamed," he said. "I dreamed we were on an empty ferry heading for the mainland . . . making love on the deck."

"Dreams!" She replaced her glasses and laughed into the

84

teeth of the wind. "Here's my dream, chum. I wake up and go out to the porch. Your friend Barry Kessler is lying on my chaise. I say, 'Why are you here?' 'I really don't know,' he says, and then crawls off the chaise and over to the door . . . in a crablike manner—arms bent at the elbows and his hands in the air like pincers." She snapped the waistband of her bikini. "What's the better dream, Devereux? Which is more telling? Where is the truth in these dreams?"

"Would you go with me?"

She laughed again, wrapped an arm around his waist, and urged him into a return walk. "I really don't know. I doubt it. But you wait and see what happens when the sky turns pitch-black and megabolts of lightning begin to zigzag over our heads. You watch, mister watchman."

When the sky did go black, all ambiguity went by the boards. Jack Vilna, man of water, had no use for and a great fear of electric discharges from the heavens. Presiding over their late afternoon supper of charcoaled fish and various alcohols, he transformed himself into a Bligh of the Outer Banks; they were gone from their campsite by the time the third visible bolt had connected the blackened cumulonimbus with the surging Atlantic below.

Storm Watch. The domestic electricity went out within an hour of their return to stilt cottage. By then, the invisible Sound was thoroughly possessed by Beaufort force-eight winds, and below the masking of rain and pitch darkness, the water level rose steadily until first the dock was submerged, the seawall breached, and soon enough the wind succeeded in rushing the water in chaotic ridges toward the cottage itself.

Inside, the revelers moved to and fro in the light from candles stuck onto saucers and strewn around the table. On Jack's orders, each person wore either rubber-soled running shoes or the rubber thongs he called "slaps." All of them had put on jackets or sweatshirts over their beach gear. The points of candlelight kept a St. Vitus rhythm with the trembling of the support stilts and thus the table on which the candles stood. Most of the windows had been closed, as had the sliding glass door through which each in turn peered for evidence of the advancing wall of water that would snatch them into oblivion. But all that actually could be seen was the occasional and quite beautiful radiance—a moment of purple-blue luminosity following each crump of thunder.

His drink clutched between his thighs, Jack occupied a rocking chair placed square in front of the door. Beside him, her straight chair turned toward the rocker as if for succor, sat Lily. Bob paced the room behind them, from time to time shooting the beam of his flashlight out one window or another in a hopeless effort to discover if his Impala had been overcome by the rising waters. Ling made trips from the kitchen to the table carrying plates of cold charbroiled fish, bottles of pepper sauce, cans of beer for Bob or for Devereux, who sprawled himself across the couch for a viewing of the show whose ending nobody could predict.

The decibel level of the wind and rain seemed to double every fifteen minutes, as did the violence of the cottage's shimmy . . . until a tall lamp near Devereux's head teetered and then fell across his chest. Without comment he laid it on the floor, where it rolled back and forth like a prone pendulum. Meanwhile, Jack and Lily whispered in the front row, Bob paced, and Ling fussed with kitchen matters. During one triple burst of lightning that lasted a crackly twenty seconds, Jack called out in nervous glee, "See there, three-foot waves. Oh mother!"

Bob bounded to the door and stood with his hands pressed against the light until blackness returned. Behind him, Lily's implacable gaze penetrated his back as if he were not there.

"Be cool, Bob," Jack said. "The cottage has been through hurricanes you wouldn't believe, and this isn't one of them."

"And how do you know that, Jackie?" Ling said.

"He knows," Lily decided.

86

Bob turned from the door and stared at her, his face twitching on the outer edge of control. "You're a miserable fuck, Lily."

Devereux sat up. "Hey—"

"It's all right," Lily said placidly. "Bob's a victim of passive aggressiveness."

"Oh come on, *girl,*" Ling said with pure exasperation.

Crump.

A plate of charred fish smeared with ocher pepper sauce slid off the table and landed upside down beside Jack's rocking chair.

The rain crashed against the siding of the cottage as if fired by cannon at random intervals.

Bob seemed to disappear within his leather jacket. "I have work to do!" he shouted.

Everyone stared. Bob's tears gleamed like BB shot in the candlelight.

"Well, Bob," Jack said. "I suppose you do."

Bob began to move in the direction of the hallway but was intercepted by Ling.

Devereux watched her overwhelm the man with a wordless affection, and then the two of them abandoned the quaking, flickery room like beings oblivious to storm or the ill will of some of those left behind.

And Devereux? What of him? Although the storm would continue, even worsen, during the next several hours, although the water beneath the cottage would rise to the level of his sedan's creased bumpers, although he would remain physically present during part of Jack's bizarre courtship of Lily Wiggins, Devereux Hoopes himself had turned off the exterior storm in favor of an inward, needful fiction in which Alice Mullins existed as the very definition of a surveyor's perfect goal, should he be able to move the boulder of his true self but two inches to the west, where—on his new map—the ferry to the mainland waited, its idling engines a burble of expectation.

*   *   *

Ominous stillness awoke Devereux at five o'clock on Saturday. A glance at the window told him the storm had
smashed its way inland, leaving behind a void that seemed
encased in cotton batting. Through his open door came a
faint but nonetheless electric glow of light, and with it, he
realized, the sound of muted weeping. In an instant he
clambered from the bed and into his robe, barely knotting its
sash by the time he reached Ling's open doorway. Bathed in
lamplight, propped up with pillows as if she might be reading late, she looked, in the sway of her tears, both miserable
and relieved. The two of them said "Hi" at the same time, a
bit of ridiculousness that brought mutual smiles.

"Where is he?" said Devereux.

"On the beach with Lily. Where else?"

"Christ. What about Bob?"

"Walking."

"Walking!"

"He woke up an hour ago," she said, "and when he found
both of them gone . . . he said he was going for a walk."

"To find them?"

She smiled. "Not without a four-wheel drive. He just
needs to walk out his jealousy. Bob's fond of long nights of
the soul." Her breath rattled. "I don't know how Jackie got
my car out of here, but he *did*. The water's mostly gone. It's
just mud." She wiped away tears with the sleeve of her robe.
"Come here, Devereux, come sit on the floor beside me."

He did so, gladness balanced against the knowledge of his
mouth's funk. Miraculously, a Granny Smith apple sat on
the bedside table like a green promise of tartness. He asked if
she minded. She handed the apple to him as he sank to the
floor, and a single bite was sufficient to cleanse his palate of
the night. She refused the unbitten side he offered. But when
he put the thing to rest on the table, she took that hand and
placed it along with hers on top of her robe beneath her

breasts. Her heart beat like a creature intent on escaping from the cavity of her chest.

At the edge of Cape Hatteras itself, beneath the clear early-morning sky, Jack Vilna lifted Lily onto the blanket spread over the hood of Ling's station wagon. When he leaned into the V made by Lily's upraised legs, they were both of them in love with the universe's glorious present tense, and they faced each other's rising and falling with the careless grace of sleek animals. Miles away, in Frisco, Bob Wiggins shadowboxed with his loss as his booted feet took him farther and farther away from the company he had sought. And in stilt cottage, above the debris-littered foundation, above two stranded crab traps, Alice Mullins laundered her face of all grief, replacing it with a fond deliberateness that Devereux Hoopes would not soon forget. They kissed like the careful lovers they would never become.

Later on this day, the sun will rise to illuminate the flotsam-strewn beaches of the Outer Banks. People will eat, glower, accuse, sleep. Some will find the manners for a proper good-bye. Alice Mullins will take her own car north to the Hatteras lighthouse beach where she will find joy in the discovery of a fossilized sand dollar and a perfect starfish. The Surveyor, having driven north along the Cape, will finally head inland in pursuit of the storm and his home.

TUSCALOOSA

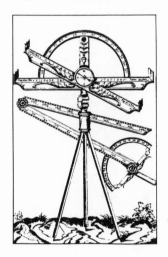

ANY INLANDERS of the southeast ignore the delights of water. That it rush from the tap after a brief descent from a looming water tower is the premium consideration; that it nurture the lives of bass and bream is a requirement of some; that it provide a transporting surface for coal is the concern of the Army Corps of Engineers, a few capitalists, and the hard-core river buffs whose habits include barge counting and the observation of lock masters. The river town of Tuscaloosa, Alabama, hard by the Black Warrior River, maintains a green neutral ground of boulevard and forest between itself and the moving waters. Some citizens will spend a lunch hour parked in the cleared area above the dock reserved for barge towboats—powerful coal-shovers with names like *Cahaba, Talledega, Elizabeth*—most of them white, all of them flying the corps' red flag with the white, hydro-building insignia. More adventurous types walk the trails along the banks, trails cut through kudzu and pine, which have been known to harbor chemically inspired villains, a murderer or two. Others might gather like penguins on the gray rocks below the fall of the dam at the William Bacon Oliver Lock, gather in sight of the great red signs that proclaim, DANGER STAY 800 FEET FROM DAM. A most rare phenomenon, upstream from the dam and lock, would be a swimmer, someone actually immersed in his city's portion of the Black Warrior. And yet it is known that a colleague and friend of Devereux Hoopes's (and an even older friend of Tessa Dixon's), one James Patrick Conover, made a daily spring and

93

summer pilgrimage to nearby Holt, where he would swim the wide river with the measured strokes of an inlander in his own spiritual element. J. P. Conover: freshwater acolyte, *married* man, father of contrary teenagers with absolutely no interest in water.

Another ritual of J.P.'s involved two cans of Coca-Cola (Classic) and a half-pint of bourbon. On Sundays, instead of churching or fishing or reading, he would drive his aging American sedan to Oliver Lock and park in the lot on the bluff above the lock works. He enjoyed the contrast between the functional, thirties architecture of the three-story concrete works and the manicured swale of the golf course that draped itself over the landscape on the other side of the road leading to the parking lot. For him, the contrast was between old-money country clubism and the government-money maintenance of a commerce helpful to the survival of his adopted state. *He* paid the lock master's salary willingly, but not one penny of his went for golf cart or pro. Fair enough for a family man who loved order, Chaucer, and the once-in-a-while ruinous sweetness of bourbon and Coca-Cola.

On this first Sunday in June he wheeled the sedan into the lot, parked, and sat with his boy's face turned toward the works, the dam, and the faint roar of water fallen over the spillway. On the opposite side of the river a bone white grain elevator poked up out of the trees like a blocky church spire designed by functionalists. From his vantage J.P. could not see the dark rocks off the opposite bank and downstream from the dam, but he well knew the trashers and the fishermen gathered there. On his side of the river were only the six pastel golfers, two lock workers, all of Tuscaloosa's structures, and himself—a slight, graying man with the swollen shoulder muscles of a swimmer lately taken to pumping iron in the university's fetid weight room. He crammed the flat bourbon bottle into the side pocket of his khakis and let himself out of the car. The Cokes—two scripted red cans that immediately beaded with moisture when introduced to the Alabama humidity—he purchased from a machine beside the lock's storage garage and fenced boat pool. Equipped, he strolled across the lot and along the grassy embankment overlooking the huge, empty lock, the high-windowed works, and the silt-brown river. He stopped when he found a spot free of fire ant mounds where he could sit cross-legged in the grass and—while his glasses flashed in the sunlight— measure out his potions.

Behind him, a police cruiser inspected the area on both sides of the road at the speed of a slow walk; its driver, Officer Buddy Kinsley, was now so used to seeing J.P. on this part of his Sunday morning beat that he ID'd him as he would any familiar citizen with regular habits, although you had to be wary of your college professor types, especially the ones from out of state, which he knew J.P. to be since his daughters went to County High with his own Jodell. He watched J.P. pour part of his cool drink into the grass, then reach himself the bottle of brown from his britches. Kinsley disapproved, especially on federal property, but what the hell. After he made his turnaround at the end of the road where the fairways were divvied by a little pond circled in pine trees, the officer mashed the accelerator. He had to pass by Ralph W. Green's to make sure the home of the black politician hadn't been blown away on the sabbath. As Kinsley left the lock area and turned right onto Thirty-fourth Avenue, he made eye contact with the sunglasses of the driver of a gray Japanese sedan, to whom Kinsley raised a forefinger, although he failed to recognize him as one of Ralph W. Green's neighbors. The driver looked as fatigued as someone just off the graveyard shift.

Devereux Hoopes, his mind a swirling of repetitive road thought, and not so much fatigued as stuck in driving mode —nineteen rain-borne hours from Hatteras to sun-blanched Tuscaloosa—motored into the lock compound in the air- conditioned embrace of his car and the John Lee Hooker blues . . . nothing more in mind than a glimpse of water in steady motion before he went to encounter the expected, even hoped- for emptiness of his house on Sixth Street.

*   *   *

"And so," J.P. was saying to Devereux on the knoll above the lock and river, "you're afraid of going home." Behind his glasses J.P.'s eyes were bright pennies.

Devereux grunted as he tried to rearrange his legs in the grass. The body had gone stiff on him in the midst of all this non-motion. "I've missed you, deacon," he said, scratching in the beard hairs of his neck. "You're smart enough not to travel."

A slug of Coke for J.P. He offered the can to Devereux, who regarded it with a bemused frown before he shook his head. "You and your river habits," he said. "I've had enough of that stuff. I'm too old."

J.P. drew the can back and leaned it against his groin. "What is yesterday?" he asked in his serious, rhetorical way. "Are you too old to go home and sleep? There's nothing to report from the river today."

Devereux waggled his head as if to shake water from an ear hole. "James Patrick," he said, "my head is so full sleep wouldn't be possible, and besides, Tessa may have set booby traps in the house. You should come over there with me just in case."

J. P. Conover considered the proposition from behind his eyeglasses. He knew Tessa Dixon might be competent in the area of setting traps, but his friend looked to be hiding behind a weary jocularity. "You have the squint of guilt on you, Hooper," he said in a kindly way.

Devereux blew air and leaned back on his hands with his face to the sun. "If you're talking about women on the road . . . not really. If you mean Tessa, you may be right. As soon as I headed inland, I began thinking she'd bolted. Why is that? Is it my fault? What claims do the two of us have on each other? Tell me, tell me the truth, my brother."

"Bolted?" said J.P. "I talked to her a week ago, right after you left. All she said was that she had the cops coming by at night to check the house."

96

Devereux turned his head to the other man and nodded. "She doesn't answer the phone, including when I called from Charlotte at four this morning. You think she's in protective custody, huh?"

"No, of course not, and don't rail at me."

"I'm not mad," Devereux said. "I'm a tired fuck whose girlfriend has apparently disappeared."

J.P. fortified himself with some of the contents of his warming can. "Maybe she left a note; maybe she's on a retreat; or"—here J.P. illuminated—"perhaps she didn't appreciate the death threats against your neighbor."

"Really?"

J.P. leaned forward. "He's running for office again; it always brings the bugs out of the woodwork."

Devereux sighed and let himself fall back on his elbows. Beyond the lock works, water flowed over the dam at a steady, boring rate. He wished for waves, for vast regularity, for the present tense attentions of travel. "She should have called me. Tessa," he grumped. "She had all the goddamn numbers."

"Not a woman who likes *shoulds*," J.P. observed, then raised two fingers of discovery. "I remember when she drove all one night to St. Augustine and lived for two days in her car at the beach. All due to 'a crinkle in the psyche,' as she called it. Then Adrian Brothers arrived to save her."

"I didn't know her then," Devereux said with sullen force.

"Do you know her now? Do you two actually connect?"

Devereux went completely supine, his prophet's nose pointing to the glare of the sky. "J.P., you're a self-righteous choirboy, and you really ought to wear black togs and a dog collar instead of those preppy rags."

J.P. gazed down upon Devereux with pained affection; the man should look to his own instead of flitting about the country. "You see," said J.P., waggling his Coke can, "drunkenness is very sepulture of man's wit and his discretion, but I am still a good fellow, and you are a fool who can nought be still . . . if you'll excuse the translation."

97

A long pause from Devereux. His scraggly beard may have hidden a multitude of responses, but finally he said, "If you're drunk, then I'm the father of triplets, and the river down there is flowing backward."

J.P. snorted. "Then solemn oaths should be sworn. First, that you will find Tessa Dixon and swear undying fealty. Second—"

Devereux lifted his torso from the grass, grabbed J.P.'s second can of Coke, shook it, and popped the tab in his friend's face, anointing him with a spray of sweetness that dappled his eyeglasses like a dark mist. J.P. did not budge. If anything, he became more still as Devereux ranted in his face: "Come off it, James Patrick, I'm not in the business of undying fucking fealty," he sputtered, "and I think you *family men* need to be shot out of your tacky ranch houses. Who's the fool here anyway?"

J.P. removed his eyeglasses, shook them daintily, and smiled. "Now that," he said, "is passionate urgency. You ought to practice it more. Emotion is so foreign to your sort." He stood up and put the glasses in a pants pocket, his face now naked, owlish, as finely formed as any youthful parson's. "Come on, Dee, we'll check out your home, we'll find some clues to Tessa's holy psyche."

Behind them, across the road, beyond the railroad tracks and pond, a pastel golfer called out, "Ah'm not holdin' this flag 'til church's out, Beidler; putt or git off the green."

Devereux Hoopes and J. P. Conover came at the house on Sixth Street from the rear; Devereux's single set of keys served only the backdoor of the one-story affair that was his home, Tessa's home. The two sedans parked nearby a drooping pear tree in a stubbly yard that gave onto other backyards and several equally seedy wooden homesteads, many of them occupied by the retired and the halt, although the most immediate neighbor was a well digger, whose family doted on white bread and the flesh it produced.

Directly opposite Devereux's backdoor sat a shotgun cottage with wrought-iron bars on the windows, the home of Mr. Horace Mum and his bedridden wife. Mr. Mum himself had the emphysema, but it did not prevent him from ceaseless yard and garden activity, as well as steadfast vigilance over all of the visible yards and houses. A diminished and bent man of seventy, he wore in all seasons a powder blue jumpsuit. He spoke gutturally, hoarsely, rationing his breath in a manner that made his words jumble together in puzzling clumps. Spit ran constantly from one corner of his mouth like tears, and he always carried a white handkerchief stuffed into one sleeve of his jumpsuit. Before Devereux had shut his car door, Mr. Mum was on his way over to account for himself and his domain, which included all the conjoined yard spaces. He called Devereux "Dan," always had, and he wouldn't be corrected. As Mr. Mum approached, his whole body in tremor, Devereux took note of the absence of Tessa's own Japanese sedan and the need to concentrate on translating Mr. Mum's husked syllables into sensible English. J.P. moved into the area to offer his own brand of gentle assistance.

"Hey, Dan, you up north?"

"Yessir, I saw my boy." Five years in the deep south and you fall right into the rhythms as soon as you reenter the territory; Devereux enjoyed it, although at the moment his vision was blurry and Mr. Mum's voice faraway.

The old man grinned and wiped his slickening chin. "That Carl!" he grunted. "How'at boy? He makin' it okay? He ain't with you that I can see, less he's shrunk up some and gone gray around the head."

J.P. acknowledged the jest by rubbing his palms over his flat stomach and smiling. Mr. Mum turned aside from them and spat into his tomato and dill garden patch.

Devereux said, "Carl is making it just fine. He's a houseboy, houseman, on Long Island in New York State."

Mr. Mum's head performed a turtlelike retraction toward

his frail collarbones. "No!" he said. "Does his momma know y'all raised up a houseboy?" He nickered.

Another uncorrectable notion held by Mr. Mum was that Tessa Dixon had given birth to Carl, an event which would have had to have occurred when she was twelve. J.P. had no knowledge of the mix-up.

"His mom knows everything," J.P. put in (he had known Carl's true mother Tracy since before she and Devereux divorced; J.P. thought her a virtuous and worthy pilgrim in this world). "She has knowing bones," he concluded for the benefit of Mr. Mum and Mr. Hoopes, both of whom now looked at J.P. as if he were an embarrassment to intelligence.

"Well," said Mr. Mum, "she has little bones, that's a fac'. . . . She's scared, that one."

Devereux's hearing improved. "Is that right?" Had he ignored more than he ever imagined? The impossible mystery of those right next to you!

J.P. looked puzzled. "Who? Tessa?"

"You said it, too," Devereux said to J.P. Then to Mr. Mum, "Are you talking about this stuff with Ralph Green?"

Now Mr. Mum leaned into an evil cough, and when he recovered, a new wheeze had added itself to his voice. "What happens out on Sixth Street don't signify back here, Dan—not the bidness of colored politicians—but that wife of yours, when she left, she told me you'd gone north, leavin' her a bitty tear-gas gun that wudn't stop a grown tomcat." The speech cost Mr. Mum plenty; tremors bore down on him. "Said she wudn't stay in your house, not a minute more. Drove outta here pale as a dog's bone."

Inside the locked house, Tessa Dixon's objects—her books, her journals, her Mexican glassware, her rolltop desk, her Georgia O'Keeffe prints, her dark clothing—stood mute, attractive only to the dust. In the kitchen at the back of the house was an oval table made of oak, its center leaf carved, like a printing block, in the shape of a stylized, Janus-headed bird, its beaks as bold as the table was bare of anything resembling a note, or a sign that might inform Devereux Hoopes of the whereabouts of baffling Tessa.

After saying "thanks" and "so long" to Mr. Mum, Devereux and J.P. trooped through the backdoor and stood facing each other across the table. When J.P. reached into his pants pocket and set the bottle of bourbon on the table, Devereux slumped into a chair and stared his way around the room.

"Aren't you going to check out the rest of the house?" asked J.P.

"I've had it," Devereux said, pinching at the sunglasses' dents on either side of the bridge of his nose. "There's no mystery here. She's just one gone dog bone."

"Ah, you're wrong, friend, there be mystery in every corner of God's world. A river of mystery." James Patrick Conover's final words on the subject. He departed, as always, happily, a man Devereux had depended on and would depend on for moral companionship of the best and truest sort.

The house was cellar cool. The kitchen opened onto a study and the living room beyond, the long space a wonder of polished wood floors and dappled light. In the study were most of Devereux's few possessions: an amplifier and tape deck now covered against thievery with a white scarf; four-foot speakers; a bookcase containing nine running feet of books, none of them recently published; and—facing into the living room and the oversize front window giving onto Sixth Street—a solid draftsman's tilting table, which Tessa kept waxed to the color of light honey. On its surface sat a vintage Selectric, garnet, covered with a swatch of patchwork quilt. The white walls displayed only a black-and-white print of Neil Armstrong in full moon-rig and a blown-up color shot of Devereux and Carl sitting beside a swimming pool in the golden, magical light of late afternoon in the Mexican Sierra Madre—Carl is studying the ground before him, Devereux is in profile, both are as serious as men in repose can be; between them is a bottle of Negra Modelo beer.

It should be noted that the one object in the room of any substance or worth did not belong to Devereux Hoopes—a 1911 Steinway upright that Tracy Hoopes (now Tracy Hannah) promised on an annual basis to remove, but she never seemed quite to produce the wherewithal to have the piano shipped from Tuscaloosa to Nova Scotia, or wherever she might be living that year. So Devereux considered the thing an eye pleaser, and did not mind that it caused Tessa to frown whenever she passed its unwaxed surfaces.

On Sixth Street, parked in the generous shade thrown by Devereux's pecan tree (his rented pecan tree, to be accurate), Officer Buddy Kinsley allowed his gaze to rotate to a visual fix on the home of Ralph W. Green. No Klaners or Aryan Nationists in sight. For sure, Green's house was the neighborhood's most spiffy, with its freshly sodded lawn, bright paint, and heavily curtained windows. In the driveway crouched a boxy purple Chrysler, one of two Kinsley knew resided at this home, the target of phoned-in threats from some dumb boys probably crazy from eating Twinkies since they was two. Kinsley yawned and checked the roadway from the railroad bridge behind him to the intersection with Thirty-second Avenue ahead of him. A black male came up from the shack blight along the railroad cut and blinked in the sun that flooded the sidewalk. Kinsley ignored the person of the wrong color for this particular situation. His shift would be over soon, and he could hit the Waysider for grits, biscuits, ham, redeye gravy, and potato skins.

Nothing would happen.

Inside, in Devereux's now-empty kitchen, the wall phone rang several times, but Devereux, enshrouded in the narrow shower, did not hear the rings (instigated by Carl in Sagaponack) from either kitchen or bedroom phones, did not in fact hear much of anything but the white roar of his own brain's exhaustion.

In the entire house not a single trap was laid.

*   *   *

"Pop!"

Carl's voice came to Devereux through a soup of dreams, and he momentarily confused his son's voice with the word "pain" murmured by Ling Mullins before she spread a mustardy balm over his entire, sunburned body. But then he knew himself to be naked in his own bed beneath a light thermal blanket, clutching at a phone, staring wide-eyed at the ceiling cracks, while Carl modulated his greeting to "Devereux, are you there?"

"I'm not sure."

"Well, wake up," Carl said, "it's four in the afternoon. I've been calling," said an older Carl, almost imperious in his tone.

"Yeah, what do you know good?"

A pause from Carl too long for glibness.

"I was wondering—" the younger, tentative Carl here— "Pop, I was wondering if you could pick me up in Atlanta?"

Devereux reached for pillows to stuff behind his head, full focus suddenly necessary. "Say it again," he said.

"Barry booked me on a flight from La Guardia to Atlanta. It leaves in two or three hours." Carl's voice caught a crab on the time part of this statement. The boy now seemed in misery, but on he went: "Barry's going to drive me to the airport . . . assuming you'll meet me at the other end. But I could—"

"Of course I will. What's happened?"

"Please don't get mad," Carl said.

"I'm not, I'm profoundly curious, old friend."

"I can tell you the story when I see you, but Barry says I'm 'terminated with affection.' "

"That sounds just like him," Devereux said. "It's Natalie, right?"

Carl made a rattling sound in his throat but said nothing.

"Okay, okay," Devereux went on. "Is Barry there?"

"No," Carl said, "he's running."

"Listen, Carl, I think we're in the same boat here."

"That can't be true, Pop, it can't be. I mean, I do Nat's laundry . . . or I did."

Devereux didn't quite understand, but he went on with it, "And I do Tessa's."

Some power found its way back into Carl's voice. "So? *She* irons your shirts and sews your tears. Besides, she's an adult, and Nat's a kid. Well, maybe not a kid exactly, but shit, *I'm* a kid. Kids shouldn't wait on other kids."

Now that sounded right.

"Granted. But I'm trying to tell you that Tessa is gone, split, flown. Take your pick."

"She left you?!"

"Not exactly," said Devereux, unsure of the truth of this. "I don't own her, and she wasn't exactly thrilled when I left here to pick you up from school, left here without her."

"She hates being alone."

"So do I, I just realized it."

"Me too." Carl's voice became urgent, "I'll help you look for her."

"How? She could be anywhere between Louisiana and South Carolina; she could be on the moon. Besides, I can't chase her all the fuck around."

"Why? It's undignified?" Carl said, right on the adult button. "Oldie pursues youthful sweetheart."

"Jesus Christ!" Devereux said. "Prep schools aren't fair to parenting, you know that?"

Carl actually snorted at him over the phone. "You sent me, Dee-Vo."

Devereux became an essentialist. "What time does the plane arrive in Atlanta? And have you talked to your mother?"

"No. I'm thinking about Tessa, Pop, I have a theory."

"Theory!" Devereux kicked off the blanket, and the sight of his own nakedness seemed to create the ghost of Tessa beside him in their bed—a sulky ghost with skin like Irish linen. He rolled away from her spirit and said into the phone, "Show me your theory."

"I mean," Carl's voice rose, "she's a fanatically private person, right?" Devereux made a noise of utter agreement. "Telephones give her the creeps. She doesn't use them. But she's a demon letter writer, she even writes *me*."

"I didn't know that. I now count two private persons."

"That's my point." Carl's breath sucked in. "She types her letters, and she uses your old typer."

"I guess," said Devereux.

"So try this. I learned it when I lost my history term paper I typed on a machine like yours. It's neat; you just get the film ribbon thing and read it. Everything is there, mistakes and everything. You have to get used to reading the two lines of letters, and there's no spaces; your eyeball just goes up and down. It works, I promise."

Devereux sat up and rested his feet on the side railing of the bed frame. The air bubbles in his knee joints crackled with the effort. "What an elegant way to invade your partner's privacy," he said.

"Well, ex-cuse me, Father, I thought you were hot to find her."

"No, no, I'll try it. You're assuming she would—"

"Yeah, I know she would."

"Would what?"

"Write Adrian Brothers. Go to him if she was . . . sad."

"Christ," said Devereux, pulling at his beard with enough force to hurt himself. "She writes to you about *him*?"

Carl let go with a most mature laugh for a boy who had been, minutes before, near tears. "The plane is a Delta, one twenty-six, and it gets in at eight twenty-two," he said. "That gives you some time."

"For what?" Certainly not even to unpack the damn car, or do some laundry.

"To read the film ribbon, Pop."

"Oh boy," Devereux groaned. He must regain parenthood, "I'm sorry you lost your job and your . . . friend."

"No, Natalie didn't lose herself," Carl said flatly. "Tessa did."

"We'll see. You call your mother and tell her what you're up to."

"Yes, sir. See you."

"For sure. Eight twenty-two tonight."

As soon as Devereux cradled the telephone, he got up and walked from the bedroom into his study, where he stood naked in front of the uncurtained windows and gazed down upon his typewriter.

Across the Black Warrior River in the town of Northport, James Patrick Conover lowered his head against the rebellious noises of his only son, a teenage prick with the soul of a mystic hermit. When J.P. could take no more, he told his boy that since they could not fight, they might as well go for a swim in the Warrior. The boy said, "I hope you don't fuck like you swim," and at that moment J.P. gave over his son to the perverse gods of family life in America.

Tuscaloosa City 5/29 Dear Adrian [Devereux read, deciphering with painful slowness the transparent letters of the unspooling black film ribbon], *Soon I will go to the roads, surely sooner than later cuz without D I'm become a gunnysack of* [illegible] *tussling fears. My night space is ambushed by fat murderous shapes, and by day I total up my obsessions like stitches in a crazy shawl. Tsk, tsk, you will say, but you can't know the full crappy silliness of my mind. D shouldn't leave me alone with it. He shouldn't romance with his friends in far-off places while I stay put with the dust, the night shapes, the bed that becomes so large I don't know where in it to put my small self . . . where to sleep, if I sleep. Tsk! I daydream now of islands, of beaches, of your lagoon and its birds, of you in your cutoffs, the sand sticking to your skinny old shanks like confectioners' sugar. I know you'll take me into your shack and tell me stories of olden times, of Ponce de León,*

Narváez, De Soto, Alvar Núñez Cabeza de Vaca, and of all the ships at sea. I want to run crazy in the moats of harbor forts at night, I want to hear your ways to happiness, see your diagrams of grace. Unless I'm murdered in my [illegible], I'll be there Saturday, for all we have in common. Love [Envelope matter:] *Mr. Adrian Brothers, 318½ St. George, St. Augustine, Florida 32084 P.S. Since I'm intendin' to charley-horse D with my absence, I'd appreciate you not acknowledging my existence to anyone, not even your crowd of loved ones.*

Wearing the sneakers that Devereux had so thoroughly repaired in Wellfleet, Carl scuffed off the airplane and up the slight incline of the access tunnel. He lugged a less-than-stuffed army duffel, and in the dimness of the tunnel he seemed to loom above the other passengers like a handsome, albeit galootish stork. He wore his trademark baggy fatigues and a spotless white T-shirt that depicted the infamous Aquaduck ("This Duck Is Different!"), invented by his roommate, the great Evces, and the skin of Carl's face and arms was a delicious golden-brown. When he came blinking into the more intense light of the gate's waiting area, he cast about for his father and found no one of that description among the decked-out to-and-froers of the Atlanta airport, Concourse C. Should he panic? Better to sit here at the gate and thumb the copy of *Great Expectations* Barry Kessler had given to him as an antidote against VCR overindulgence. Carl took a seat and rummaged in the duffel for the odd little book about love and disappointment, or at least he thought these might be the grand themes after reading along to the introduction of Estella—where Pip observes, "She seemed much older than I, of course, being a girl, and beautiful and self-possessed; and she was as scornful of me as if she had been one-and-twenty, and a queen."

Natalie.

Terminated with affection. Shit.

What if Devereux were dead on the interstate, his radar detector cord wrapped around his neck like a Ubangi necklace? Carl saw himself supporting his tiny mother through the flapdoodle of the grim funeral.

" 'Don't be ridiculous, boy,' " Estella said to Carl from the page in front of him. Carl's cream-pitcher ears reddened, and he slouched down in the chair, bringing the book within inches of his face, as if to hide from the airport public the fact that he wasn't properly grief-stricken over the possible death of his reckless pa. Actually, it was to disguise the fact that this was the first time in his life he had ever even considered the notion of Devereux ceasing to exist. How very unglorious. How awful. He turned hopefully to the last page of the novel, an act he had so far avoided—his last semester's English teacher would have termed it "dodging around the art in a pedestrian search for fact"—and was relieved to discover that weary Pip "saw no shadow of another parting from her."

Ha!

Still, something ominous in the tone . . . and why in the world was he, Carl, mixing up death and love, Natalie and Estella, Pip and himself? If Devereux didn't come pretty soon, he would run screaming along the concourses until he ended up in prison with all the horrid convicts of the world. Well, that wouldn't be so bad, a prison hulk on the sea marshes of the Georgia coast! He could sin no more, whatever that meant.

Outside, in the humid night, passenger jets came at the concourses like famished, light-eating submarines. Carl gazed over the top of his book and out of the high, narrow window . . . where he saw a fiendish Godzilla chomp a jet pod from the rear end of Carl's own Delta craft. Carl yawned mightily. Such hunger he felt, yet was afraid to move from this one spot on the planet where Devereux knew him to be.

On a moving sidewalk not half a mile from where Carl sat, the former mistress of Newburyport's leftist philosopher was swept away from Carl in a manner more stately than she felt. She carried with her, in a shopping bag from Lord & Taylor, the small Seth Thomas clock stolen in New- buryport, which she intended to use for a grubstake when she reached Key West. She took no notice of the rumpled, grizzled man who rushed past her in the opposite direction, the only person to be using the walking space between the two flanking ribbons of moving sidewalk. At the moment, Devereux was cursing the endlessness of the Atlanta airport as he pressed on with his rolling gait, and he did not know or care about stolen clocks, abandoned mistresses, or even the slow rise of the world's seas. On the final up-escalator he did become conscious—escalators do this—of an Indian woman in full sari descending opposite him. Her caste mark was as bright as arterial blood, and her beauty was such that Devereux thought of a polished jade boulder he had once seen in someone's courtyard. When they drew even with each other, Devereux offered small worship for the perfect brownness of her glimpsed belly, for the opacity of her proud eyes.

We are all a bit crazed in airports.

He found Carl asleep, his face covered by Dickens. His boy's sockless feet in their colorless sneakers looked like upside-down skiffs, and on the whole he presented an aspect so wonderfully unkempt and innocent that Devereux found himself near weeping with the pleasure of discovering such a sight at the end of his swift journey from Tuscaloosa. He stood behind Carl, his eyes glistening. The boy's head hung over the seat back at an awkward angle, and the novel threatened to topple to the floor with every breath Carl took. When Devereux reached out and tugged at a lock of Carl's hair, the book did slide off his face, but Devereux caught it neatly and stuck it in his back pocket as Carl looked at him from below—a look that combined startlement, fear, and more than a little pain, whether from his neck or from his recent life, Devereux did not yet know.

"Oh . . . hey," Carl said, aware of his father's smile and

the untamed underside of his salt-and-pepper beard. The guy was actually here! Carl armed himself out of the chair, and by the time he was up on his tingly legs, Devereux had come around the bank of chairs, and the two of them embraced and neck-kissed with some fervor.

"Here, now," Devereux said, handing Carl the book, "wot yer readin'?"

Carl looked at the floor, leaned back on one leg, and mock-kicked a hacky-sack with the free foot. "The book of Pip," he said, coordinating the kick with the statement. "Barry gave it to me."

Devereux nodded. "I'll bet he did." He himself approved of unassigned reading in any form, and Carl had never been one to pick up the unassigned book. Carl's comic-book collection, stored in special boxes in Tuscaloosa, each book-let in its separate plastic sleeve, could probably provide the boy with an embarrassingly large dowry by the time he reached the age of twenty-five, when no doubt he would finally be capable of marrying the likes of Natalie (please, no). What a vast difference between Aquaduck and Philip Pirrip, yet here stood Carl, with Aquaduck grinning from his chest, and with Pip's book in his meaty, adolescent hand. "You hungry?" asked Devereux.

"You could put it that way," Carl confirmed, reaching his duffel from the floor. "Where're we going, Pop?" He stuffed the book into the bag.

Devereux wrapped an arm around Carl's shoulders, and they began the long hike to the sedan. "To eat?" he said. "I have no idea. Let's get out on the highway, find a Cracker Barrel. Steak 'n peas and unsweetened icetea."

"That's cool. But I mean, where are we headed?"

"Beaches," said Devereux, squeezing hard the muscles his son had never had before (had he?).

Carl cast a sharp, questioning glance at the tip of Devereux's nose. "Tessa?" he said, "my theory worked? There was stuff on the ribbon?" But he was already certain of the answer, already certain life again had a clear purpose.

"Yes, thanks, thanks a lot," Devereux said. "I took *my* trip; now, you and me, we'll take *hers*."

In room number eight of the only motel in Bland Villa, Georgia, they came to ground for the night. Carl immediately labeled the place a roach ranch and went about stomping the creatures who had been caught out in the light. Devereux unloaded their gear from the sedan, then walked up the road to see about a six-pack that the motel clerk had assured him could be purchased on a Sunday from Danny Craddock at the Getty station. In Devereux's absence, Carl showered—secure in the knowledge no freaked-out burglar alarm would set the roaches into a frenzy or awaken the few pickup denizens of this low-rent place. Carl's stomach was pleasantly full of the red-meat meal they'd eaten south of Atlanta, and although he suspected he would soon enough have to tell his dad the full story of Natalie, he dreaded it much less than he had in Sagaponack or on the plane, because Devereux's sheer presence assured Carl of what he sometimes forgot: you could tell the old guy anything, even the sex stuff (oh sweet Christ), as long as you looked him in the eye and spoke up straight and true. He could spot fibs by the color of your ears or the pitch of your voice. Even Carl's mother admitted this, and she wasn't always kind on the subject of her former husband; yet even so, Carl figured they loved each other like war buddies. Or, as Tessa once put it to Carl in a letter, "Dev'ro's soul is a jumble-box of all the women he's known, and never really let go, and probably never will, bless him." This had always seemed to Carl a difficult proposition, a dangerous juggling act for his father to maintain; but then Natalie had taught him one rather sharp lesson: a girl can bounce you from one end of the universe to the other. As he slicked back his hair in front of the cracked motel mirror, he tried on his best, close-mouthed smile. He was out of it, he was safe!

In the bedroom Devereux cracked a Pabst and reclined himself against the headboard of one of the double beds. His eyes were still widened and red from the night-driving south, as well as from the effort to convince Danny Craddock to sell beer to a stranger, but in his body Devereux knew a fair peace, a letting go of tension, that made him feel pleasured to be alone with Carl in this air-conditioned nowhere called Bland Villa. Now if he could just provoke Carl to speech beyond unanswerable car and restaurant questions about Tessa and St. Augustine, he could enter sleep with his curiosity satisfied and his son fully known.

Such utter impossibility.

Carl came from the bathroom securely wrapped in a thin white towel. "You scored," he said, approaching the foot of the bed and gazing at his father with an expression that suggested tolerant affection or bemused knowledge. Before Devereux could reply, Carl leaned forward and removed the leather moccasins from Devereux's feet, dropping them to the floor space between the two beds. Carl then tweaked one of his father's hot toes and sat down on the other bed, hugging himself above the tiny fold of his belly button.

Devereux reached to the bed table and pushed the necklaced beer cans toward Carl. "Have one," he said, "you deserve it."

Carl sent rays of nonchalance in the direction of the cans. "I don't mind if I do," he said, smacking his lips and freeing one of the beers. He opened it, swallowed a long draught with his eyes closed, and then frowned. "Deserve it? Why?"

Devereux took a pull of his own beer and for it received rivulets of the swill water in his chin whiskers, which he brushed away with an easy curse. "Because," he said, "you're here, you survived, and you don't look much the worse for wear."

In the dim light from the bedside lamp Carl's hazel eyes sought distant places. You handsome boy, Devereux thought. What's going on underneath that slick hair, that wrinkled brow?

"So you talked to your mother yesterday?"

Carl's eyes returned to the room. "Yeah, I told you, she thought Kessler's was too 'fast' for me anyway. She was glad."

"She always wanted you to be with kids your own age."

Carl zeroed his father with his clear eyes. "Natalie is fifteen going on thirty-five, Pop." His voice, so matter-of-fact, surprised both of them into a silence finally punctuated by the sounds of beer being swallowed. Carl went on, "Sometimes, like now, I think I prefer grown-up romances, no matter how fucked-up, to the games of 'normal' kids."

"Tell me," said Devereux.

Carl put down his beer can, folded his arms across his belly, and leaned forward on the edge of the bed. During the beginning of the story his gaze traveled from the floor to Devereux's face in a rhythm that had more to do with self-consciousness and relief than Devereux could ever know.

"There's Jer . . . Natalie's mother . . . Barry's girlfriend," Carl began. "She has fake eyebrows and looks kind of starved. She edits in New York City, but every once in a while she bombs out to Sagaponack in her SX-7 to take Nat in hand."

Devereux smiled, thinking of Pip. "You mean she's being raised up by hand?"

Carl's head snapped up from its floor gaze. "Yes, right! but only on the weekends. The rest of the time she could hang out with the beach freaks, or bug Barry, or watch videos, or run me around like a slavey, or"—the color rose up through Carl's ears like cranberry juice poured into clear pitchers—"take saunas until I thought we might die."

Ahhh. The ex-surveyor finally understood why Kessler had threatened Natalie with forty whacks for leaving the sauna running the night of the alarm malfunction. "It's dangerous to make out in saunas," Devereux said prissily, "something about extreme heat, heart rate, and respiratory difficulty."

With a look of extreme vexation, Carl allowed this paternal remark to pass away into the half-cool air of the motel room. Make out, indeed! Might as well call it schmoozing inside a furnace . . . but don't, Pop, ever call it fucking.

"It's good I have my driver's license," Carl continued. "I got to take the beater Mustang of Barry's to every store and veggie stand on the end of the island. What an eater Barry is! And then, when I wasn't washing clothes or pots or bathrooms, I could ferry Nat to the beach or the video store . . . or sometimes a party. A couple at any rate." He drew breath and shivered.

Devereux finished his beer and opened another. If only the good James Patrick Conover could witness this divorced parent and child confrontation in Bland Villa, Georgia.

"Why don't you get under the covers," he said to Carl.

"When I'm cold, I will."

Damn. Time to stop such habitual solicitude, Devereux thought. "Great," he said. "Go on with your story."

"This party was in Sag Harbor last Friday night," Carl said. "Jer called at dinnertime to say she wouldn't be out from the city until Saturday. She told Nat I could drive her to the party as long as we were both home by eleven and I 'keep Nat-lee out of mis-chief.' Now that is a pretty heavy joke—Houseboy Keeps Mistress Out of Mischief."

"So Barry sent you off to this party with a pat and a wink?"

Carl scrunched up his eyes like a seer in difficulty. "I think Barry is . . . amused by Jer's kid . . . or by me with Jer's kid. It's hard to know, but, yeah, he sent us off. He was having a dinner for eight—I had to clean the gross squid—and he sort of waved at us from the head of the table when we left.

"So this place in Sag Harbor is full of druggies, rich ones, and for an hour or so after we got there, I didn't see Nat."

Devereux bestirred himself. "What'd you do?"

"I went to the beach, the Gardiner's Bay beach, and I thought about calling you up and asking for help."

Devereux said nothing. God help us all.

Carl shrugged in the silence. "Big deal. I was being jacked around by a spoiled girl with smoky eyes . . . and I loved every minute of it." He looked hard at Devereux, who nodded once with no irony whatsoever, and Carl fell back onto the bed and continued talking to the ceiling. Devereux saw his jaw muscles contract as he swallowed twice. He did not see that Carl's eyes were closed as if he were watching a video of the remainder of these events. "I walked back to the house and found her in a bedroom with a bunch of whacks and a crack pipe."

"Oh—"

"Don't worry, this is not about crack. It's my big moment. Natalie was, you know, on the edges—these guys are eighteen, nineteen—and I got her by the upper arm and said, 'Let's go, Nat, it's over our heads here.' She looked relieved for about a second before she told me, pretty loud, to go take a flying fuck at the moon. These whacked-out people got into some boom-boom laughs . . . and that's when she stuck her face in my ear, kissed it, licked the earring, and whispered, 'Car, five minutes, sodjer boy.' "

"I'll be damned," said Devereux. "Did she—was she—?"

"Nope," Carl said, laying a hand across his groin. "She got into the car as straight as I am now, and we had a nice time driving back to Barry's house." Something clicked in Carl's throat. "See how she is!"

"I think you done good," Devereux said, his face slack with the knowledge of Carl's stymied grief.

"Right, good," Carl growled, rolling his body toward the headboard and pillows at the same time he yanked a section of the spread over himself. He worked the towel off, removed it from under the spread, and flung it toward the air conditioner embedded in the wall. When he had done this, he turned to Devereux, supporting his head with one hand, and said, "Jer told me I think with my dick."

Carl's pupils had enlarged to black, glistening holes. This frightened Devereux into jokiness. "In sixteen years I haven't observed such a thing. Why would she ever say it?"

Carl raised his other hand as a promise of delivery. "Well, you're right, that's the real funny part of the story."

"I know this isn't funny . . . except I'm betting that it might be later . . . down the road."

Carl allowed his lips to sound a distinct raspberry. "Later's later. Like Tessa and all that. Like a hot, *boring* summer in Tuscaloosa. Right, Devereux, right?" Devereux had to assent. Carl went on, "Anyway, at Barry's the dinner party was in full roar. Nobody noticing us come in, nobody noticing me lift the bottle of Medoc from the bar, nobody noticing us drinking it in the pool . . . or in the VCR room while we watched something fucky like *Hansel and Gretel Get Down.*"

"She drank?"

"She said she was celebrating her liberation from the sick world of drugs."

"Of course. You're now drunk in the sauna, you both have seizures—"

"Shut up!" Carl said, flopping back in his pillows. "You should talk."

"You're right, I'm sorry," said Devereux, meaning it. Equality with your child comes in strange and unexpected ways. "Then?"

Carl covered his ears with his hands. The skin over his cheekbones seemed mottled. "We made love in the sauna."

Jesus Christ . . . he'd said this phrase to no other human being before. Even Natalie gave it no name when it applied to herself, to her own precious body. And here he was saying the words to his dear, impossible dad, who wrapped his hands securely around the beer can set on his chest and said, "Was it good?"

Carl gave out with a loud incoherence. "It was always good! It was incredible! Isn't it supposed to be, you old fart?"

Carl could not see Devereux's grimace. "You bet," he said so quietly as not to be heard.

"That's established," Carl said after several beats of silence. He removed his hands from his ears. "Good father or

116

not, you can be very hard to talk to. You should have told me some of this stuff, not about plumbing or shitty infidelity . . . but about the way people *feel,* or don't feel, the games they play, the things they need, or want, or have to have. All of it. You should have told me, Dee-Vo."

"I'm not sure it can be told," said Devereux. "I'm still doing research."

"Great, swell," Carl moaned, but not painfully. "You're right about saunas and booze and sex, though. We got all stupid and ended up in her bed."

"And you both passed out?"

Drawing a deep, sobby breath, Carl said, "Yes, we did."

"And Jer found you?"

"Yup."

There it was: *caught.* Sin . . . Guilt . . . Punishment . . . Confession. Were these things biological? So far as Devereux Hoopes knew, he had never given instruction in any of these matters, either by word or example, and yet, of course, he had.

"But you didn't do anything wrong, Carl."

"Bullshit," said the boy. "The sun woke me up, and I lay there listening to Nat breathe, listening to what you call a hangover, and when the door opened all I could think to do was cover my head with the sheet and whimper, which woke Nat up. I could feel her start to sit up, then lie back, and swear under her breath. From the end of the bed, Jer said, 'Who's that?' "

In spite of himself, Devereux laughed, but Carl was past the point of caring; in truth, he suddenly realized it *was* funny in a shameful sort of way.

"Then Nat said"—he put on a perfect Upper East Side accent, awash in sarcasm—"'I don't know, Mother.' I couldn't help it, my whole body drew up like I'd been busted in the balls, and that was when Jer came around my side of the bed and whacked me on the ass."

"No!"

"It hurt. Then she kind of screamed, 'It's that guttersnipe!'

It was ridiculous, it was awful. Nat kept saying, 'You don't know *anything*, Mother,' and Jer would poke at me and hiss like a snake. But finally she got her act together and told us to be downstairs, dressed, in twenty minutes, for a *discussion*." Carl sat up in bed and looked directly at Devereux. Carl's face was wild. "Guttersnipe! What the hell is that?"

"Pip," said Devereux. "Jer sounds like quite the lady."

Carl blinked. "When Jer left, Nat told me to go on, then she giggles and says, 'Thanks, Carlos, I don't have to pretend to be a virgin anymore.' "

"How sweet. Then you got fired . . . I mean, terminated with affection."

Misery crossed Carl's face. "The affection was Barry's. I think Jer wanted me crucified in a potato field."

"Ah," Devereux said, "and Mr. Ya would place the cross in the perfect place."

Carl tried out a smile. "When Jer began the little discussion by saying I thought with my dick, Barry hollered from the kitchen, 'Jer, babe, I've been called a five-foot-eight-inch walking penis, and you *live* with me.' "

"Good for Barry," Devereux said. "A member that doesn't reason ain't worth having." He paused. "How'd you leave it with Nat?"

"I didn't. Jer took her right off to the city, took her for what she called a morning-after shot. Shit. Then Barry and I spent the weekend together. He was nice to me."

"Of course he was," said Devereux. "Look, friend, I think I know what you've lost, but you gained a couple things too."

Carl flopped back down on the pillows. "Such as?"

Devereux kept his tongue still.

Up the road at the Getty station, Danny Craddock opened a bag of Ruffles and decided not to go abroad as a mercenary, after all. In Tuscaloosa, J. P. Conover dreamed of his children crucified on the cross of modern life, and in Cape Hatteras, Ling Mullins took Jack Vilna into her arms and, in the absence of any cowboy resistance or struggle, fell deeply in love with him once again. To the southeast, in St. Augustine, Adrian Brothers read on into the night, Tessa Dixon sleeping like a stone in the next room where he kept his single bed.

In the motel, in room number eight, Devereux switched off the light.

"I love you," he said to his son.

"I love ya too, baby," Carl returned, echoing perfectly the tones of ass-gazing Kit McGuffy, dead to the world near the grand dunes of Wellfleet.

ST. AUGUSTINE

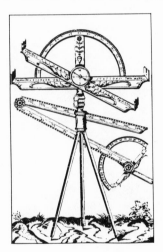

COQUINA: a soft, gray-whitish rock, a sedimented glomerate of marine shells and coral. In the history of northeastern Florida, a material used by men for walls, for pillars, for roadbeds; a material resilient but easy to crumble, easy to expose the basic ingredients of sand, calcareous bones, and seashells.

Co-kee-na.

Carl savored the word as if the three melodic syllables held the taste of a mystery solved, or a game understood— reduced to its sensible essence. Would that the rest of his life would pass as simply as this word passed his lips. While Devereux steered the sedan along St. Augustine's harbor boulevard, noontime, Carl allowed the word to ricochet off the walls of his brain until all other thoughts were forced to take refuge in the back recesses, where he could now keep Natalie, the older wounds of his parents' divorce, and the minor fear there might after all be a God. Coquina. Our father who art in coquina, hallowed be thy date palms.

"Check out that fort," said Devereux, forcing Carl once again to come out to the world of geography, structure, history, color . . . and the incredible, squat date palms.

A gray-black fort with walls that curved outward to a moat, the Castillo de San Marcos looked to be six-sided, and so low to the ground Carl wondered how people might make use of it—to defend or bombard or repulse. Still, in its obvious solidity, its there-ness, it looked capable of saying, "Go Away," although thanks to his efficient prep school, Carl knew full well that the town had been burned and sacked and pillaged by the likes of Sir Francis Drake and others who swashbuckled about in their galleons. "Pure coquina," he said of the fort to his father, who seemed remarkably calm for a fellow in hot pursuit of his sweetheart.

"What's that? Say it again." Devereux cocked an ear in Carl's direction. The old man's hearing suffered in cars, especially with the tape deck moaning out country music through the rear speakers, but Carl couldn't seem to learn to speak up when he was riding shotgun, a failing to be ranked with not wearing socks or forgetting to write thank-you notes.

"A lot of this town is made out of it, Pop, coquina. It's like your true sea rock."

"I appreciate your erudition. Wanna mint?"

Carl did not.

They passed through the old city gates—more coquina—on their left the harbor, to the right, shops, a square, horse-drawn tourist jitneys, the red towers of Flagler College. Nothing special here but for the sight of salt water, shrimping vessels, and the Bridge of Lions (two marble lions gloaming each other on either side of the entrance), leading from the mainland to Anastasia Island, the mass that separates St. Augustine from the Atlantic. The town itself sits on a narrow, board-flat peninsula between two rivers, the narrow San Sebastian and the broad Mantanzas, but neither Carl nor Devereux as yet understood the geography to which they had come. What struck them both, as they forked away from the harbor boulevard and into the region of homes, was the dominance of walls—gray, tan, light green—the narrowness of the streets, the live oaks with their furbelows of Spanish moss overhanging everything with a thickness of vegetation, and the sweet gloom of age and well-protected housing. After several blocks Carl decided that Devereux's turnings were arbitrary, his muttering indicative of the stubborn male game called Find It by Feel.

"What street?" Carl said.

"St. George."

"Let me ask someone," Carl offered, even though the populace seemed walled-off from travelers like themselves.

"I'm looking, I think, for a lagoon or a small lake," Devereux said. "Adrian will live by a lagoon."

"I hope he lives in one of these crumbly coquina palaces with a wooden second story. Do you think he'll speak to us?"

"Eh?" Devereux glanced at Carl. The boy looked rested, eager, the cantilever of his hair seeming to point the way to a great adventure on this strange coast, or a great pain. "I hope Tessa will speak to us first," Devereux said. "I hope to hell she'll say, 'Hey, y'all, where've you been all this time?' Then Adrian will offer us some shoofly pie and a crock of whiskey."

Carl studied this wishful proposition while the sedan re-negotiated a street of small, colorful bungalows, peopleless but spiffy. "I have my doubts about that," he said. "Now take a left here, and go on up to where there's that gap in the tree line. I have a sense of water, Pop."

Devereux obeyed. After all, they were both operating on faith here, were they not? Although Carl seemed to possess more faith in water than he did in Devereux's hope for discovering Tessa's precise location on this earth. "And from where do you dredge up these doubts?" he asked, slowing the sedan to a child's pace.

Carl's thoughtfulness filled the sedan like a benign smoke. His broad forehead seemed to contract until it centered itself at a power point an inch above the center of his eyebrows. "Because of what you told me her letter said, because of the sentence about going to the roads."

"Yeah, what about it?"

"It's what she wrote me in May. She said, 'Sometimes bold resolves and going the roads are the only solutions.' Then in big letters, 'I need islands.' This is no island, Dee-Vo. Look!"

They emerged from a block of pastel walls into an open

space that did in fact contain between low, grassy embankments and sentinel palms a brownish lagoon, roughly rectangular and perhaps a quarter-mile in length. The side opposite them was lined with wooden frame houses. The side closest—St. George, into which they turned left—curved slightly in front of a long line of more rambling, more vegetated structures—the riffling lagoon appeared to be the dividing line between two sorts of folk. In the distance a low bridge indicated where the lagoon joined with the San Sebastian River.

Devereux wrinkled his nose as he searched in vain for number 318½. "Maybe you're right," he said, "maybe she will have moved on, and if so, you and I will have to take Mr. Adrian Brothers in hand and shake him upside down until he gives out with her goddamn whereabouts."

Startled by his father's tone, Carl gaped at his whitened knuckles on the steering wheel. Violence, however funnily threatened, had not been in Carl's bag of possible adventures. "He'd uhh . . . cover for Tessa?"

"She told him to," Devereux snapped. "I know him some. His first loyalty is to her . . . is always to women."

About three quarters of the way along this more ramshackle and wild side of the lagoon, they spotted a youth in cutoffs, unloading a dirt motorcycle from a small pickup parked askew in front of a two-story garage with a decided sideward list to its structural integrity.

"It's a real St. Augustinian," said Carl, then noticed the truck's New Jersey plates. The kid muscled the bike from the truck bed and allowed it to drop to the sand where it bounced on its knobby tires.

Devereux stopped the sedan just beyond him, turned off the tape, and rolled down his window. "Excuse me," he said.

The one addressed turned around and unfurled a beatific smile over a set of snaggly teeth. His earring was a duplicate of Carl's green malachite nib, but this kid's hair hung to his shoulders in graceful wavelets that stirred in the warm breeze. "What's up?" he said to Devereux, staring at the rear of the sedan, the bike resting against his hip like a heeled beast.

"Looking for three eighteen and a half."

"So who you want?"

"Adrian Brothers."

The youth moved himself and his machine until he could see around the corner of the garage in the direction of a concrete path, a bicycle leaned against the garage wall, and two shadowed houses beyond. "Aid!" he yelled out nasally, "ya got more visitors from Alabamee."

Directly across the expanse of the lagoon, in the neat yellow house surrounded by dogwood, the house with the large picture window that at this moment reflected the over-flight of a great blue heron, sat a woman playing idle chords on her black baby grand. A chesty woman, gone handsome in her early forties, she wore her dark hair in a mispinned Gibson-Girl bun and looked prepared to pounce over the piano and out the window at the slightest provocation from across the waters. Her name was Emily Overton Mills, and the day before she had forever banished Adrian Brothers from her life—this time (it was the seventh or eighth) for harboring the curly-headed Dixon bimbo in his own monk-ish bed. Now, Emily felt a sick headache coming on, and she knew it was for lack of love, her daily bread. She watched the gray sedan back into the space beside Adrian's garage-apartment walkway, and when she saw a bearded man and a rangy adolescent alight from the car and begin to speak to the motorcycle boy, she reached behind her for the phone and dialed the number of the pantywaist Adrian Brothers.

"Why aren't you at work?" she said when he answered. His silence might have shucked an oyster, but she let it pass. "You're about to have Don Q and Sancho Jr. at your door."

The two people so-identified had already disappeared from her sight. She heard Adrian say, in his sweetest tones,

"Just a minute, Dev-row." And then he positively dumped in her ear, "Emily, you are a bitch."

"Are they from Tuscaloosa? You shouldn't call me names, A. If that's the Dixon girl's man, I want to meet him."

"Not possible, sugar."

Emily drew herself into full-bosomed posture and smote some of the piano's bass keys with her free hand. "I will meet him, I will have him to my house . . . I'll tell him everything about you. And also, I want my oil portrait back."

Adrian blew cigarette smoke into the phone. "You're so full of it," he said quite sadly—or so she wanted to believe as she smiled to herself. He asked, "You have a headache, don't you?"

"Just the tiniest, A," she cooed into the instrument.

"Good," said Adrian, then venomously, "tough!" And the nerd hung up on her.

Emily Overton Mills, free-lance amanuensis and amateur folklorist, sat with her liver-spotted hands on the ivories and stared across the water at Adrian's hovel until a plan of sorts took the place of her throbbing anger, and until the adolescent came out of Adrian's to chat with the motorcycle boy, who lived on the second floor and always addressed Emily as "Em-O," even when she drove up to the hovel in her Dart wearing a formal linen suit and her most impressive hairdo. The plan was so simple she knew it would work. Adrian must bike back to work at the historical association by one o'clock, not twenty minutes from now, and when he did, Emily would strike; she could not allow Adrian Brothers to be so easily banished from her daily life.

Meanwhile, on the same side of the lagoon as Emily, eleven houses away, a delicately veined, youngish woman named Belinda Ruffin was unloading her dishwasher and hoping that her husband, Holt, wouldn't return early from his trip to Tallahassee where he was lately involved in religious endeavors of a nature Belinda seldom, and then barely, understood. In fact, if she were to cast down deep for the truth, she hoped he wouldn't return at all, that perhaps

128

he might be born again in Tallahassee and find himself blinded and wandering on the road to Denton, Texas, where he'd been born in the first place. Belinda entertained such thoughts because yesterday morning, Sunday, before departing on his journey, Holt had discovered—at the bottom of her sewing basket, for pity's sake—the three passionate love letters she had in the past month received from Adrian Brothers. In addition, Holt had brandished at her (in his controlled way) a photograph of Adrian taken at Vilano Beach when he was wearing only his Brooks Brothers underwear and the unbuttoned red flannel shirt that smelled like cedar. The photograph seemed to perturb Holt far more than the letters, which were handwritten, mystically orientated, and covered with charts and graphs of his passion for her, a passion that had *not* been consummated, but it might not look like this in the letters. Holt had seemed to agree when he called her a fornicator and an un-Christian bum. With Holt promising to return today and "settle the matter once and forever," Belinda wondered how Adrian's principles would respond.

A month ago, those principles had compelled him to take his friend Holt to dinner and, over black bean soup at Scudder's, declare his love for Belinda—nothing untoward, underhanded, sneaky, or illicit for Adrian Brothers—but then he wrote the fateful letters (she worshipped the letters) and easily seduced her into long bike rides, poor Holt wondering all the while what in tarnation had gotten into frail Adrian that he would announce such a thing over dinner, a dinner Adrian insisted on *paying for,* when he had about as much money as a sea gull. And now, now, with Holt off in Tallahassee with the letters and the photograph, reading into them fornication and ruin, Belinda had promised to meet Adrian at the beach for one final go-round of lingering, swoony looks; she had promised to meet him in less than an hour. But of course, if she left now, and then Holt returned, the self-righteous goon wouldn't know where she was unless he hired a helicopter. Once she left Holt in a formal sort of way—should such a decision zing into her flotsamy life—wouldn't Adrian's nonfornicatory principles melt into bliss like ice cream in the June sun.

Finished with the dishwasher, she ran her fingers through her cropped mantle of brown hair, gave the whole business a determined flip, and headed for the backdoor, a slim figure in green bermuda shorts and simple white blouse.

Outside, above the lagoon, a gliding osprey might well have registered the movement of Belinda's bicycle as she pedaled it out of her driveway and made the leftward turn for the center of town. In general, however, the lagoon's ecology paid scant attention to the nearby humans, including Emily Overton Mills, Peter Crow (the motorcycle boy), the Hoopeses, Adrian Brothers, and his landlady, the brooding Lorna Crow, who at this moment was reclining on a mildewed divan on the second-floor sun porch of her house, close behind the rickety garage apartment in which a conversation between men was under way.

Lorna had no wish to overhear such hooey, but the screened windows of Adrian's "sitting room" stopped no sound from rising through the small space—darkened by bougainvillea, coral vine, and overhanging oaks—which separated her house from the garage where lived her sometime bed partner Brothers and, upstairs, her son, Peter, lately returned from New Jersey.

Lorna had about her the look of a southwestern horsewoman too long in the sun. At fifty, she was neither a horsewoman, nor had she lived in the Southwest, but after years in New Orleans as a consort of the low life, she had come to St. Augustine to stay clean, and eventually to become as brown and well-crinkled about the face as a carefully preserved grocery sack. Her bangs were pure white, her eyes were as blank as two huckleberries, and she wore every day of her St. Augustine life a pair of summer-weight sailor pants and a near-matching T-shirt, its pocket always adroop with a smushed pack of mentholated cigarettes and a miniature butane lighter. She believed in nothing, Lorna Crow, except the value of property and the momentary un-deadness of the orgasm. Yet it pleased her to watch such airheads as Brothers attempt to please *her,* attempt to startle her from her neutral life with gestures of empty romance, or foolish rushes into the vanity of thinking some matters more worthy than others. When Brothers had introduced Lorna to the coon-ass Tessa Dixon, a woman he claimed to admire for the gracefulness of her fears, for the power of her mental equipage, Lorna had reveled in her own ironclad silence, the same silence she now contributed to the parley going on in the apartment below her. She knew the exchange had for its dead center the matter of Ms. Dixon's whereabouts on the ever-spinning planet. As if it mattered. So help me, she thought, men are an endangered species.

Adrian's thin, hug-me voice seemed to be playing footsie with the other man's tough-guy rumble. Certain it was that this particular Jack-O was Devereux Hoopes, or Whoopes, called by the Dixon woman "a guy too much in the present tense . . . a floater." To Lorna he sounded like any bozo in search of his property.

Adrian was saying, ". . . and if you'll just have a seat, I'll bring you some Irish stew and a glass of whiskey. Life shouldn't be as quick as it is, but I've got to go back to work, there are appointments. We'll have a long talk at suppertime when the light becomes so extraordinary. You should see this town, it's a living breathing museum. Every century is—"

"You're serious . . . you really won't tell me where Tessa is?" said the Hoopes voice in a friendly way, as if he were in the thick of an easy game of hide-and-seek and didn't quite believe he'd been tapped "it."

"Hoopes," Adrian said manfully, "I've said I can't do that. You can be certain she was here until this morning. You can take my word she's physically and spiritually sound. I just wish you and your child would accept my meager hospitality and not go putting me in this god-awkward position."

Light and shadow tricked over the seams of Lorna's face as

she blindly reached herself a smoke and blew streams of bored knowledge into the soft air of her sun porch: a threat would now be in order, if she knew her boys at all.

"Adrian," Hoopes breathed, "what fuck-all difference could it make? Did she go north or south?"

Several beats of silence.

"Hey!" Adrian yelped. "That hurts. You've got to be kidding me! A grown man doesn't . . . uh!"

Even Lorna could not resist rising from her divan and peering through one of the screened windows overlooking Adrian's apartment. She made out a section of green plastic couch and the back of Adrian's head sliding out of sight as if, sitting on the couch, he had decided to scrooch himself down in it. Then she saw the head again, this time upside down in the space between the couch back and the top of the window. Hoopes was apparently holding his tormentor by the ankles and shaking the change out of his pockets (Lorna did not see any change fall, but forever after she said she had). Adrian began to laugh, a breathless ha-ha-ha-ing, just his sort of stylized response to the vicissitudes of his made-up and various life. If Lorna had been in the habit, she too would have joined in.

"All right," Adrian snortled, "I see how serious you are. I want down, please."

Lorna watched his slight body fall all aheap onto the couch where he lay with his rosy face in a shaft of sunlight, looking directly up at her. Perhaps he winked—it would have been in character—but certainly he saw her. Behind his head were the corduroyed Hoopes knees. She shook her head at Adrian, and her white bangs lifted from her forehead in the breeze she created. Oh, the funny little men of her life.

Suddenly, Adrian disappeared from the couch; his apartment's door banged open; and out he flew in his khakis and white button-down, a red flannel shirt tied about his waist. He yelled over his shoulder as he headed for the bicycle leaned against the sidewall, "Lorna darling, keep an eye on my guests." And, humping the bicycle, he was off in his usual clashing of sprockety gears. He had chutzpah, even Lorna could admit. She waited for Hoopes to appear in the doorway or to give chase, but he did neither. Perhaps living in the present tense made the pursuit of a man on a bicycle unnecessary. Lorna moved back to the divan, prepared to wait however long it would take Adrian to deliver up the Hoopes to her.

In front of the garage, Carl and Lorna's son, Peter Crow, continued their conversation after the brief interruption of Adrian's rather speedy departure. For a skimpy guy, Adrian could sure make the old racer skim the pavement. When he leaned right into the lagoon road, he had called out to Carl, "Your pa's a Tartar!"

A sentiment that Carl hadn't time to dispute, but since he detected no visible wounds on the fleeing bicyclist, he figured everything was more or less all right. Certainly Peter Crow was all right, with his queer teeth and anachronistic head of long squeaky-clean hair. Peter now spat into the crushed coquina behind his truck and, again taking up the subject of his motorcycle, still leaned against his hip, said, "I even rode your daddy's mainsqueeze."

Carl gazed across the lagoon. He saw a fish rise and belly flop; he saw a silverish car backing out of a driveway. What in hell was a "mainsqueeze"? He stuck his hands deep into his fatigue pockets and fluttered his hands against his thighs. "You did? Where to?" he said.

The silver car was moving toward the bridge at a stately rate, as if driven by an impaired ancient on the lookout for a limpkin bird—that amazing, cranelike creature that hobbles jerkily over its territory giving out the wailing cry of a maniac. Carl smiled while he waited for Peter's response. It was good to be back in such slow-motion exchange with someone his own age. He'd just about had enough of life with the desperate middle-aged and the loud of voice.

Peter took hold of the handlebars of his machine, tilted it away from his body, and began to swivel his nonexistent hips as if he were schussing a fast slope. "Yeah, we went beachin' all the way to focking South Ponte Vedra."

After crossing the bridge, the silver car made a left and came on toward Carl and Peter.

"If you mean Tessa," Carl said to Peter's bare feet, "she's an island sort of person. Likes to lose herself."

"I dunno about that," Peter allowed with a toss of his hair, "but she grooves riding beaches on this here—" he whapped the seat of his bike—"and my mutha called her a water-baby."

Before Carl could adequately deal with this questionable observation, or the idea of Peter Crow possessing a mother in the area, the silver car had sighed to a halt beside them, a great ship of a woman at the wheel.

She tootled the horn at them once before saying, actually gushing the words, "U-who, boys, how they hanging?"

"Banana barf," muttered Peter Crow, then raising his voice, "Em-O, how you doin'? We're hangin' loose here. This's Carlo from Bama."

The woman leaned over for a gander at Carl. Perhaps her bright makeup was on crooked, but to Carl she looked like a ship's figurehead carved and painted by a demented genius. She was beautiful, but *all wrong*.

"I'm Emily Overton Mills," she sang out. "I thought I'd stop by and see if you and your father have all you need. Adrian can be lackadaisical in that department." She knitted her powdered brow for a second. "Have you all seen the Fountain of Youth or Ripley's or the fort?"

Carl scuffed his sneaker in the coquina dust. "No ma'am. We passed the fort."

"They's chasin' that waterbaby," Peter said with a snaggly grin.

Emily's entire (and substantial) nose seemed to fold in upon itself like an apple turnover. "That's neither here nor there," she said in a tight voice, then sweetening, "but, Carlo, honey, I'd love to meet your father and show you around. Is he in A's little place?"

134

"My name is Carl," he said, unaware that Devereux was only ten feet away, standing behind the drawn shade of Adrian Brothers's bathroom and wondering who in blazes might be the somehow familiar harridan he could see through the light crack between shade and window frame. One of Adrian's "crowd of loved ones," as Tessa had written? Carl continued in the manner of a laid-back impertinent, "My dad's indisposed with coquina fever."

Emily, taken in for a moment, placed a spotty hand over the broad reaches where her breasts began to swell beneath her white linen suit jacket. "Well, God, let's wash him down with cool cloths." As Devereux flinched in the bathroom, Emily forced gasoline into her automobile's engine, and the vehicle dipped and groaned into a position parallel to the Hoopes sedan.

While she performed this elegant maneuver, Peter Crow peered up at Carl with a certain awe. "You're shittin' her man, aren't you? I hope so. That scuzz is Aid's sweetie."

Hearing this, Devereux left the bathroom, walked past Adrian's bed, where he could easily imagine several of Tessa's dark hairs curled up on the pale blue pillowcase. In the sitting room, he took a good look at the oil portrait on the wall. What before had been only a blur of smeared greens now became a Wicked Witch of the West version of Emily Overton Mills—the painter had not been kind. Devereux left the apartment in time to present himself in a healthy light to the real Emily, now emerging from her Dart like a blowsy, sun-drenched protectress . . . far more huge and comely than the portrait let on.

When Carl saw Devereux walking up the pathway to the cars, he said to Peter, "Is there gas in this thing?" Peter shook the motorcycle back and forth, liquid sloshed, and both young men silently agreed that a summer afternoon could be spent better at the beach than listening politely to the rumba these two oldies were about to perform. Already, Carl could see on Devereux's face the sharp, alert look that meant, or might mean, "What *is* this creature hauled before me? If she can direct me to Tessa, perhaps the Fountain of Youth wouldn't be so bad after all." Or so Carl reasoned while Peter Crow jumped the kick starter once, twice—then a half-muffled blatting came into being, and they were off along the lagoon road before Devereux could raise a finger of warning to "Hold!"

To reach St. Augustine from the open sea, it is necessary to shoot through St. Augustine inlet, a narrow passageway between Conch Island and the peninsula, whose tail end is called Vilano Beach. The inlet itself is a frothing roil of confluent waters, perilous, and today—from Carl's perspective at the easternmost tip of Vilano Beach—inky green. He and Peter had shrieked across the intracoastal waterway on the low bridge, crossed the peninsula, and entered the beach proper through a restaurant parking lot. Peter maneuvered the bike over the minor dunes, avoiding the saw palmetto, and soon they had bombed their way here, to land's end, a tiny finger of flatness covered with medium-grained sand the color of unfinished pine, a mini-cape pointing casually to the east under a cloudless blue sky. Although Peter kept revving his engine, its blats were nearly lost in the combined sounds of wind and disturbed water. Behind them a herd of pickups had gathered for lunch; several of the drivers clustered around a man with a large pair of binoculars stuck to his face. The other men seemed to be cheering him on to new heights of magnified sight. Sitting on the rump of the motorcycle, Carl twisted his body to the left so that he might look north and discover what so fascinated the pickup contingent, but he could see nothing more than a tiny figure, a man without a shirt hunkered down in the sand and staring into the easy, rolling combers.

"So, Carl baby," Peter was barking over his shoulder, "you wanna head up toward Vedra or what?" He began to spin his machine in the sand using one leg for a pivot. Carl lifted his own feet to the rear pegs and held on with both hands to the underside of the seat.

"Let's check out the rednecks," Carl said as the bike slewed around to face the trucks and began to plow forward in the humpy sand.

"They not rednecks. Maybe cracker surf casters. I dunno."

Another man, this one wearing a blue gimme cap, now had hold of the binoculars and was extending a connoisseur's hand in the direction of the solitary figure.

Carl and Peter circumnavigated the truck folk and, as they did so, were not offered even a glance. The door of one cab was open and from it thumped and wailed a music impossible to identify. All of the men wore jeans, T-shirts, and neatly trimmed beards, and each one sported fisherman's skin like a dark olive layer of weather.

"They're casters," said Peter. "Mean ones. My mutha used to hang with one." He angled the bike toward the water, and when the knobby tires hit the harder wet sand, he upped the speed for the run north. Carl set himself to enjoy the speed, the wind, Peter's fine hair whipping at his own cheeks, the surf foam that spat at his right ankle whenever Peter veered the bike toward the raggedy edge of the oncoming water.

And then he saw the naked woman rise up out of the surf as if air-sprung from a small submarine specially designed for the purpose of landing beautifully nippled women on the continent. Peter saw her at nearly the same moment, and as they shot past her, his seasoned response was to cut power, hit brakes, lean left with a pivot foot extended, and wait for the bike to reverse itself. Carl, however, was still twisted to the right . . . in the thrall of his receding vision. Thus the balancing agents of the motorcycle were at war, and the beast went down hard on the wet sand, but not before Carl was launched into the shallow surf at the same time Peter was tucking and rolling to the left, away from the thing before the killed engine could crush his leg.

Whoa!

Knowing himself to be all right if scraped about the nose and one elbow, Carl thrashed in the warm water until his head entered the air once again, and he could begin to laugh. Then he remembered to look to Peter, who by now was huddled in dry sand and cursing this failure of dirt-bike prowess. Because Carl thought him hurt—he could not hear the obscenities—he tried to rise up from the foam and swirl, only to feel his shoulder seized, as a voice said urgently, "Are you okay?"

Carl looked first at the small hand gripping his shoulder, then raised his eyes to the woman who was not all naked, now, although her sheer white man's shirt and bikini underwear beneath clung to her with such pink, brown, and chocolate dampness that Carl immediately shifted his eyes seaward before answering, "Yeah, sure," and scrambling to his sneaker-heavy feet, certain that the two of them were in the focused center of the binocular's field of vision. With self-conscious aplomb, and maintaining eye contact only with the heaving sea, he waded a half-circle around her until—he believed, he hoped—his own bulk would cut her off from the squinchy eyes of the so-called surf casters. A kindly act, of which, of course, the woman was unaware, at least until Carl blurted, "Some guys are watching you from down the beach. Don't look." He felt safe in gazing at the top of her head, the hair boy-short and clinging to her skull like wet seal fur. He sensed that she cringed. Her forehead reddened, then she turned her back to him and did something to the front of the shirt.

"I knew this was dumb," she said, "but he insisted on a last swim for his sea nymph."

Carl glanced up at the beach where Peter now had the bike upright, his head down close to the engine. Behind him, the shirtless solitary strolled toward them carrying in one hand a red shirt that blew in the wind like a gay banner, in the other a bundle of clothing. Goddamn, Carl thought, that's Adrian Brothers. What is this? Adult life was a labyrinth of saw palmetto stuck into deep, sucking sand. When the not-naked woman turned and began to head inland, Carl moved along with her, a living screen whose own sneakers had to fight the suction efforts of the sand beneath the restless water.

"Here he comes," said the woman of Adrian. "Isn't he darling?"

Carl did not feel her odd question wanted an answer. When they left the water, his side vision fell past her turned-up nose, her slender neck, and came to an embarrassed halt at the lovely up-curve of her left breast. Immediately he cut his eyes away. The peepers were still huddled near the bed of one turquoise pickup, and to this bunch Carl raised the middle finger of his left hand, a gesture seen by Adrian (over whose face played a rainbow of emotions, from bafflement to recognition to fear) and by kneeling Peter (who muttered "Oh, *fock*," before ducking back to the engine he reckoned they would soon need).

The four of them came together in the proximity of the motorcycle. Adrian, now looking peeved, stared along the beach at the pickups. The bunch had disbanded, each man now in the process of mounting his own cab. While Adrian considered this apparent decisiveness on their part, Carl reached out and took from his hand the red flannel shirt. This he put around the woman's shoulders and was relieved when she used one hand to close the material over the transparent source of the probable trouble.

"Carl?" Adrian affirmed, his blonde hair so pale it was invisible in the sunlight. "Thank you. I hope you and Peter aren't injured." Peter was hopping the kick starter to no avail. The pickups had formed up in tandem, six of them, and they appeared to be awaiting the turquoise's leader's order to move out. Adrian said, "I see you're a chip off the old impulsive block."

Carl gripped his scraped elbow and wrinkled up his smarting nose. Piss on this twerp. "We left my father with Emily Overton Mills," he said.

As Carl suspected would happen, Adrian exhibited more

perturbation than he had before, but he only said, "Bully for him. She'll swallow him like a wad of brie."

"Adrian," the woman said, performing some sort of wriggling action underneath the red shirt. "For Christ's sake, give me my clothes and get me out of here."

Adrian handed over her green shorts, white blouse, and shoes. She placed the pile on the sand, and the pickups came on at the speed of a slow walk. Peter Crow rose in the air over his machine and came down with a grunt. After a series of hiccups, it died. He leaned over and tickled the carburetor, his face grim.

"If I can start this suckah," he said, "I say that Carlo and this lady ride it into the dunes where them casters can't take their trucks."

For the first time, Carl took fear; he had never in his life driven a motorcycle. They would perish. Better to stand pat.

Adrian said to Peter, "And we'll face the mob, right?"

Peter didn't answer. Again, he went up and swung down on the kick starter, his hair flying out like feathered wings. The woman had by now turned away from them to fumble beneath the red shirt. Carl watched the graceful stoop necessary to rid herself of her bikini underwear, which she dropped on top of the rest of her things. What self-possession. With a momentous blatting, the motorcycle engine caught and stayed caught. Peter looked around at them with a triumphant display of snaggled teeth . . . until he saw that the turquoise truck had now come even with them, had stopped fifty yards off, between them and the dunes. The other trucks joined up, snouts to tails, and the blockade was complete.

Amid a flurry of flannel-covered elbows, the woman removed the wet shirt and tossed it to Adrian, who still had his back to the trucks. Then she reached her arms through the sleeves of the flannel shirt and buttoned it.

Peter revved the bike until the engine screamed. "Come on, Carlo!" he shouted.

Carl looked at him and shook his head. He decided then

and there that it was time for some of Tessa's bold resolve. "Ma'am," he said to the woman who was now fluffing her hair in a distracted way.

"Her name is Belinda," said Adrian as if he were imparting wisdom.

The tinted side window of the lead truck whizzed down and out popped the swarthy face of the man in the blue gimme cap.

"All right," Carl said, "Belinda . . . would you please make a rude gesture at that man in the pickup."

Instead of protesting, as Carl had half-supposed she would, Belinda moved away from him with a purposeful air. She went past the post that was Adrian, and when she had sufficiently separated herself from her defenders, she planted her feet wide apart in the sand and stood with her red arms akimbo—staring down the trucks it would seem—a slender woman in a shirt whose tail barely covered her own. The motorcycle had gone quiet. A gull swooped through the airspace between Belinda and the trucks. The gimme cap leader had cocked his chin, perhaps signaling for the next move in the drama. Not only did Adrian still have his back turned on the scene, but his eyes were also closed in prayerful avoidance, and his soft belly trembled with either amusement or terror, Carl really didn't care which.

With a quick, pure motion, Belinda turned her back on the trucks, bent at the waist, and with her two hands raised the tail of Adrian's red flannel shirt.

The first female mooning Carl had ever seen.

Delicious.

Whatever happened next, Carl's admiration for Belinda's simple act could not be beaten out of him. And, in his way, he had provoked it. Even Natalie would approve of this.

Peter Crow was sucking on pieces of his own hair.

"What *is* she doing?" said Adrian, still playing the blind man. Belinda raised her head and glared at his khaki backside. Then she smiled at Carl. The gimme cap's mouth seemed to open like the tilting door of a postal box. An air horn on the top of one of the pickups sounded shave-and-a-haircut. As soon as the notes died away, the gimme cap raised a thumb and waggled it. Carl, seeing this, nodded once at Belinda, and she allowed the shirttail to settle back over her most effective posterior. By the time she had brushed past Adrian in order to kiss Carl's cheek, the trucks had moved on like a convoy of Tonka toys in search of new seascapes to conquer.

Emily Overton Mills decided to seduce Devereux Hoopes when she bit into the perception—three quarters of the way through their tour of St. Augustine—that she had in her clutches an obliging if bristly character with whom she might do some carnal business of an innocent sort. In exchange for his relieving her headache, she would tell him the whereabouts of his Cajun princess. But wait a minute, Em, that's far too crass for an old bobby-soxer of your upbringing. It's downright gross. She must include additional delicate morsels before the entire snack would taste acceptably scrumptuous. No doubt that Mr. D. Hoopes of New Jersey and Tuscaloosa was an attractive, no-nonsense sort, with back-curving, aristocratic thumbs that reminded her of swaybacked monks. And when he watched her lips move in presentation of purified historical information, his blue eyes sparkled with wit and attentive energy. That he said little, even when she showed him the Fountain of Youth, must be a mark of an elegant taciturnity, and not merely the glum reticence of a man taken on tour against his will. The chest hairs sprouting from his shirt V were so silky white she wanted to harvest them one by one. This is more like it, Em. He was attractive, physical, and more eligible than he knew. The Dixon girl was far too brittle and cerebral for him. Here, then, was the challenge; she would show him a thing or two about femininity and the erotic potentials of congress with her. And, if she was successful, he could well take it into his head to leave off his pursuit, and then it would not be necessary to exchange stolen information for his necessary favors. Perhaps he would even spend the summer in her spare bedroom, and every day she could flaunt his presence across the lagoon.

Oh Adrian, you feather merchant schmuck!

"Would you like to go to a bistro?" she said to Devereux as the silver Dart passed by the Beacon of Faith Cross, a 208-foot stainless steel cross, marking the exact place where Christianity began in the United States.

"First I'd like to find my son," he said from the passenger seat. "Then it would be nice to visit Adrian where the little dodger works."

Emily pressed her substantial mouth into a prim arch. She realized her new plan had a ways to go to reach fruition. "How 'bout the Coquina Café? We can sit and visit," she said, slowing and gesturing at the place with its rambling roof and a waterwheel sticking up behind. She moved her arm again in order to hear the starchy sound of fresh white linen.

Devereux watched her as he might watch a great actress rehearsing the role of Cleopatra as the eccentric driver of her own barge. "No thanks," he said.

Emily pouted. The car swayed on past the fort, the bay, and through the bright pastels of the town's center, where the Ponce de León statue pointed an accusing finger at Emily, as if to say, "In four hundred seventy-five years, nothing has changed. We wrinkle and die, still chasing ephemera; and look at you, *vieja,* still using the small death as a physic for the brain pain. Shame!"

"I must say," lied Emily, "Adrian won't be found at work. He gads about." She looked over at Devereux and fluttered her mascara-laden eyelashes.

"Then let's go to your house and fuck."

He was looking through the windshield like any handsome tourist. It couldn't be true. She swerved the car back across the midline and said, "Excuse me?"

He laughed in a way that was robust, ominous, and more

143

than a little uncharacteristic of the person she thought she'd met—a kind of heh-heh-heh, drawn back into his larynx before it fully escaped. "You heard me, Emily," he said, reaching along the back of the seat and touching her shoulder blade with the insistent tips of his fingers. As she performed a double take, madly striving to learn, from his uncoopera- tive face, his *attitude,* she noticed in her peripheral vision his gracefully curved thumb, rising from behind her right shoul- der like a pink totem of all that she could not know. "But really," he said, twinkling, "let's do go to your place. You say you can see Adrian's from there. Fine. I'll know when Carl gets back; I'll know when Adrian's through gadding; and in the meantime you can pour me a drink. We'll just visit our heads off." He squeezed her shoulder.

Here Emily developed a healthy suspicion she was being had, and by an expert. All thoughts of erotic commerce, as well as her headache, had been driven from her mind; replac- ing them was a melancholy expectancy that somehow had entered her through his fingers, which had now gone from her shoulder and were draped casually across his corduroy groin.

Oh, Adrian . . . why must you believe my silly guff?!

The Dart swept on along Charlotte Street.

Within the home of Belinda and Holt Ruffin a curious event had taken place. Holt had returned from Tallahassee to find the dishwasher still alive with the drying heat of its final cycle. A tall, jug-eared, and spectacled man of thirty-six, wearing a glen-plaid suit, he had bent down to the door of the machine, touched its heat with his cheek, and then im- mediately he had unlatched and opened the door, pulled out the lower rack, and broken on the kitchen floor every single ceramic plate, cup, and bowl. The stainless steel flatware he had bent into metallic puzzles; the glasses and sharp knives he had (with foresightful precaution) left in the dishwasher.

Now, surrounded by a rubble field of tan and white shards and winking twists of cutlery, he sat at the kitchen table and awaited his faithless helpmeet. Before him on the table were the three love letters and a photograph of the jackass Adrian Brothers, a man so patently misnamed that Holt Ruffin had a great deal of trouble breathing God's air. Already an hour or more had passed, but he was determined that Belinda should see the results of his well-considered rage. Yet he had not prepared himself for her to walk into the kitchen through the backdoor wearing the very same red flannel rag that Brothers wore in the infernal photograph on the table in front of him. Not only that. Her hair was damp, spiky, whorish; in one hand she carried a ball of what must be unmentionables; and the Jezebel was *smiling* . . . at least until her bare feet struck the rubble field. Then, then she stopped and laughed like a brazen person he'd never before encountered in his life.

This is called unchristian, unforgivable goading.

Lorna Crow had yet to move from the divan on her smoky sun porch. She languished here, a slight blue-clad heap, quite intent on her toenails, which peeped above the cuffs of her sailor pants and were painted the color of wet cork. She had heard the Hoopes drive off with Emily Overton Mills, a woman too suited to Adrian's ridiculous fancies. And Lorna was also aware of her son Peter's absence, thanks to the small engine screechings that had preceded Emily's departure with the Hoopes. All of this, including Adrian's escape on the bicycle, registered in Lorna's mind as being of no more importance than the bunions on either great toe—minor blebs, whose horny surfaces she now rubbed together, producing a sandpapery sound that gave her enough pleasure to make it to the next cigarette, or to the moment she might choose to walk downstairs for a jelly glass of this clever, new wine-cooler gimmick.

Purple martins conversed in the shadows of her largest live oak. From down the block came the gay-drag of some New Orleans funeral music, unnecessarily reminding her of the subject. Perhaps Adrian would come into her bed tonight— he did so, by her arrangement, not more than twice a week—and poke away in her roux long enough to dilute the vapors of the grim reaper's breath. Lorna ran a finger down one wrinkled cheek and coughed, a drawn-out affair that must have covered the sound of Adrian's dainty step on the inside stairway . . . because when she'd done racking herself, when she'd made her eyes all bulgy and bloodshot, there he stood above her in the doorway to the sun porch, wearing a damp white shirt and his boy's moody face. Men aged far too well; she felt they should let go as fast as a cut apple in the sun.

She wiped her mouth and croaked, "Fell in the lagoon, did ya?"

He never looked abashed, this Adrian. No, he was more a bedraggled, potbellied lotus-eater with wispy, platinum hair. "Wha'zat?" he said, cruelly imitating what was left of her New Orleans inner-city accent.

Lorna did not rise to the provocation; she never did. "Come here, baby," she crooned. "I bet you hid your bike in my bushes. Tell Momma what happened."

"I swear, Lorna, you're the most sensitive woman I know."

He stepped from the doorway and crossed in front of her to the screen windows overlooking his own apartment. Bending slightly, he peered like any Jack-O caught up in the stickiness of anxiety, of trying to please the entire, ungrateful world. Lorna knew very well he considered he had three women, or more, to look after—although Lorna hardly thought herself in the same category with an arrogant tomato like Emily Overton Mills, or with the new one, this Belinda monkey she had never laid eyes on. How could skinny, butt-less Adrian contain so much passionate nonsense?

She said, "You think there's an ambush down there?"

"Do you?" Adrian turned and fixed his soulful faded-blues on her heaped self. "Tessa Dixon deserves better than that crude—"

"Horsepucky," said Lorna. "She loves the bugger, wants

him to believe enough in the future to commit, connect, cohabit . . . and die."

"You amaze me. You don't believe in love. How can you—"

"No, no. I just don't give two lit farts in hell for it, it's always doomed. But I'm not so foolish to deny it sends nervous Nellies like T. Dixon on long trips to see the endless and stupid ocean. Don't *you* love the fair Belinda?"

For a moment Adrian looked gut-shot, a good trick for someone with the face of a degenerate angel. "I don't—" he began, but was interrupted by a bass cry from the direction of the lagoon.

"BROTHERS!" And, now closer, delivered in tones approximating fire and brimstone, "A-drian Brothers!"

"My lord," whispered Adrian, "it's Holt Ruffin, it's Belinda's husband."

. Lorna wriggled her painted toes, as close as she would come to ecstasy on this day.

Across the lagoon, behind the plate glass of her front window, Emily Overton Mills placed a silver tray atop her piano and turned to her guest. "Would you sit," she said, indicating a campaign chair just next to the piano bench. She handed him one of the moisture-beaded glasses and watched while his thin lips, so sensually circumscribed by beard hair, captured the rim of the glass and formed a passage down which the lime seltzer water might travel. His eyes were not on her. Hooded, they ignored the alcove, the piano, the white bastion of herself. Instead, they must be taking in the lagoon, the palms, and the hovel belonging to her belovéd Adrian. The liquid in Devereux's glass never did reach his delicious lips.

He moved the glass into the still air between them, the skin closest to his nostrils whitened, and he said, "A man with a baseball bat just broke out the taillight of my car."

Emily turned to the window. Fate had such gall . . . her plan skewered from every side. She saw a tallish man in a dark suit disappearing into the vegetation beside the garage.

He did seem to be carrying a thick length of blonde wood. The rear of the gray sedan appeared unscathed, but then the midafternoon glint of sunlight on the lagoon made her sure of nothing. The silence around the piano was broken by the clicking of his glass on the tray.

The last slow moment.

"I suppose," he said, "we should do something about this." He took her linen arm above the elbow and applied steady pressure. "Unless you know something I don't."

Did she? Yes indeed.

Now a woman in red loped along the lagoon road on the other side of the waters. When she came even with the garage, she stopped and stood with her back to them, her arms akimbo.

"All I know," said Emily, "is that that *person* there is wearing Adrian's shirt." She tried to smile.

"In that case," Devereux said, "let's you and me go over there and socialize."

Emily bowed before the idiot wisdom of his determination and led him forthwith to her car.

So much for erotic blackmail.

Ignorant of the vectors of event and emotion in the proximity of the lagoon, Peter Crow and Carl Hoopes had done with feeding their faces at Cuzzin's Sandwich Shoppe and were now heading up Charlotte at an easy blat. Carl's scalp tingled with the sun-fry of their long beach run following Belinda's amazing moon, and the rest of his head felt pleasantly empty of all save the coquina streets through which they passed. He was comfortable in this aged, mossy place, so comfortable that perhaps he should urge Devereux to erect a silken tent on Vedra Beach—well away from the likes of Adrian Brothers and Emily Overton Mills—and in it wait like serene Buddhas for Tessa Dixon to come to *them*. But, fat chance. His pop was no waiter. You got to move, you got to go after them to prove your abiding interest, saith

Big Daddy Sternmouth, who by now, Carl figured, had either heard Emily's life story or had enlisted her aid in the wresting of information from old fool-around Brothers— some such nonsense of grown-up conspiring. Right now, leaning into a right-hand turn behind silent Peter Crow, none of it seemed to much matter. For him, it was, and would be, far more important that the San Sebastian River gleamed like an alligator's wet back in the hot afternoon light: the extraordinary eye-food of the edge of America, Florida brand.

When they cut into St. George Street and came in sight of the garage, Peter shouted over his shoulder, "Jeez, man, look there, it's the mooner!"

Carl, who had been studying the lagoon for signs of waterfowl, looked forward past the whippings of Peter's hair and saw that Belinda truly was standing behind his dad's sedan with her hands over her ears, as if to drown out some horrible caterwauling. Across the lagoon, Carl noted, the silver Dart was once again beginning a circumnavigation of the waterway, this time at a more urgent speed. "Hit it!" he said into Peter's ear.

With a grunt, Peter wristed the accelerator, and the front end of the bike lifted from the pavement so that they covered the remaining distance to Belinda at a more or less full wheelie, an action that caused Carl to clutch Peter's waist in small terror of falling on his ass. The larger terror seemed to be Belinda's. She turned to face the advancing machine as if it were a maddened bear coming at her at a full stand. Her hands flew away from her ears and conjured an invisible screen between herself and her attacker. At that moment, Peter hit the kill button and the rear brake at once. In the sudden, blatless silence the front tire came down with a soft *thwap* on the crushed coquina in front of Peter's pickup. Belinda's face had already moved through several phases, now stopping at grateful recognition, even though her hands remained outstretched.

Behind her, Carl saw the smashed taillight of the Alabama

sedan. "What is it?" he said, putting his feet to the ground and backing off the bike. Belinda's mouth opened for breath and speech, but before a word could be uttered, there came from within Adrian's apartment a sound that much resembled a heavy stick striking an empty wooden barrel. Now a harder blow, a strangled cry; the person dealing out these whacks was not achieving the effect he wanted. Belinda lowered her arms and looked from Peter to Carl as though she expected them to interpret the noises and put them to a stop.

"Lady, what's wrong?" Peter said, dismounting from the bike and leaning it against the pickup. He tugged at his earring. "Is Aid in there? Did one a those casters follow you guys here?"

She used both hands to yank at her hair with throat-gurgling frustration. "It's my jerk of a husband," she finally said. "I don't know if Adrian's in there, I'm afraid to find out."

A voice called out from the bathroom window eight feet from where they stood. "I'm very much here," said Adrian. "I've decided to wait in the bathroom while he smashes my apartment. A passive response is best in these cases. Belinda, I tried to reason with him. I did."

Adrian's bizarre-O declaration was punctuated by first a terrific wallop to a major appliance, then glassware singing the sounds of their own destruction. Carl rolled his eyes away from Belinda's look of mingled disgust and relief.

"You're a wimp, Adrian," she said. "You're lame."

Carl gave silent assent. Turning away from the shaded bathroom window, he discovered that the Dart was nearly upon them, his own dear father riding shotgun. Good, Carl thought, maybe now we can get untangled from this water opera and hit the simple road. Boy!

Peter was saying, "Does my mutha know about this, Aid? It's her property bein' wrecked."

"Your mother knows everything, Pete." The sound of

150

window screening being torn from its moorings. "It's all the same to her."

True.

The Dart bobbled into the space next to Devereux's sedan, and by the time it stopped, Carl was bending into the passenger window to present his father with the simple (!) facts of the situation. But before he could introduce words of his own into the perfumed interior of the Dart, Emily said, "Who is that woman in A's shirt?" With her hair all wisped out and sweat dotting her pancaked upper lip, she looked like Katharine Hepburn's oversize cousin undergoing a ladylike fit.

Devereux turned his face toward Carl and allowed the closest eyelid to fall shut; otherwise he remained as impassive and sincere as the wall of a fort.

"Her name is Belinda something," Carl offered. "Her husband's inside trashing Adrian's apartment." Carl slipped sideways into a welcome perversity. "Now Adrian, he's in the loo chatting with Belinda through the window there," he piped. His sense of unreality had the feel of overwhelming humidity, especially when Emily began to hyperventilate, one hand splayed across the foothill of her bosom.

"Ch-ch-chatting!" she managed.

Carl watched Devereux place a comforting hand on her shoulder, a hand he had to clap down hard when a deep male voice from within the apartment pleaded, "Brothers, you lechering pirate, please come out of there," and Emily began to show signs of a major palsy in her upper body.

"He's f-f-fucking her!" she cried. "Both of us!"

At this, Carl withdrew from the car window and looked over to Belinda and Peter, both of whom now regarded the trembling Dart as if it might harbor a ticking, explosive device. Belinda's face seemed to pop with revelation. She whipped her head in the direction of the window and said loudly, "Your principles suck, Adrian. I hope Holt brains you."

Any response Adrian might have made was creamed by the blaring of the Dart's horn, a lunatic herald sounding notice of Emily's emergence from her silver carriage. Before Carl could quite comprehend, she had swished past him, headed for Belinda with sufficient fierce momentum to plow through the front wall of the rickety garage and crush Adrian in his hideout. But this did not happen. Peter Crow retreated in the face of her onslaught, in fact looked to be preparing to remount his bike and ride away. Instead, while slight Belinda held her ground, Peter disappeared around the far corner of the garage.

Carl fisted his hands in his pockets and squinted into the brightness that surrounded the coming together of the two women . . . as if they were being harshly illuminated by a malevolent fashion photographer—Emily in pure, rumpled white; Belinda in the worn red flannel of her alleged lover. Carl supposed they might go at each other with small swords, if someone had only thought to bring them along.

Devereux was at Carl's back now, a truly comforting presence who whispered, "I think we've fetched up in a nest of hotheaded beach mice."

Out of the side of his mouth, Carl said, "Right, Pop, but—"

Emily and Belinda were only staring at the shaded window, ignoring each other, as if each could not possibly recognize the other as a species allowed on the planet.

Not a sound came from the apartment. Perhaps the destructive husband had by now brained Adrian, or had marched off some back way, or was even now slumped against the bathroom door counting his tears while Peter Crow watched him through a smashed window screen.

Belinda leaned toward the bathroom window and said, "I want to see your face, Adrian."

"Right now, little man," said Emily, her breathing under control. "If *I* don't, I swear on the head of Ponce de León I'll tell this Hoopes what you did with his girlfriend."

Behind him, Carl heard the in-suck of Devereux's breath. "Don't worry," he said. "We're closer."

Carl shrugged. What's to worry?

Belinda shook her fist at the window. "I don't believe this! *What* girlfriend?"

The shade snapped upward, and behind the window's screening appeared a shadowy version of Adrian Brothers's face. He did not in any way look like a man encircled by several problems. As far as Carl could tell, his face was that of a florid saint doing good works left and right.

Adrian said, "Belinda, I think you should come inside and care for Holt. I've told him the truth, but he doesn't believe me. He's desperately unhappy and needs your attention."

Belinda stomped her bare foot in the coquina dust. "You are so full of shit, Adrian Brothers."

Emily gave no sign that she agreed or disagreed; she just stood there with her arms folded across her chest, perhaps waiting (Carl thought, hopefully) for Adrian to set her off like a rocket.

Instead, Adrian said, "Emily, I did nothing to or with Tessa Dixon. So don't threaten me, you hear, sugar. Why don't you just go on home and diddle your piano."

That did the trick. Emily's mouth contracted to the point of invisibility. She turned on Belinda and, for want of any other reachable target, like a beleaguered kid hounded by a bully, Emily clutched at the front of the red flannel shirt in an effort to rip the offending garment from Belinda's body.

Flailing at Emily's clawed hand, crying, "Cut it out!" Belinda lurched backward.

And here and now, within sight of the sentinel palms, the indifferent lagoon, the lazily circling osprey, and the brooding live oaks, Devereux Hoopes—winker, ironist, waiter— made his first spontaneous move of the day, if not the last ten days. He ran, this Hoopes, past his stalwart son and, once he reached the grappling women, encircled Emily's upper body with his arms, bringing his hands together beneath her breasts and—simultaneously—squeezing her diaphragm and jerking her off her feet and away from Belinda Ruffin. Since the jerk-back occurred while Emily's hand had firm hold of an expanse of red flannel, the shirt's buttons flew into the air like black gumdrops. Devereux tucked his chin into the softness of Emily's neck and turned about, turned the struggling sack of Emily away from Belinda and began to propel Emily toward her car like a kidnapper with his victim, or a man practicing the Heimlich maneuver under combat conditions. In one hand Emily clutched a victorious swatch of flannel, and as they moved, she roared out in the voice of the old bawd she must want to be, "Fuck you, A!"

The woman had the specific gravity of a hundred-pound sack of flour, yet her neck skin smelled of lilac and was the texture of a young girl's. Behind them, Adrian's voice said, "I think, Mr. Hoopes, you should throw her in the lagoon."

Emily sputtered, seemed to shimmy in Devereux's arms, but he pressed on with his load. Carl's face floated past them, its affectionate startlement as clearly exhibited as the bright sunlight would allow. Good, swell fellow Carl, taking it all in like his personal video. What a summer!

Devereux swerved around the rear of Emily's car and leaned her against the driver's door, his own loins pressed tight to her buttocks, pinning her while he spoke into her baroque ear, at the same time noting the appearance on the path from Adrian's apartment of the dark-suited Holt Ruffin, who carried his baseball bat dangling from one wrist.

"Emily," said Devereux, "tell me where Tessa is, tell me right now." She made a sound, a cross between a humming and a gasp, and then her pillowy rear moved even more tightly against him, cleaving to him with a lasciviousness to which he only half-pretended to respond. He saw, when she arched back her head, her lips, lips redder by far than the cloth she still clutched in the hand that now seemed to be reaching up from below to caress his cheek, or scratch out his eyes.

She said, "I love your thumbs."

Mother of us all! What foolishness is this?

Carl, in the middle distance, began to move toward Holt Ruffin, perhaps to protect tattered Belinda, perhaps to demand reparation for the busted taillight, perhaps both.

"My thumbs aren't the issue here," Devereux said, aware that these same appendages lay curved against the bottom swells of her breasts. He flexed his arm muscles, squeezing her, the thumbs again pressuring her diaphragm. Now, at the risk of her offense and his own dignity, he would expel the morsel of simple knowledge from her trachea. Emily's breath flew from her mouth like a sweet wind.

"Cumberland Island," she gasped—syllables borne on the same wind. "Georgia. She took A's little tent—his tepee. I saw her."

Of course! An island! An endless circle of empty beach! Tessa's vision of perfection.

Devereux released his swooning captive, but not before brushing with his lips her tender neck and murmuring, "Thanks, you're swell."

Meanwhile, Carl stared into the haggard face of Holt Ruffin. He looked—with his pinched nostrils, his horn-rim glasses, his wrinkly, dark green suit—more like a Ralph or a Dave recently defeated in a bid to become a Boy Scout troop leader; no way had this man just made a havoc of the Brothers pad. Carl knew that Belinda, who stood calmly in front of the bathroom window, was in no danger. The baseball bat in Holt's hand might as well be a length of wet pasta. Carl stepped aside to permit Holt to continue on to his wife, but the man seemed inclined to speak through his chapped lips, to issue Carl some bit of wise misery— perhaps a warning against the tomfoolery of the world, perhaps a theorem as to the counterproductiveness of wanton, baseball-bat destruction.

The engine of Emily Overton Mills's Dart cranked, caught, began to tick the sedated rhythms of its owner, a ripper of shirts, but now apparently retired from the fray, and content (maybe) to back the car into the lagoon so that Devereux could rescue her once again from her impulses.

Still, Holt said nothing, continued to stand in the heat glare like a stoned Mormon. Carl glanced at Belinda. She was holding one hand over the squarish hole in her shirt above her heart, and she looked like a patriotic if dazed reciter of the pledge of allegiance, though a ribbon of her fine torso was exposed to Carl, thanks to the shirt's missing buttons.

And Adrian? Had he crawled into the linen cabinet for a snooze, in hopes these players in the lagoon drama would go away for lack of someone to diddle them into their various frenzies? Carl would bet that Peter Crow was upstairs in his own apartment reading *Motorcycle Madness,* oblivious to the grown-ups below. Carl cleared his throat of the whole business and looked to Devereux for the next move.

The old cock was bowing Emily's car out of its parking space and into the road, on his face the look of a happy man, which in his case meant a kind of jagged crack of pleasure or triumph, laid over the harsh landscape of his face.

"Son," Holt finally said in the modulated voice of a reasonable man, "forget about growing up." He handed Carl the bat and a fifty-dollar bill, smoothed his suit jacket, and walked over to Belinda at the same time Emily's car gained the road and began a slow acceleration. When she came abreast of Holt and Belinda, Emily turned her head to them—her hair an undone fright—and produced a smile that would have dazzled a zombie; in front of this message, one hand fluttered her red flannel souvenir.

Belinda removed her hand from Adrian's torn shirt and waved her whole arm in the swimming air. The moving hand nearly knocked off Holt's glasses as she called out to Emily, "You've got it all wrong, sister! I thank you from the bottom of my heart." And, for sure, the rent in her shirt revealed even more of that thankful heart, at least until Holt formally removed his jacket and—just as Carl had done on the beach—placed it around his wife's shoulders, buttoning her into modesty . . . while Emily Overton Mills motored into the rest of her life by the bitter lagoon.

Devereux came and stood beside Carl. Together they watched the married couple begin to walk up the road with the purposeful air of ordinary folk out for exercise and companionship.

"Nice to have met you," called Devereux; and when Carl flashed him the fifty-dollar bill, he added, "we'll put the money to good use."

Belinda looked back over her shoulder and offered Carl a steady gaze full of what he considered beach rapport. "I say buy Adrian a new shirt," she said. "He'll never see this one again. Take care."

Holt picked up the pace and soon enough they became any distant pedestrians, slightly distorted by the pavement's radiant heat waves.

Carl placed an arm across Devereux's back and rubbed his palm against the trusted material of his father's shirt. "Well, Pop," he said, "did you score? Are we on our way?"

Devereux smiled, glanced at the empty bathroom window, and nodded with all the certainty of a master scout back from a long reconnoiter. "Apparently," he drawled, "loyalty to women has its difficulties." He looked up at Carl, his gray-blues as calm as the lagoon. "What's wrong with your face? Your nose is scraped."

Carl flashed a wicked, no-teeth smile of his own, but only said, "Where we headed?"

"One of the sea islands," Devereux said. "Right now, old friend."

They embraced. Carl's sneakers dug into the coquina dust, and as he hoisted Devereux into the air, he dropped the bat into that good, powdery stuff. His father smelled of lilac and sweat.

On the second floor of the main house, Lorna Crow's sun porch contained its afternoon share of stippled shadows, still contained Lorna herself, who lay upon the divan like the grand dame of wrinkled patience. Her earlier ecstasy at the arrival of Holt Ruffin had given way to a reverie of Adrian's muddled fate, a reverie punctuated by the rising sounds of domestic farce: of crashing, of tinkling glass, of pointless exclamations that came to her like fragments of a vanishing dream, but a dream that did not belong in any way to her as she reclined, smoked, sipped from her wine cooler—secure in her knowledge that when all was done, Adrian would come to her for his dose of world-weary comfort, her secret potion.

But he never came.

For, in the aftermath of the Hoopes departure, Adrian Brothers had emerged from his bathroom into the wreckage of his apartment, had stood in the midst of it—bereft now of all his women—and decided that fate's revised map of grace had no room for anyone but the sublime, unreachable Tessa Dixon. At first, this certainty of a perpetual monogamy came to him with a tickle of whimsy (after all, he had no real choice here, had he?), but when he saw that Holt Ruffin had dislodged from the wall of his sitting room the greenish and murky portrait of Emily Overton Mills, Adrian seized upon a ceremonial way of marking his liberation from the heady exertions of his flesh. The overpainted horror of a portrait lay across his desk, a piece of ripped-out screening covering Emily's features like a gray, distorting mask. Flushed with the prospect of action, he stepped around the ruin of his bed—Holt had ripped Adrian's sole pair of sheets into bandagelike strips, fastidious even in his short-lived rage—and took the yard-square painting by its off-kilter stretchers. The screening slid away from Emily's face and fell to the floor. Adrian bore her image out the door and along the path; all the while her headachey eyes watched his progress toward the road and the lagoon beyond . . . into which he threw her . . . and on which she floated until the water penetrated the canvas, she tilted, and slipped down into the darkness.

Adrian, his white shirt now perfectly dry, watched her become invisible, and when he looked toward her house, toward Belinda's house as well, he appeared a man at peace with his own guiltlessness.

North, on Cumberland Island, under a cloudless sky, good weather thus guaranteed in the visible, perfect world, Tessa Dixon smiled with delight at all she surveyed. Also pointed north—its direction commanded by Tessa and Tessa alone—the gray Japanese sedan followed the sea road to Jacksonville, out of the world of coquina, saw palmetto, and the unseen limpkin bird. Carl drove.

CUMBERLAND ISLAND

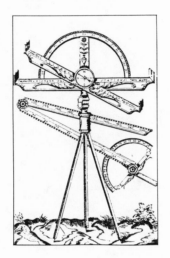

FOR SOME there is keen relief in leaving behind the gaudy constructs of tourism. No matter that a few of these sites possess proved souls, are "true" to history—every pot, pillar, and beam authentic, each tale-bearing plaque certified by a historical society or a local antiquarian; the larger "truth" is that the sites spawn your horse-jitneys, your Ripley's, your Info Booths, your Fountains of Youth; and these, some cannot abide. If the very Spanish moss seems to serve commercial greed, then it is time to move north in search of the unbesmirched coast, even if such regions are likely controlled by the United States government's National Park Service and its able rangers, the watchmen of the National Seashores.

St. Marys, in the extreme southeastern corner of Georgia, is the drowsy embarcation point for the government ferry to Cumberland Island. On any morning—May to October—it's possible to breakfast at the local café catercorner to the ferry's ticket office, which itself is part of a wooden pier that juts out over the quiet, uncluttered waters of the St. Marys River. Enter this café at around eight o'clock, after purchasing round-trip tickets to the island, and find dozens upon dozens of others who have chosen the same way to pass the time before boarding the vessel awaiting them at the end of the pier. Tourists, yes, all of them, whether dressed like jungle birds or in the khaki and rough-out leather of those who have hiked the Appalachian Trail or the bowels of the Grand Canyon. In the middle of the short main street, parked side by side, the cars of these breakfasters contain sunglasses, lotions, coolers, straw caps, cameras, and—a few of them—the bright nylon cylinders and packs of camping gear, for it is possible to sojourn on Cumberland from one to seven nights so long as each camper is willing to tote his or her own grub, potable water, repellent against the dread gnats, a source of light, and perhaps a book or two. ("Campers will not be permitted to use the ferry boat to resupply themselves.")

On this Tuesday morning in June, a day that already promised outlandish heat beneath a scattering of fibery, heaven-reaching cirrus clouds, two Japanese automobiles were paired in the designated parking area—one gray; the other, the older and the smaller, sun-bleached yellow, its hood rippled by accident, its windshield smeary with travel crud, its rear bumper a billboard possibly more assertive than its owner on such public issues as nuclear war and abortion. The freshest sticker—"Wild Women Don't Get the Blues"—looked to have been mounted slapdash by someone anxious to blot out parts of the more righteous messages. On the dash of the yellow car, barely to be seen through the windshield grime, were a miniature, pink-mouthed conch shell and a slim paperback copy of *Los naufragios* (The Shipwrecked), A. N. Cabeza de Vaca's recounting of disasters and amazing survivals on the lower extremities of the North American continent. Otherwise, the car's interior was empty of personal objects.

After a motel night in Kingsland, Georgia, Devereux and Carl Hoopes had had no trouble covering the eight miles to St. Marys, where they discovered the yellow car with all the nonchalance of two guys running into an old friend in the supermarket parking lot. Or so Carl thought when they spotted the car, Tessa's car, and Devereux, beside him in the passenger seat, simply nodded his head once and said, "Awlright." Still, Devereux's right leg had been jiggling against the underside of the dash all the way from Kingsland, and Carl had to figure a fair number of repetitions of Will She?/ Won't She? in the rainbow mind of this father he would probably never fully know. Had not Carl asked, after they'd turned off the light in the motel last night, "If we find her, Pop, what then?"

"We have either a long or a short period of . . . decompression," Devereux had said, and then commenced to snore with impressive fervor.

Now, they stood at the back end of Tessa's car and gazed upon the new bumper sticker with more bewilderment than nonchalance.

"Weird," said Carl. "She's about as wild as me."

Devereux adjusted his sunglasses, the better to fathom what they beheld. "No, it's not *her*, is it?" he said finally.

Behind them, people made passes at the ticket office and then either headed for the café or strolled to the end of the pier where they might check out the fittings of the boat that would diesel them to the island. Devereux and Carl crossed the road to the office: the father in light corduroy trousers, once-white leather court shoes, and blue-going-white cotton shirt; the son in fatigues cut off as mock-Bermudas, the resurrected and colorless sneakers, and a bright yellow Bama-Bino T-shirt from a well-known chain of Tuscaloosa pizza stores where Carl had once worked the duration of a sweltering summer.

Patriarch as grizzled beach scout.

His male issue as a tall, fair boy with well-turned calves the color of cinnamon sugar, or the sand of Cape Hatteras.

Carl hung around outside regarding the sparseness of the town and the riverfront, while Devereux entered the crisp air-conditioning of the office and lucked into two no-show tickets that he paid for with Holt Ruffin's fifty-dollar bill. (The bat-struck sedan would continue to collect and endure unrepaired wounds for years to come; Devereux did not believe in cosmetic bodywork.) Behind the counter, several feet away from the female ranger who had provided the tickets, a male ranger in acorn brown uniform occupied his swivel desk chair like a golden-haired and amiable preacher, the desk a pulpit from which he might issue homilies having to do with island visiting. Devereux had not recently felt so drawn to an official of the United States government, and as he tucked away his change and thanked the ticket seller, the male ranger rose from his chair and advanced to the counter, a handsome, smooth-skinned, immaculate definition of blue-eyed authority if there ever was one. He could not have been more than twenty-six. After lifting the counter flap, he entered the public's realm and smiled openly at Devereux, for whom he then held open the street door, and the two of them passed from the cool office into the hotting Georgia morning.

The ranger's plastic name tag read "Bevan Smith."

"Been to the island before?" he asked. No southern cadences here—say, Des Moines, Iowa . . . some placid and bland center of rectitude.

"No." Devereux swallowed the "sir." Silly reflex for a grown man. "I've been knowing about it for years."

At the bottom of the stairs, Bevan Smith stopped and gave Carl a look that immediately made the connection between the beach scout and his tall boy. "You ought to camp," Smith said to Carl. "You can't know the island until you hear its night."

Both Devereux and Carl stared at the ranger as though his graceful conceit had violated the protocol for officialdom. Smith pulled a billed cap from his belt, fixed it squarely on his head, and flashed them his solid, midwestern teeth.

"Are there animals and stuff?" Carl said.

"Alligators and mink in the saltwater marshes. That's a fact. Pretty little feral horses. Loggerhead turtles in the dunes, sometimes. The most savvy raccoons in the world, and a whole host of your diamondback rattlers and cottonmouth moccasins." Smith perfected the placement of his cap. "Still, if you're careful, the place is a soul cleanser. It's full of the benevolent magic of solitude. Most people understand this; only a few behave like numskulls," he went on in his sober, informational way. "I don't imagine I'll have that problem with you folks."

Devereux took off his sunglasses and arranged for Bevan Smith a forthright expression. Did uncovering the eyes signify sincerity, openness? It might. "Are you talking vandalism, littering, drinking, what?"

Smith took a long breath and sank his massive hands into his trouser pockets. "Oh no, I'm talking botheration of other human beings. You see, most campers prefer to be left completely to themselves, so alone they're liable to be startled by their own footprints."

"I understand," said Devereux, aware that he was frowning, his empty stomach more hollow than it should be. "Do that many people camp alone?"

Smith returned the frown, and his blue eyes flattened. "It's not so rare. There's an eco-biologist out there now, a fellow with the university. There's a photographer been on for days. And the woman who belongs to that yellow car you gentlemen were looking over so thoroughly a few minutes ago. A nice woman." He smiled, but his eyes remained cold and alert.

Carl stepped on the suspicion with alacrity. "She's a good friend of ours, sir," he said, his hands held out to the ranger, palms up, the hands of a human being who hadn't lied, so far as Devereux knew, since he was five years old, and then, disastrously. Good Carl continued, "We're bringing her a few things."

Such as themselves.

"Her name is Tessa Dixon," Devereux said.

"I know that," said Smith, visibly relaxing. "She's a sweetheart."

Yes, but whose?

Devereux asked Bevan Smith how much time they had until the ferry departed. "Right," he said, in charge, "my spiel begins in fifteen minutes. You wouldn't want to miss that. Best go to the café and chow down; it's a long day over there." He touched two fingers of his left hand to the bill of his cap and began to stride toward the pier.

Carl glanced at Devereux, found his father fiddling with

his sunglasses, and so took it upon himself to say to the ranger, "I was wondering if you know where Ms. Dixon is camped."

Ah, foresight in the young—one of the rarer virtuous qualities.

Bevan Smith stopped, half-turned, his billed head silhouetted against the sun-drenched gleam of the river beyond him. "The Sea Camp, near the showers," he said. "An orange tent more or less like a tepee"—his cheek muscle twitched—"as you must know."

Smith's Wellington boots sounded on the cross boards of the pier as he approached his audience of island-goers.

After a breakfast of sausage biscuits and hot tea, Devereux and Carl returned to the gray sedan and from its backseat removed a small canvas sack that had been hopefully prepared the night before. In it were Devereux's colorless shorts, a flashlight, a plastic bottle of number six sunscreen, Carl's black Swiss army knife, repellent, and—now transferred from Devereux's back pocket—the map/brochure of the island given to him along with the tickets. They then crossed the street and joined with the other passengers at the end of the pier where Bevan Smith stood a few feet up the ferry's gangway, already in the midst of his spiel.

". . . folks, we expect that what you truck onto Cumberland you'll truck off. We expect you to keep to the paths, or to the main road we call Grand Avenue, others call Interstate Zero." Chuckles from the crowd, a rapt bunch in the face of information and warning so well mixed by this handsome (and large) public employee. "Sections of the island are privately owned; there are families of some eccentricity. Please respect fences and posted signs.

"With forty square miles of marsh, live oak forest, estuary, and dune, with eighteen or more miles of spotless beach, most of you should have no trouble staying out of trouble, no trouble avoiding the islanders, who are not always so friendly. But your real enemies are the ticks and the gnats, the sun and the snake."

A boy-child in a camouflage jumpsuit said, "I hate a snake!" only to be shushed by his father.

Bevan Smith smiled upon them all before proceeding to rap out the rules of the ferry, urging that they return to Sea Camp Dock and Visitor Center by 4:15 in the afternoon, else they would be spending the night buried in the sand like loggerhead eggs, because the mosquitoes and gnats wouldn't allow those without proper equipment any other form of sleeping. "And believe me," he said, "the gnats, especially, control the forest at night. They seek the dark, moist places of the body"—he smiled like an innocent schoolboy and provoked scattered tittering among the assembled passengers—" and should you venture off the paths or away from the camping area, the ticks will literally jump off of the forest floor to secure the services of your person.

"But the island will return love for love. All aboard!"

Once they had clambered onto the white, broad-beamed ferry, Devereux and Carl mounted to the upper deck and stood behind the flat-roofed box of the wheelhouse. Positioned in the bow below them, Bevan Smith chatted with a group of earnest backpackers with knotty, soccer-player thigh muscles. Voices floated over the diesel burble of the engines.

Once they were under way, at a distance from the brownish docks and the few snouty shrimpers of St. Marys, the river began to widen, and after twenty minutes of cruising, they emerged into Cumberland Sound, leaving behind a mainland of scrub pine, salt flats, and cord grass. Soon enough, Cumberland's lower self could be seen—a jungle-like mass of greenery stretching north on the horizon.

Tessa's island!

On a good map the island resembles the silhouette of a moronically grinning shark, its huge and deformed fin veined by the meanderings of the Brickhill River. But focus on the shark's tail area to the south, marked on the southwest by Sea Camp Visitor Center. Eastward, across this shank of the island, lies Sea Camp itself. Find the seashore boundary of the kinked and embrangled live oak forest that creates for the pilgrim the revelation of passing from holy twilight into the overwhelming white glare that washes a double set of low dunes and, beyond, a beach of such magnitude that human figures appear of no more consequence than the terns, the pelicans, the sanderlings, or the mother loggerheads intent in their season on sculpting nests in the dunes for the eggs of their horizon-seeking young.

On this day, the morning winds from the pressing breath of the sea had whorled the fine sand into miniature and exquisite ridges, perfect topographic maps of a terrain that because of the wind would last not much longer than the time it might take a pursuer to walk a mile or so north of Sea Camp, either on the dirt-and-shell Interstate Zero, or on the firm, wet sand of low tide, the surf in temporary retreat from any footprints that might have been made by an individual advancing into the perspective with the determination of a starving Cabeza de Vaca bent on conquering the perimeter of the island, an individual near-naked and alone, willfully alone.

But now, at 10:30 A.M., Tessa Dixon sat cross-legged on her folded shirt midway between the sea and the double set of dunes backed up by the live oak forest that here in its northern progress offered a gap or portal in its façade wide enough to drive a jeep through, as if Bevan Smith or one of his colleagues might need such access to the beach at just this point in order to ensure the safety of such as Ms. Dixon— given to bare-breasted solitude. Her mass of dark curls had been flattened by the wind and now clung to her head like an everchanging netting, and this gave prominence to her nose, her rounded chin, the blue eyes that narrowed eastward as if the wind were a tonic to be savored. This 102-pound woman in jade green shorts, her skin a dark honey except for the small, pinked breasts, from a distance those of an adolescent girl's; this woman so still on the sand she might have been a piece of driftwood sculpture.

The terns paid her no mind. No camper debris here, no scraps of white bread flung into the air for the swooping catch. And her hair held no interest for them, no more interest than the moving clouds above or the hot yellow star of the sun, which had turned the air of this deserted portion of the beach into a shimmying dance-field of rising thermals that supported the terns in their disdain of the pacific woman with the ribbon of jade across her narrow loins. If she owned the island, if she sat there in full possession of its life, its aspects, its magical soul . . . they could care less, these graceful scavengers with their cool side eyes, their deeply forked tails, and snowy breasts so unlike the twin swellings of the still figure below them.

In the perspective now: human movement.

Trouble, she would have thought had she known, she who didn't favor any but the most necessary movement, and only then movement toward grace, purity, bliss—the many impossibilities a starving cerebralist's life offers up like food encased in unbreakable glass. Her breakfast had consisted of four carrots and a swig of water from her canteen.

From the gap in the live oak forest emerged three figures on foot, figures that came on over the dune humps toward the rising sea as if they might be the true owners of all they looked upon. Not tourists agog with what they had seen of palmetto and sea myrtle; not booted trekkers intent on the conquest of distance in the shortest possible time; not Devereux, Carl, or Bevan Smith; no, these three—a mother and her two sturdy teenage boys—were residents of the privately owned part of the island marked on the west by the red-roofed Grayfield Inn, an inn that provided mail and social intercourse to, among others, these three members of the family Vesuvio who were striding through the hot sugar of the sand in the direction of Tessa Dixon's well-aligned back.

Ahead of her sun-darkened offspring, Marni Vesuvio swung a straw carryall in one hand, in the other an Indian print bedspread. She had some height to her, this forty-one-year-old veteran of the Georgia sun, a height accentuated by the length of her neck, a supple stalk supporting a close-cropped head—the face a collection of narrownesses, as if she'd been too quickly sketched. Even her sunglasses were as narrow as a strip of film. Her bikini was handmade from red calico bandannas, bits of cloth carelessly protecting the modesty of a muscular body, with skin like the carapace of an oiled leather purse. On her feet were thongs that slapped her heels as she led her boys in the direction of the fickle ocean. These adolescents—come to be named Pell and Mell by their father, Pierre—carried between them a yellow rubber dinghy, which they hefted by the gunwale safety lines as if they were both intent on leaving the island and their mother as soon as the surf could be reached. Although Pell's suit was orange and Mell's dirty white, they were identical twins. Each fourteen-year-old cheek bedded a pinch of smokeless tobacco, the spit from which dotted the white sand of their passage with gobbets of amber.

When Marni emerged from the dunes into the great, whorled topography of the open beach, she also entered the thermal dance-field of diffraction in which light seemed to puddle, shimmy, or elongate all moving objects. Conscious only of her curiosity about the woman meditating on the sand in the distance like a naked stele, Marni was unaware of her own transformation into a swan-necked sylph . . . followed by two stubby trolls bearing an oval platter of liquid butter. Yet once she had come abreast of the meditator, once she had thrown down her bedspread ten feet away, once she had overseen Pell and Mell's march to the sea, once she had removed the bandanna from her pendant breasts, and once she had pressed her body to the spread and the hot sand below, Marni Vesuvio knew she was being secretly regarded by the other woman as an apparition, a Cumberland mirage arrived from the dunescape.

With her arms crossed above her head and her face turned to the left, Marni peeked through the V of her armpit and wondered if the meditator wondered why her space had been invaded when she, Marni, could easily have chosen six of a million other square feet of unoccupied, wind-dictated sand.

In the bashing waters of the surf, Pell and Mell worked as one at launching their dinghy in the direction of Bermuda where, thanks to their father's home-teachings, they fancied they might find a mountainside cave overlooking endless fields of red onions. Both of them, however, were reluctant to depart with the single paddle they had between them. Their mom had promised another, yet she was notorious for her "after while's," her "someday's," her general spaciness. Even now, they knew, she was trying to drive the bare-titted lady nuts, or at least a little sunstrokey. With a deal of spitting, and no conversation, they managed the boat beyond the breakers and rolled aboard, Pell paddling with practiced vigor, the aluminum blade flashing in the sunlight like Poseidon's silvery eye.

To Tessa's distorted eyes, the boys in their fragile craft became her own brother disappearing into the morning sun of Grand Isle, Louisiana, land's end, the day it became clear their mother had given over her mind and heart to God. No surf at Grand Isle, no wind—only religious ecstasy, and the young boy rowing away from it into the hazy hot light of sanity. Tessa curled her fingers into her kneecaps and breathed with the wind in hopes that the woman on the bedspread would ascend to heaven as Tessa's mother had already done. Begone, calico cunt, and stop watching me from the hairy cave of your armpit—a single black eye beaming its message of invasion and desire. Tessa shrugged from under the paranoia of contact, uncrossed her legs, and got to her feet, careful to give the bedspread woman her back. She would move on north, the best of all directions. But a voice said, "I went down like a willow," and her nose narrowed in disbelief that this could be the voice of her mother speaking from somewhere above the heaven-reaching clouds. "I gave myself over to Him and went down like a willow, Teresa, you must do this. There are Catchers, you won't be hurt. Listen to your Mamere . . ."

Empty, dry, sunstruck, Tessa Dixon swooned and crumpled onto the sand like a suddenly abandoned cloak dyed brown, white, green, her face upturned to the clouds as peaceful as if she were listening to a music of oceanic grace.

The witness, Marni Vesuvio, believed, first, that the slender woman had been downed by the wind, and then— spying her boneless inertness—that malaria or tick fever might have been smuggled into her bloodstream. In any event, Marni roused herself to render what aid she could.

Offshore, in the minds of Pell and Mell, the world had become the illuminated horizon beyond which anything could be waiting. Their mom would have a bodacious time calling them back now!

On Interstate Zero, not quite a mile north of Sea Camp, Carl Hoopes (per agreement with his father) reconnoitered the island's nifty interior, or at least the parts resplendent to either side of the arrow-straight, dirt-and-shell roadway on which his sneakers crunched so pleasantly. Beneath the seemingly man-thinned pine and oak, the chartreuse palmetto plants and the woody vines thick as hawsers gathered like a psychedelic florist's idea of garnishing for indoor trees. Under the live-oak canopy of branches reaching out to impossible lengths, the sense of being *inside,* in a controlled domain, was manifest; and Carl found it hard to believe that this innocent arboretum so reminiscent of a movie set could harbor the various lethal snakes colorfully depicted on the poster he and Devereux had found fixed to a shed next to the showers in Sea Camp. But Carl sure as hell wouldn't leave the roadway, not even if he spotted a whitetail deer, one of the feral horses, a brace of hogs, a trumpeting pileated woodpecker, Guale indian hatchet markings on a tree trunk, or the carved initials of General James Edward Oglethorpe himself . . . and other such island lore as Carl had read in the brochure during the ferry ride with silent Devereux.

A Devereux, Carl imagined now, striding the outer beach like Captain Nemo deprived of his Nautilus (the Kings Bay Submarine Support Base was not far to the west in the mainland marshes), but certain, this Nemo, that at any moment his craft would surface and bob in the shoals like a sleek, beautiful dolphin. Whichever of them first made contact with Tessa—assuming she favored northerly movement—was to return with her—assuming she favored return—to the pint-size orange tepee they had found so well pitched on the outskirts of Sea Camp, and where they had left their kit.

Carl walked on through the jigsaw shadows, his hands well down in the pockets of his fatigue cutoffs, his yellow T-shirt an advancing beacon that might be seen a half-mile up the roadway, although on the icinglike perfection of the roadway he could see no one. He felt pretty sure he would not encounter Tessa; that she would hold to the outer beach, not this arranged interior; and that Devereux would be the one fated to make the prime connection with his skittish lover. So Carl scuffed his sneakers through the crumbly shells to the place on the roadway where a plain dirt trail led off to the right, toward the beach. A short way down this trail was parked a topless, dark brown jeep that looked both empty and vaguely official. To his left he could see through a thinning of the trees what he felt certain to be a fenced pasture full of thoroughbred horses, a pasture so clipped, so green that it could be a mirage visiting from rural Kentucky. The dozen or so horses were as still as cutouts. Forgetting snakes, ticks, gnats he had yet to meet, Carl abandoned the roadway and struck out across the floor of the forest, intent on disproving the evidence of his eyeballs. Among the fern, palmetto, and vine he zigzagged, his sneakers leaving exact impressions in the spongy earth. A hundred yards from the roadway, he stopped beneath a giant grandfather of a live oak, its branches festooned with Spanish moss. In front of him, the pasture fencing was of ancient split rail; the horses were indeed svelte enough to be racers, and they nibbled at the grasses with all the dumb nervelessness of sheep.

From the tree branches above, a voice turned Carl's insides blue with startlement, "Ours is a country of contrasts."

Up snapped Carl's head and he beheld—in the crook of one great branch—a man who wore dark shorts covered with yellow moons and stars, a man with sleepy, liquid eyes that were not at all threatening. He was reclining in the crook as if he might live in the tree trunk itself, the branch his front yard, the pasture and its horses his fields and chattels. "Do I know you?" he said.

Carl gulped and offered a smile suitable for authority. "No. I was just curious about the horses. They're so . . . out of place, in the midst of all this."

The man shook his head—the hair was long, blonde, a frame for the gentle face of a fifty-year-old with peeling skin across his nose and cheekbones. "Not if you live here," he said, "but I know what you mean. This tree, now"— he patted the rough bark next to his thigh—"I'm married to her." Carl blinked. "We should all marry trees," the man went on. "Or you and the wife can form a ménage. It's a perfect sort of harmless communion. Do you like the circus?"

"Sure."

"I was ringmaster of the Tree of Life Circus out of St. Pete. You know it? I doubt you're old enough."

"Can't say that I do," said Carl, a little spooked and inclined to back off the way he had come.

"Oh, it was a powerful and magic bunch we had. Airwalkers and the like, elephants juggling heads of lettuce. Mantric clowns. All gone now." He smiled radiantly and tossed his hands into the air like an evangelist of trees and circuses. "Tell me, am I right? You're a youngster without guile, you're—almost—above reproach. You walk this enchanted isle alone because you're a seeker, because you dig beauty. You're open to horses, to all the mysteries. You could possibly marry a knobby-kneed cypress, or become engaged to some modest loblolly, or a red-berried cassava, or—best, and I've got your number, kid—a youthful magnolia with gleaming, voluptuous leaves. Excuse me, your earring suggests all this."

"Well," said Carl, thinking, *loony,* and touching a finger self-consciously to his bit of malachite, "I am looking for a friend, and I do think this place is pretty special."

"A friend!" He sat up and swung his ropy legs around so that they dangled from the branch, his high-topped sneakers not far from Carl's head. From this position he peered down at Carl with all the intensity of an aged ringmaster in search of a new act, as though Carl might be the advance man for a troupe of well-formed, cosmic seekers.

"My father and I are looking for a small woman with dark dark hair and blue eyes who's been camping on the island by herself."

The loony's eyes glided toward Interstate Zero, then came back and settled on Carl like perfect indigo marbles. "You're the first to pass this way today," he said. "The first un-islander."

"My father's looking on the beach."

Another starburst smile. "He's correct, he's in the right place, he'll find her there, for that is where you go (or most of us). I sometimes keep my entire family there."

"You do? I thought you were married to this tree."

"There are levels of everything, dear boy," observed the loony. "Hasn't your daddy taught you that?"

Carl pondered his summer thus far. Prep school seemed farther away than the Sea of Tranquillity. *Oh Natalie, oh cosmic bouncing!* And here he was in an allegedly magical, tick-infested forest, within sight of a posh field of thoroughbreds, staring at the black and tattered sneaks of some sort of whip-muscled yogi married to both this hefty tree and a mortal woman kept, sometimes, on the outer beach.

"He's trying. My dad's *deep*," Carl admitted—or joked— as the yogi dropped from the branch and stood in front of him with all the dignity of a shirtless man who came to the level of Carl's sternum.

"Pierre Vesuvio, at your service," he said. "You see, look there, no more horses. Poof!"

Carl turned, followed Pierre's pointing arm, and found the pasture deserted, ragged, abandoned, although still a definite contradiction to the forest that curved around it. "So you can disappear horses," said Carl with a cool he did not quite feel. When he looked again at Pierre Vesuvio, he had adopted the guise of a wise, sunburned turtle, his blonde head pulled convincingly down between his hunched shoulders, his jaw unhinged.

"I'm quite sure there's a sensible, e-quine explanation," Pierre mouthed, "they being the horses of Atlanta Coca-Cola money, you'll understand, given to flights of Pegasus, created from the blood that is the secret formula syrup invented by Asa Griggs Candler. Something like that. You'll have to excuse me, island life can be boring, can lead to piles of lies. Am I confusing you?"

Carl grinned his tight-lipped version of a beholder's pleasure, conscious of the performance being perpetrated by this man in the moon-and-star pants, and of a growing awareness that his own cutoffs were being invaded by a host of phantom (he hoped) ticks, as though the hard-backed creatures were leaping for his thighs from the pockets of Pierre's shorts. Carl submerged his fists in his pockets and gave the garment a precautionary shake, all the while casting his head down in order to see into the fluent eyes of his interlocutor, who now snapped out of turtle mode and began to hum from somewhere in the center of his chest.

After a few bars of what sounded like a perfect-pitch version of any number of blues songs, Pierre sang a couple of lines owned by B. B. King, "Nobody loves me but my mother . . . and she could be jivin' too," then he reached up and for a second laid a finger against Carl's earring, an act of such quick simplicity that the younger man failed to pull away in alarm. Pierre Vesuvio smelled of tree, a sunny mixture of living dust and oakness, and when he began to speak again, his breath carried molecules of fertile sea marsh: oysters, shrimps, conch. Impossible!

"I have a sense," he said, "that we've had enough of my mumbo jumbo. You shouldn't listen to thirty-five-hundred-year-old men any longer than you have to, eh? What's your name, then?"

"Carl Hoopes." The disturbances beneath his cutoffs had quit.

"You're a handsome lunk, Carl. Do you take after your pa or your ma?"

Carl hesitated. His mother's face was so rare *nobody* could look like her: Tracy Hannah of Bear River, Nova Scotia, his soul's other half; no, his soul's best half. Damn Devereux, damn prep school, for splitting him from his natural mother. He said, to defend himself from what was happening in his heart: "My father looks like Ulysses S. Grant before he got fat."

The deep smile furrows that curved down from Pierre's nose and bracketed his mouth twitched. "Ha, your dad looks like a killer. So your mother must have control over your karma."

Carl shrugged powerfully. "I doubt my father would kill a tick," he said, visualizing one of the little suckers attached to his testicles like a barnacle. Thank God his sex life had begun and ended so quickly. This forest was too still, too perfect, too creepy to allow for any more standing about, trading chat with an ancient who was cluttering Carl's brain with matter that had nothing to do with his purpose for being on Cumberland, or at least with Devereux's purpose. Still, Carl knew in his bones that Pierre possessed the eyes, wrinkles, and bandy legs of a righteous being, and so he offered to this man of presumed character the gift of his own heart's truth: "My mother is so *good* I can't believe it. Nobody can. She's like . . . the smallest, wisest creature . . . in a perfect forest."

As unexpected as Pierre's voice from the tree branch long

minutes before, tears embarrassed Carl's eyes. He turned his head away from Pierre's gaze and bit his lip. This wouldn't do—his goddamn chin was trembling like a tapioca pudding. Inside himself he went limp.

"I sense divorce," said Pierre after a pause. "The genuine, true-blue curse of this century." Carl shuddered. "Why don't we walk to the beach, change the perspective, perhaps scare up my family." He reached up and encircled Carl's shoulders with one arm, turning him away from the deserted horse pasture and in the direction of Interstate Zero. "I have sons, you know, wicked saplings that they are. Come along, old sport. The beach is made new twice each day. The world may be full of random disease and fatal mistakes . . . but there are no yesterdays on Cumberland Island! She's a she, you know, there for the having."

Beach Report. The pale, red-bearded man with the telephoto lens screwed into the body of his Japanese camera snapped off two quick ones of the most enticing tableau he had witnessed in his two hours of hunting this blanched sand-waste for what he liked to term "Zeit Shots," that is, human beings unaware their shimmering, sequential images were being snatched by the solitary figure standing a good hundred yards off, the lens transforming him into a spread-legged unicorn, until he lowered the camera and pretended to be checking the sky for evidence of weather. Developed, his most recent shots (and perhaps others) would prove out his powers of found composition: a tall, bare-chested woman with a silver paddle in her hand like a biblical staff is bowsprit and figurehead for a yellow rubber boat hefted on either side by strapping boys with sea-wet hair; in the boat, her head snoozing against the rounded stern, a younger woman, also bare of torso. This allegorical beach party is tramping purposefully away from the sea, oblivious to the fact that they've provided someone else his crafty art—the best sort of thievery, to the mind of Carter Donner, who stood on a rising of dune and hoped his women would not burn their poor, puckery nipples. Again, he raised the camera from his chest to his knowing eye, focused, then crouched so that the procession would be more silhouetted against the purpling sky, would be perhaps more mythic in its aspect of primitive sea rescue, for surely the woman in the boat was sunstroked, jelly-fish bit, or drowned. Before he could snap off his third panel, a voice punched through the surf's sullen roar: "Don't," it said with all the authority of a beach master.

Devereux gave the hunkered shootist a small push at the shoulder joint, and he toppled over into the sand where he remained fetal, his camera still attached to his eye like a cumbersome, black spyglass. The grizzled beach scout stood for a moment over the form of his newfound antagonist, stood long enough to make sure the fellow had really turned pasty ostrich, and then Devereux hurried on to discover why in the world a woman resembling Tessa Dixon was being carried into the dunes on a yellow litter.

Above him, in the cloud-rich welkin, the sun burned down upon them all, indiscriminate, with neither affection nor malice, although before this day was done some would know pain, but none more than the scrooched-up photographer, parts of his epidermis already beginning to pinken and contract in the aftermath of his assault by the man whose back was now cross-haired in his lens.

Devereux intercepted the litter party as they were about to breach the first line of dunes. The boys paid him no mind. The woman, to be known to him later as Marni Vesuvio, gave him a cursory, unabashed once-over, and Tessa—for by Christ's elbow, it was she—languished in the dinghy, her dry weight sagging its soft bottom almost to the sand, which caused her two bearers a certain bulging and straining of the arm muscles. With her eyes closed, with the fine points of her face in repose, with her exposed breasts flattened like a boy's, she appeared a hobbledehoy playing possum. Although his troublesome reason brought up other possibilities—siriasis, metaecstasy, encephalitis—his heart refused to panic. Above all, the rescue party looked so calm, especially their buxom leader to whom he now spoke.

"Excuse me," he said. "I know her."

The boys, their identical faces smeared with relief, set down the dinghy and put their hands to their hips while Marni came back to Devereux with all the aplomb of a tall and self-possessed Valkyrie. She pointed at him with the business end of her paddle.

"In that case, Prince Charming," she said in a vaguely froglike way, "I think you should kneel down and kiss the lady awake. Elsewise, me and my sons will take her on home and call the ranger. She was meditating, or something, and just keeled over. There's pulse, no fever, and I bet she's just dreaming. The island does that."

One of the boys spat a dark substance into the sand and cheerfully called out, "Marn, she's down here smiling like she knows secrets." His twin bent over and said something to Tessa that Devereux could not hear.

Time to move.

Devereux approached the stern of the dinghy and knelt beside Tessa's head. The twins moved off a way but their mother stayed put, all three appearing as solemn pickets assigned to protect the moment from rogue terns, curious sanderlings, or felonious photographers. And it is true that just then Mr. Carter Donner, the red-bearded worthy, did invade the space of strangers for the third time. Then he scrambled to his feet and fled south with his art.

In Newburyport, at that moment, the leftist philosopher underwent a simple but deadly infarction in the privacy of his boudoir; time had finally stolen his clock. Jessica's girl-child Laura decided—in the excitement of a sudden, bath-warm rain shower—to dart from her mother and cross, without *looking both ways,* the intersection of two real busy streets; she almost made it, she did make it! But a red truck came tooting and skidding into the crosswalk and clipped her knee with a rusty bumper, which made blood all the way to the emergency room; the man drove Jess and Laura in his red truck, and he looked whiter than Caspar the Friendly Ghost. Out above the elbow of Cape Cod, in Wellfleet, Kit and Ellen McGuffy paced the gritty beach and came (neither quite knew how) to the decision that would uproot them from their homeplace and set them down in a new scholarly life in Tuscaloosa, Alabama, and only a mile or two from the house where Devereux Hoopes sometimes rested his sweet posterior. Surrounded by the potato fields of Sagaponack, Mr. Ya's crew struggled with Barry Kessler's boulder, while inside the farmhouse Barry himself did battle with the surreptitious harassments of his former lover Jer; he went into battle armed with police telephone taps and a new double-barreled shotgun with which he intended to blow out the windshield of the louts Jer had hired to spew his driveway gravel with their tires every midnight for a week running. Already done violence to, Willy Liebling lay on a hospital bed in Paterson, New Jersey, a small-caliber bullet lodged forever in his neck, a victim of the mistaken notion that one should stop for a red light in deepest Newark. Beside him, Miriam Shore laughed with the sheer joy of his survival in this world of capricious harm. By way of contrast, Jack Vilna hauled his crab traps from Pamlico Sound, and it came to his morning mind that he would, by fuck, marry Ling Mullins. With an inbreath of satisfaction Ling would consent.

On Cumberland's outer beach, Devereux placed his hands on the wet tubing of the dinghy and prepared himself to practice the minor form of first aid recommended by Marni Vesuvio. He did not find Tessa to be smiling, knowingly or otherwise, but her face in repose radiated an elf's keenness that belied the possibility she might be addled in the brain. He bent down and kissed her lips, such welcome familiars tasting of salt and dry heat—not slack, not fevered—and when he drew away, she opened her eyes and said, without a trace of astonishment, "Hey, so you're my Catcher," an obscure Tessa-remark if there ever was one. He had come so far to this gentle meeting, he had come home. Begone, uncertainty.

"No," he said, taking off his sunglasses and smiling more truly than he had in weeks, months, "I just stumbled on a rescue operation." Her eyes, half a foot from his own, seemed to be absorbing their deep blue from the sky. She reached up and took hold of a handful of his beard.

"Just a stumbling sort of guy, huh?" she said.

"You bet. Are you as all right as you seem? Won't you get out of this boat. Do you have a shirt?" He saw she was lying on the thing, little protection against the sheen of sea water in the bilge.

"Fusspot," she said, pulling him closer until he blocked the sun from her face. "Where are those people?" With his eyes he signaled that the boys and their mother were behind her, watching. Tessa whispered, "Do you think she's some sort of conjure-woman?"

"No, just a Samaritan. She said you keeled over. Her boys were carrying you home, Tessa."

"No, I went down like a willow," she said as if she were stating a languid truth. "I've been fasting without quite knowing it."

He grunted. "Great. The old carrots and water trick? Flush out the poisons. We found your tepee, your pitiful victuals up in the raccoon box."

"We? Is sweet baby Carl here?! Where?"

"He's right here," said a voice remarkably like Carl's, amused and matter-of-fact, coming from above the bow of the dinghy. Devereux withdrew from Tessa's field of force, looked to his left, and saw Carl's wretched sneakers, the blonde curlicues of leg hair, the billowing cutoff fatigues. Between his son's legs he could see as well the stubby figure of a man approaching across the sand glare like a hard-gutted old goat bent on mischief.

What next, oh Providence?

As Devereux stood up, Tessa raised her torso from the bottom of the dinghy and, in a quick sequence of motions, donned and buttoned her briny shirt. Marni Vesuvio, her own breasts now covered with the linked bandannas, moved for the dinghy, but as soon as Tessa stepped out of it, obviously as healthy as a yearling, Pell and Mell unweighted from their picket stances, rushed to their vessel, lofted it between them, grabbed the paddle from Marni, and made for the frivolous ocean they had been deprived of far too long. Let the elders and the young twanger sort out the physics of beach life; Pell and Mell would put some leagues under their invisible keel, the Bermudas before them like a dream of wisdom and chaos.

Meanwhile, the beached five performed the rituals of harmony and grace always prescribed by the existence of happenstance on the planet. Carl embraced and lifted clear off the sand his friend Tessa Dixon, who whispered, while elevated, "How did you find me? Did you betray me? You geek. I'm sooo glad!" When he set her back down, grinning uncertainly over whether he had or not, or something in between (Oh Jesus, the ribbon-read letter from Tessa to Brothers), Carl introduced Devereux to Pierre Vesuvio, now become some sort of mysterious godfather to Carl.

To Devereux, Pierre said, as they gripped palms, "So now I meet the *pop* to this clear-headed chap I found mooning at horses in the forest. You do take after Ulley Grant in a sunny sort of way."

To this, Devereux mounted up his sunglasses, the very things that made him look so mean and nasty (wrongly), and said, with uncharacteristic zest, "I did. I fathered *him*." Then Carl, Tessa, and Devereux were offered Marni's name by the raw-boned woman herself.

Said Tessa, "I appreciate y'all helping me."

Marni shrugged, "Babe, the boys and me have come here full-moon nights and found barnacly, mother loggerheads so weighed down with eggs and their old selves, and seeming to weep brine because of it, that they could hardly make it beyond the tide line without a little help from us. You, you were an easy creature, thin as you are." She handed Tessa a honey-flavored granola bar from her carryall.

Pierre jigged his high-tops in the sand. "It's a white hell out here," he said, then gazed out to sea in a proprietary fashion. "And my wee lads embarked once again. I tell you, they're nautical mules!"

"It's your blood in their veins," said Marni, her strip of black sunglass making her appear to Carl a monocular priestess of the dunes. He wanted for these assembled seniors, now gone quiet in their not-knowing of one another, all the peace of spirit the world, or at least the island, might have to offer. If not, he would jump off the continent and join with the Vesuvio brothers on their impossible voyage to never-never land. He watched his father, whose left hand rested against the small of Tessa's back, whose reddening face—despite the concealing beard and glasses—had developed a bad case of open curiosity and even fondness for whatever was going on among this circle of beachites. Only Tessa showed signs of a wandering attention; her expression might be called pensive alertness, as if her amazingly blue eyes loved the visible world at the same time they feared it.

"Well," said Devereux, looking to Tessa, "I guess we should head for Sea Camp. Maybe you'll share your carrots."

"It's possible," she said, biting into the granola bar in a most seductive way.

Carl thought, They want to be alone in the tepee. Of course! Love must always come to this going-off. How could he have forgotten? Good old un-grim American fucking.

Now Pierre reached up and laid an astute, firm hand on Carl's shoulder. "I tell you what," he said to Devereux and Tessa. "Since Carl is a man after my clown's heart, and since you two clearly need a walkabout, a sweat-lodge, a shower under the live oaks, Marni and I and the urchins will take Carl along to our place and show him a thing or two, and—if you like—I can come for you in my jeep, say two or three hours from now. Bring you to a luncheon of mullet and marsh oysters. Am I right, Marn? Some rich tidal fodder from Christmas Creek we get from our friend Bailey Wilks."

"Aren't you always?" said Marni. "But Bailey delivers the goods."

Devereux unhanded Tessa, put his hands on his hips, and lowered his head to her as if she might signal her permission or her refusal. She sent along only what Carl recognized as a mugwump smile—his old man would have to parse this out on his lonesome. Carl himself willed that the offer be accepted like a shot; Pierre might just have a fully equipped alchemist's lab, or fantastic circus artifacts. And besides, Carl was horse-hungry, though he had about as much affection for raw carrots as he did for saltwater critters. Surely the urchins sucked in the occasional hot dog and can of soda pop. He hadn't been so excited about a household since Barry Kessler's.

Devereux said, finally, "What about the ferry?" more in the way of a private question for Tessa, it seemed.

Her face darkened. Only for an instant, but it was pure wordless contempt for the poor ferry; Carl's father (the lover) needed no further signification than this. "All right," he said, with his version of a hospitality-accepting smile, "let's just do that. All of it, Mr. Vesuvio."

Midday beach heat is not erotic. At its zenith the sun may be said to belch forth solar winds whose natural purpose is to create austerity, salt loss, and goose bumps millions of miles below. But at least the searing incandescence will dry a brine-wet shirt until it is stiff and itchy with its residue of salt; at least the baking atmosphere will shirr the brain to a perfection of celibate emptiness—and yet . . .

Devereux longed to enter the live oak forest whose presence to their right was an endless weavery of trunk and branch deformed by wind to create the sense of an impenetrable and cockeyed rampart crowned with parapets of grit-dusted green leaves. To find a breach in this marvel would be to escape into a world of thought, of question and response, of cool observation and the recovery (perhaps) of the familiar rhythms of two long-separated bodies. But here and now, sand-stepping south through a bleached and deserted beach world—though the long-lens man must lurk somewhere, chewing his beard hairs—Devereux Hoopes and Tessa Dixon could easily be two shipwrecked persons just met, one from Illyria, the other from Phoenicia.

She said, "You've had adventures. You reek of adventure like a wet old dog."

Her trekking face remained neutral. They had come perhaps a quarter-mile in silence. He begged his brain to fill with a spectacular language that would rend the heavens, or at least blow apart this vast igloo of heat under which they hiked. Either he was stricken to a sunstruck vacuum (as Tessa had been), or guilt coated his brainpan like a thin layer of green facial mud.

He said, without thought, "Adrian Brothers." And shuddered like a man hearing from his lover the details of her abortion.

Surveyor as ignorant oaf.

Her response to the syllables of the St. Augustinian's name came from her mouth like rude truth. "He helped me. I was afraid. He comforted me. You should know me better, Dev'ro. This is more than a diddly romance you and I have. If you don't trust me, I think I'll sign up for the goddamn nunnery in Plaquemine." She stopped their progress with a hand on his forearm, a hand as insistent as a come-along. "Marry me, you dope."

While he gazed down at her face beneath the wind-stirred aureole of her dark curls, her blue-black eyes penetrating his own features in search of he-knew-not-what awful absence or concealed pith, his mind rediscovered discovering itself—language and its boon companion desire were well in sight. Giddy with relief, he saw superimposed between them the bumper sticker on her car—"Wild Women Don't Get the Blues"—and it was all he could do not to shout, "Blue Women Don't Get Married! Blue Women Thrive on Deadly Night Shapes & Fast on Mystical Islands!" But, fortunately for Devereux Hoopes, choice-maker and seeker after the most stately dune, the grittiest sand, the most inevitable breakers, he said nothing . . . until the surface tension of her eyes threatened tears of ire, or a swift kick in the shins.

"I'd be a fool not to," he said. "You can't turn yourself over to a nunnery. The food is lousy, the beds are single, and they'd snatch your lovely hair."

Behind her the sea broke with a heartening regularity, and beyond the roll of froth and spume a full-rigged sloop, heeled-over and fat-bellied with sail, headed north for a possible rendezvous with the Vesuvio twins.

"That's what you call an answer?" said Tessa, smiling— the eyes now full of light. "You proposed to me almost exactly one year ago today. And nuthin' happened. So what's new, Beachman? An interstate vision? Tempted to sin? Death snuck up and breathed on you? You discovered that love is more daily work than nighttime boogie? Come on now"—she poked him in the stomach with a forefinger— "tell Tessa where you're at. Have you been *bad*?"

Some find it difficult to answer such truthful seashore speakings, such poking into the protected recesses of the heart where motive and event, sin and hope, fear and love, can be as madly interwoven as the Atlantic-facing ramparts of Cumberland's live oak forest. No exception, Devereux stared at the wild blue woman so fresh from her yellow litter, and now he considered with care that she made the citizens of his recent travels seem players in a grim comic film by Barry Kessler, made them—all except Ling Mullins, God help him—about as insubstantial as ice sculptures planted in the sand of this island—colorless pastiches, melting in the aftermath of a solar wind.

"If you want me to confess—" he began.

"Oh boy," said Tessa, hooking her right hand in the crook

of his elbow and heading them again southward, her head bent and listening, for all the world like the female priest she might have been had authority and the flesh permitted it.

"I haven't been bad," he began, as ridiculous as it sounded to his ears. "Aroused . . . yeah, sure . . . by friends along the coast. As you say, I have too many female friends for it not to happen. On Hatteras I was badly tempted by someone real. But I never entered where I didn't belong. Maybe Carl did, but not me."

Goodness, is that sunburn or blush on the cheeks of the prophet?

"Yup," she said, "it's a moral swamp out there all right." She benedicted the fingers of her left hand in the fiery air. "Carl's too *new* to know much about it."

He ignored this. He had to make some declaration. He'd better. "Tessa, I've left you alone too much, I know it. But here I am, ready to work. I'll help you fight off the night shapes. I'll help you draw a map of grace every day for the rest of my life. There's nothing more to fear."

After a long silence from her, during which his eardrums and heart were battered by the sand-screak of their footsteps, by the bombast of the wind, and by the constancy of the surf's smash and ebb, Tessa said, in her most knowing way, "What d'you know about grace, buddy? You read my letter to Adrian."

"How else—"

"I would have been in Tuscaloosa tomorrow," she said. "Now I'm thinking I'll go back to Florida . . . or stay here with Bevan Smith. I won't go down like a willow again."

He was aghast. "The ranger?"

Be cool, accommodator.

"If you think you're the only one who can be aroused by friends along the coast, you are full of algae and muck and everything else," she cried.

"Wait a minute," Devereux said, stopping her and setting his hands on her shoulders, "aren't you hearing me? I will marry you."

And he would.

But not before she cocked her head, smiled a confusion of shyness and clear-eyed resolve, and said, "*Guud,*" in that way she had of pepping up moments of ambiguity, argument, fear, and (maybe) the victory of her own will, and the vanishment of her fears, forever. She went on, "Say three hail mollys, one in the shower, one in the sweat-lodge, one during this weird luncheon you got me into, and then we'll both be more or less absolved, and you might even know somethin' about grace."

He would.

But not before they together worked out the mechanics of an unambiguous kiss beneath the spilling eye of the noonday sun. And while they were at this pleasure, the great whorled track of beach to the south began to reveal its small population of beach mavens. Some clustered around their plastic cold boxes; some searched for cockles, starfish, and whelks; some stood foursquare in the face of the merciless surf; some drifted hither and yon stoned on atavistic chemicals; a few (despite the heat) were lost in spiritual fugue with the soul of the island; a couple, hidden in the lee between the dune rows, sought to diagram their prehistories of infidelity and lust with a map drawn in the innocent sand between their outspread and burning legs; and one grudgeful artist made to change the film in his camera blindly by thrusting it into the maw of the drawstring ditty bag he had earlier buried in the sand near Sea Camp, the bag's whereabouts marked for him with an upright piece of driftwood shaped like an Easter Island head (only this one sported a sea-drilled hole through the cranium area), the demarcation accomplished before he had wended his way north in search of perfect human compositions to burgle with his trusty telephoto lens. Now, he spotted the kissers and sighed.

Long since, Pell and Mell Vesuvio, responding to their father's shore acrobatics and especially to his awesome wind- and surf-conquering voice, had once again turned back from their voyage to the Bermudas, where they believed certain otherworldy beings might be in earnest parley over the fate of the seabound world.

Tessa and Devereux entered the live oak forest and walked the root-heaved path to Sea Camp. Moving through the coolness of the canopied space splashed with shadow and light, they fell into the silence of those who know enough, for the moment, to believe they are at one, impossible as this may be. They nodded their way past the family with the boy-child who hated snakes, and soon came to the series of clearings linked by the path which made up the camp. Each clearing contained a raccoon- and squirrel-proof box on a tall pole, a concrete hearth (the difficult quest for firewood was a constant subject among the campers, according to Tessa), and, erected on several sites, tents of varied shapes and colors, including one like a scarlet igloo. No one was about. Tessa's miniature orange tepee occupied a clearing within sight of the crude showers, the toilets, and the shed that displayed the snake chart. Tessa unzipped the fly of the tepee, and on her knees reached within and removed a thick white towel, two opaque plastic bottles, and a soap dish. Before she zipped up again, Devereux tossed in his shoes and his shirt, and they went along to the showers—really a wooden platform with adjoining stalls open to the sky, open at floor level so that the feet and calves of bathers might be seen, had there been any besides these two, who now climbed the worn steps to the platform and chose a cubicle in which they could begin married life.

Shy of each other in the closeness of a space bounded by slick, warped siding that exuded a permanent soapy dampness, they removed their clothing, draped it over the ill-hung door, and at the second Tessa turned on the irregular stream of cool, fresh water, their bodies joined—the one, trim, muscled, perhaps a little droopy in the butt; the other, attenuated, sure, yet with small, fond breasts, a girl's narrow swatch of pubic hair, and skin over which a hand might glide as easily as over combed sea island cotton. He reached behind her and took from its container on the board shelf the coconut-oil soap, which he wetted, lathered, and spread in circles of foam over her back and the slender span of her ass. Then he crouched before her, unaware his thigh and risen testes could be seen by any passerby, and with the intensity of a ritualist he soaped her legs, her feet, and rising, her labia, belly, breasts, and all the planes of her streaming face, its eyes closed to him as against an unfamiliar masseur, at least until she had rinsed away the bubbly lather and taken up his task herself. Done, the blood red of his erection standing between them like a satirical interruption of both symmetry and the color scheme of pale white and deep tan, she washed and conditioned her hair with liquids from the two bottles.

In the hazy apricot light of the tepee's interior, he lay on her sleeping bag and pallet and watched her make a towel headdress to cover her damp, now-straight hair. She sat cross-legged on the nylon flooring, her raised arms bracketing the stillness of her naked face. She had walked back from the showers with the towel attending to her modesty, he carrying her shorts and shirt, and now her breasts, shadowed crotch, and dimpled navel dominated his inland vision. The tepee, more alive with heat than the forest outside, smelled of the skin softener in a bottle by her foot, the very lotion— she told him—that Adrian Brothers and Bevan Smith had guaranteed would keep the island gnats from the dark and moist places of her body.

He laughed without rhyme or reason, and she uncrossed her legs in order to make possible the eventual conjoining of their two bodies on the down bag and pallet.

What can be said about honest fucking?

That it's a moist, entrancing business; that tongues play swift games of thrust and parry; that nipples collide, swell, call for lips and teeth; that skin heats, flushes, offers up sweat for the purifying purpose of confluence; that the slow and agonizing connection of genitals is the dumb, sensual answer to all language of slap and tickle, tension and relief, especially when human heads—bone to bone above—are in the possession of beings intent on making this act a metaphor for the value of love.

But enough can never be said. Best to know that time passed, cries were muted for the sake of Sea Camp decorum, that Tessa's search for silence and solitude came to an end in this Cumberland sweat-lodge, and that Devereux had no more in mind than to remain suspended out of time in this cone of apricot light.

Of course, the world of the island had nowhere ceased its constant groping for renewal. As the tide rose and the wind played its shaping games with sand, foliage, and branch, and as the westering sun drew invisible evaporate upward to join with the monster bodies of clouds, the red-bearded Carter Donner hunkered in the door-hole of his scarlet igloo tent and tripped his shutter at a speed intended to capture with perfect fidelity the silhouetted, groaning shadows behind the tepee's wall of love. Donner would brook no beachy "Don't."

Up Interstate Zero, in the private sector, Carl Hoopes found himself at the kitchen sink in what he had begun to call Vesuvio Center—a manticore of a structure assembled willy-nilly from equal parts yurt, dome (the kitchen), A-frame, and rural American shack (bathrooms?), the entire kit and caboodle set in a clearing and surrounded by fern, palmetto, and Spartina cordgrass, the clearing itself bounded on one side by a shallow and brackish creek, on the other by a jeep trail leading east to the interstate. Carl had been set to the task of cleaning caked mud and tidal yuck off dozens of marsh oysters all stuck together in clusters like mounds of misshapen, black plantains on the wet newspaper in front of him. With a wooden mallet he whacked at each cluster until the individual "ersters," as Pierre called them, fell away from one another, and Carl could run them under the tap, using a wire brush to de-muck the little devils he wouldn't suck down his gullet for all the éclairs in God's pastry kitchen.

Just outside the screened porthole above the sink, he could see Pierre Vesuvio and the twins cleaning round gray mullet at a table made from an upended cable spool. Beside them was a firepit, a piece of rusty and warped sheet metal laid across it. Beyond them, the black fisherman Bailey Wilks disappeared into the forest as he had come—silent, scowling, a cast net over one shoulder, his only words, "I ain't clean 'em, Cap, you clean 'em"—but now, unburdened of his croaker sack of Cumberland's dubious cuisine.

From the A-frame part of the house, an area of comfortable chaos containing a small trampoline and a rafter-hung trapeze, came the breathy sounds of Marni Vesuvio's silver flute on which she seemed to be playing her own somber-sweet version of "The Condor Passes."

Carl felt as if he were undergoing an out-of-body experience his life had not quite prepared him for. These people, these Vesuvios, might be exactly what they seemed—that is, weird and pretty wonderful, certainly kind and given to attentive flakiness—but what did they *do* in the world? Were the elders the king and queen of the island? And why were Pell and Mell always as silent as these oysters, as fey in the eyes as Siamese cats? Oh well, Devereux was big in the reality department; surely he would bop in here for a late lunch and make sense of the whole thing. Or maybe not. Perhaps Tessa had already rendered him indifferent to all but her powerful self. Did any of this make any difference in the great scheme of things? Nope. He bashed and washed the last cluster of oysters, setting the entire clicky mess in a basket Pierre had given him, which he then carried out of doors to where the Vesuvio males were wielding their knives, and after placing the basket on the sheet metal, Carl stood in the fierce sunlight and waited to be recognized. Flute music filled the clearing like a silvery rain of fish scales.

Pierre wiped sweat from his brow with the inside of his

bicep, pointed at the sky with his knife, and said, "Hey there, Carl, it must be time to fetch the chaps from the sweat-lodge. Will you go with me to make sure I don't bother the wrong tent?" He dropped his knife beside the mullet pile on the spool, directing his kids to fillet the things into "fingers," which Pell and Mell commenced to do as if they'd been born to the work. "Give them to Marn when you're done," Pierre said. "And put this basket of ersters in the shade so they won't start to yawn. Carl and I, we'll be back soon." He wiped scale bits from his hands on some nearby fern leaves.

Pell or Mell raised his fuzzy, blonde head, nodded at his father, then turned and expertly ptooeed into the low scrub behind him. Carl had already decided they existed on smokeless tobacco and unsullen silence, only coming to life when their dinghy had broached the surf. He also knew that their room, the yurt part of the hybrid structure shown to him by Pierre, was a wonderland of dried diamondback rattlesnake skins, loggerhead penis bones, giant conch shells, Lilliputian deer racks, egret feathers, an ancient gravestone bearing the name "Stafford," and flotsam and jetsam well marred by the sea, notably a greenly barnacled airplane propeller and the bleached, beaky jaw of a dolphin. Many of these treasures had been hung like model airplanes from the roof supports below the octagonal skylight. The dinghy they had a special rack for in one corner, and on a table beneath the skylight were piled bricks of fresh green clay wrapped in wax paper. To Carl, who had had no room of his own since entering the spartan cells of prep school, these Vesuvio guys had a real deal. And they slept on futons like the padded armor of Chinese warlords!

Carl followed Pierre along the path that led away from Marni's flutings and from the queer house whose siding in the midafternoon light was the color of Colby cheese, though the great end window of the A-frame was a smoked mirror for the surrounding jungle-shapes. The jeep, a genuine Willys veteran of the Korean conflict, with its windshield prone on the hood, sat just off the interstate like a chocolate brown dream of efficiency.

"What's next?" said Pierre, nimbly mounting the driver's seat, Carl soon beside him, watching Pierre's leg strain to reach the starter mushroom.

"Excuse me?" Carl said. The engine whined, caught, throbbed.

"How will you pass the summer? With your ma or your pa?"

This Pierre must either be a psychic or the best guesser who had ever paid attention to Carl. As they chugged onto the interstate, he sucked a deep breath and realized he had been avoiding the subject of his summer future like a monster term paper. He plucked at the front of his Bama-Bino T-shirt, saying into his chest, "I suppose I could twirl pizza dough for my friends the Visellis. I worked for them before, and now I think I'm old enough to handle food, but—"

Pierre sang out, " 'I gots those topping blues and Tuscaloosa is callin' me . . . but I ain't answerin'.' Something like that?"

Carl threw the man a grin, and they rolled south over the crushed shells. "My mom lives in a one-room cabin in Nova Scotia with a serious man who believes in outhouses and thinks teenagers are dangerous to privacy or something."

The dried-out skin next to Pierre's right eye crinkled into the map of a river delta. "I hear you," he said, peering ahead between the spokes of the steering wheel; he could be a wizened kid, a jeep thief, a marsh magician. "Guess what, Carl?"

Perhaps Pierre was about to have the thoroughbreds thunder up the roadbed and trample the vehicle like a tin can. "What?"

"In one sense, you look like you'd make the ideal mailman, Cumberland's postboy."

Carl went along with the joke. "I've been a houseboy, a kitchenboy, and a promoboy for pizza. I could use a rise in status."

"I'm not really putting you on," Pierre said above the burbling noise of the engine. Carl stared at him. The moons and stars on his shorts must be his license to create great and silly expectations everywhere he went in his island domain.

"So, do I have to put on new clothes?" said Carl, warily thinking of being bitten by water moccasins as he made his appointed rounds dressed in horrid gray-blue.

"No," Pierre said. "My sister, Nancy, runs a private post for some of the more . . . umm . . . remote families who don't like to go to Grayfield and run into their foes in front of the postboxes. Nancy's had a stroke. It really did her down. You could fill in for a while, bunk with the urchins, civilize them a bit. Or, if the postboy dream is too farfetched for you, just stay here and call yourself the Tutor of Missoe, which is the real name of this isle."

Was *that* it? Was Carl to bend his back beneath the turtle bones and teach the twins the rules and habits of the mainland? Not credible. "This is for real?" he asked.

Pierre gripped Carl's knee with a hand still gummy with mullet. "I'll teach you tricks never dreamt of in Alabam or the ivy-dream of your boarding school. I liked you instantly we met. You *need* this island. Come, boy, I know you've got mischief in your bones." The hand squeezed to the edge of pain.

Bizarre, even frightening. Carl looked at the shaman with alarm. "I'll have to ask my pop," he said lamely.

Without removing his hand from Carl's knee, Pierre kicked the brake pedal all the way to the floor, the wheels of the jeep locked, slewed in the shell roadbed, and while Pierre's forward arc was stopped by the steering wheel, Carl's didn't halt until his right ear whomped into the downed windshield. In the stillness and the pain, he felt the hot mumble of the engine beneath his head. He raised up slowly, his head full of what seemed like piercing flute music, his eyes gone stingy, their focus smeared, and he cried out, "What the fuck?"

"A deer," said Pierre, a little less ruddy about the jowls,

but still as calm as a mullet finger. "Are you all right?" He examined Carl's ear with probing, scale-flecked fingers while Carl cast his eyes sidewards into the forest for any sign of such a ghost-creature. Nothing. Pierre blew a cool stream of air over the ear, surely turned cauliflower-size, and murmured what sounded to Carl like, "On your mother, the deer," although it could just as well have been, "Your mother is dear," and he didn't try to find out when Pierre let him loose, shifted into first, and soon had them chugging along the interstate as if nothing had happened to his quickened, smarting godson.

Sea Camp was full of late-in-the-day voices:

"Come on, Bubba, the ferryboat leaves in a half-hour. Git your butt in gear."

"Who's on firewood for tonight's supper? Someone stole the whole damn pile."

"Where's them heat-seekin' gnats anyway?"

"Julie, if you don't stop that noise I'm gonna whip your fanny 'til it looks like a candy cane. . . . What?"

"His camera got et by a wave, looks like."

"The coons musta done it while we wuz at the beach."

"My brain is a wok, Marcelline. Lead me to the boat, little darling."

Languid in the tepee, the listeners enjoyed the lazy aftermath of their second journey to and from the showers—where a man in an adjoining cubicle had sung with bass resonance his own version of "Old Man River," including the immortal stanza, "Tote that barge, lift that bale . . . Get a little nookie and you land in jail," a sentiment that caused in the listeners their fair share of noisy delight. And their mirth squared itself when, on leaving the cubicle, they saw that the singer's rather elegant feet—and only the feet—were sunburned crimson, as though number six sunscreen had failed him at the ankles.

Now, dressed and lying together atop the sleeping bag,

Tessa and Devereux practiced the declension of their lives thus far, the kind of task that comes easily to the tongues of lovers closeted together in a magical forest, even if the forest is populated with testy sightseers, burned-footed warblers, and serious snapshootists hairy about the jaw. The round, glowing wall of the tepee was sufficient barrier against the folderol and larceny of the world. But just in case, the two lovers wore on their skin a piquant layer of Tessa's invincible skin softener, and she had covered her legs with a pair of black, pegged jeans that together with her equally black T-shirt made her look, to Devereux, like an anorexic street priest, though an impudent one at the moment—her eyes in this carroty light a deep and merciless blue-green, her bare foot rising to stroke its instep on the center pole of the tepee.

"Tell me stories," she said, nuzzling into his shoulder. "You're supposed to tell me stories. We've had confession and proposal, yea-saying and this other good stuff. Now I want tales of a traveling man." She pinched his left nipple through the material of his shirt, an action that added pain to his languor.

"Fiddlesticks," he said into the muffling dampness of her hair. "My memory is gone. Get Carl to sing for you. He's the one with stories up the butt. Ask him about the wonders of Wellfleet. Hell, ask him about the wonders of Natalie. Ask him about your crazed friends in St. Augustine. The kid is one big story. And right now he's probably learning some new moves from Mr. Pierre Vesuvio."

"You're a slippery boy," she said, caressing the gnat-proofed skin of the arm that embraced her. "I love Carl's moves. He dudn't have much more to learn . . . except that his father is mortal, frail as a toothpick, and no more God's gift to wimin."

He scratched his whitening beard with a monogamist's deliberation. "You have a point there."

Outside, a male voice rasped, "This island may's well be hell-struck for all the good it's done me today."

Tessa laughed. "You know," she said, her breath playing

over his throat, "Bevan Smith told me, he said, 'Cumberland bites the wicked.'"

"Did he? The most pithy Fed I ever met."

She raised her head and gave him the full eye treatment. "Well, Dev'ro, in case I didn't say, I'm real glad you went to all the trouble to find me."

"Me too," he said, palming one of her breasts, "even if I had to be wicked to get it done. And manipulative, as they say. Whoo, I picked up Adrian by the ankles and just shook him 'til the Kleenex fell out of his pockets."

The narrow bridge of her nose seemed even narrower with knowing conviction. "But he didn't say one word, did he." His hand fell away from her breast. She insisted, "Did he?"

"No . . . it was Emily Overton Mills."

"Just, please, keep the hurtful out of my life," she said.

He saw himself in Tuscaloosa, in the company of J. P. Conover. Together they were erecting around and over the Sixth Street house a gigantic tepee, its cloth specially resistant to invasion, even to the bullets of any killers who might be stalking Ralph W. Green.

"I'll do my best," said Devereux Hoopes, meaning it.

Startlingly close to the actual, completely vulnerable tepee wall, the melodic voice of Pierre Vesuvio cracked into being: "Best to amscram now, Captain, the forest is full of tiresome knotheads, and we're not quite sure whether Om has yet blessed National Seashores."

Neither Tessa nor Devereux noticed the angry redness of Carl's ear, which was fine with him because while the oldsters prepared to decamp, he preferred to consider his fate, as he had been ever since Pierre's questionable offers and the subsequent bashing of his ear. Somehow the two matters were connected. For every seductive proposition—whether houseboy in Sagaponack or postboy/tutor on Cumberland—there may well be an equally intense punishment to follow.

It could blow your mind if you weren't careful. It could make you limp and draggy, so much contrary thought. Or it could be as glorious as plunging your racing brain into the liquid ice of the Cape Cod Atlantic. A boy really can't lay back circling his sneaker toe in the dust—as he was doing now, musing away—he had to choose. Come on, pizzas or the daily post? Stinky toppings or sublime flute music? Houseguest to his father and his blue-eyed sweetie, or yurt-mates with two identical fellows who may well have come ashore on the backs of loggerheads. And shoot, he'd have to consult and discuss with Devereux this time around. It seemed pretty obvious his dad had gone off the vino for now, and thus there would be no hangover to caper before, as he had on the Sagaponack beach, so easily getting his lovesick way. His heart sang out for Natalie and her smoky grays, right here in the live oak forest, but for all the others knew, he was only thinking of the fishy meal to come. Life. Somebody must be back of it, ready to crank the level way up if a guy tried to stand around just looking at it. Judging by Devereux's flushed, eager, Tessa-gazing face, even he was not immune.

Pierre moved them out, the bowlegged circus master leading a poodle-headed chimney sweep in cowboy boots and a red-nosed, middle-aged English teacher with a compelling ass borne by hips that didn't move when he walked. What a bunch. Carl lingered for a moment surveying the camp, now empty of all but the tepee and a scarlet igloo tent not far away. Centered in the igloo's door-port he saw a winking of sunlight on ground glass, then the dark, telescopic barrel of a long lens, its shaft supported by a hand the color of pizza dough, the winking eye in the act of panning away from Carl and the tepee, pretending avid interest in empty camp sites or the convoluted asymmetry of the reaching oak branches. Thinking of the surf casters of St. Augustine, the dolts in their pickups feasting upon Belinda Ruffin of the perfect breasts, imagining that this lout in the igloo might have snatched something precious from Tessa and

Devereux (to love privately, without fear of the eyes and ears of mothers or strangers), Carl hollered out, without a crack or shimmy in his voice, "Hey scumbag, why don't you stick that toy somewhere the sun don't shine!" And even though he immediately felt foolish at his anal wit, he also enjoyed the surge of adrenaline that turned him on his heels and away up the path to the west before the pasty lurker could haul up a response, assuming he could talk.

Carl caught up with the others at the intersection of the path and Interstate Zero, where Pierre had left the jeep. Carl and Tessa rode the metal benches over the rear wheels of the jeep, Pierre and Devereux like two old beachcombers on the front seats, their gab covered by engine noise and the steady crunching of road shells. With her hands clamped between her black knees, Tessa sat across from Carl and seemed to be searching his face for signs of acne or recent sin. Since he thought himself guilty of neither, he forked over his best smile, and together they contrived a pleasant trip of small talk about the island—she too had seen the vanishing thoroughbreds—all the way to Vesuvio Center. She didn't, fortunately, ask about the letter-reading ploy, nor did he volunteer. What a wonderful, dark person she was. She did offer him some skin balm from a bottle she had in her back pocket. He politely refused.

In the fern and palmetto dooryard, they found that a fire had been built beneath the sheet metal grill, a fire tended by no one. It struck Carl as odd that these people seemed to have no alarm-sounding pets. As if in answer, Marni strolled around the yurt portion of the house followed by two plump white ducks, their gabbling beaks a bold tangerine. Dressed in a long batik skirt and matching halter, minus her aloof sunglasses, Marni seemed a warmer human, and the ducks waddled behind her like fussy, possessive children with an important case to make if their mother would only stop moving away from them all the livelong day. Such a heartless giantess, who now went among the new arrivals with a plate of scallions, radishes, and goat cheese, which all nibbled at while the sheet metal poppled from fireheat, and the ducks—named, Marni said, Madge and Milly—shuffled impatiently from webfoot to webfoot.

Pierre, as host, explained his philosophy of hybrid-houses ("Leave the miracle of consistency to nature"); Tessa put her hands in her back pockets and rose up on the toes of her red boots, thus managing to look down upon the spieling host; Devereux frowned doubtfully, at the peak of the A-frame, then bit into a radish; and when Pierre went for the basket of oysters sitting in the shade beside the door of the kitchen-dome like a delivery of marsh rubble, Carl abandoned the dooryard group and went around to the creek side of the yurt where, as hoped, he found the rear entrance to the twins' hideout.

Inside, washed in the ginger-ale radiance from the octagonal skylight, he found bare-torsoed Pell and Mell concocting upon the door-and-sawhorse table what looked to be a mountainous island of bright green clay. Surrounding the island was an ocean made of rumpled blue cloth.

"Hi," said Carl from the doorway, believing that the moments to come might be crucial for his summer future.

Crouched on either side of the table like overgrown aquaboys rising from the ocean depths to check out the island, neither twin said a word, although the one on the left reached out to the island with his mullet knife and carved the mouth of a cave partway up the principal peak. Carl watched the care with which he worked, then tried again to break the spell, "So, tell me, are you two as weird as you seem?"

In unison they turned to him with expressions of delight, and the cave maker said, in a surprisingly reedy way, "You better believe it, Jack. Does a marsh pig glow in the dark?"

"Yeah, Jack, does loggerhead babies have wings?" echoed the other in the same tones, but his eyes didn't flash so much with the excitement of having an older kid at their mercy.

Carl folded his arms across his chest, rocked back on his heels, and feigned the expression of a sage dorm-proctor not quite sure which side to choose in the authority wars. "Must be interesting to be twins," he said, cocking his chin at their project, which resembled Bali more than, say, one of the Bermudas.

"We're a whole gang," said Cavemaker, taking up a corner of the sea-cloth and flipping it so that half of it rippled over and covered the island like a gentle tidal wave.

"My name's Carl Hoopes."

"Where'd ya get your earring, Jack?"

"In the Combat Zone in Boston."

Unaccountably, they hooted like young owls. "Poppa says trees got souls. You believe that?"

Was this a test? "Here they do," Carl said. The twins did not look at each other, but across their face passed identical looks of contentment that approached bliss.

"Just checking," said Cavemaker, now identified as the leader of the gang. "You go to school."

"Don't you?"

"Never ever," said Follower. "Poppa, he says he's our Harvard and our Yell."

"And Mom's in charge of ABC's, if she can ever remember. Mostly she tootles, or pens out stories for her duck-book. We're all of us here stories."

Carl unfolded his arms and stepped toward them. "Listen," he said, "what would you think of my staying here for a while when my dad and his friend go back to the mainland?" He stopped at the edge of the table. The leader was smiling and rubbing the taut muscles of his belly.

"Mainland?" he said, spitting into and ringing an unseen spittoon.

His brother chimed in, "Poppa says mainland is—"

"—a circus gone nuts," the other finished. "So why would you even think of goin' there now you're here?" He narrowed his eyes slyly. " 'Course if you stayed, you could tell us some about the Combat Zone, Mount St. Helens, stuff like that. And you can come with us in the dinghy . . . if you'll get your poppa to send back another paddle or two. What we can show you! We'll even throw in—"

"The dickbone of the biggest loggerhead on this coast," Follower promised with intense sweetness. "You can keep it under your futon, Jack."

Who's in charge here? Carl wondered. But damn all if it mattered! These guys were about as far from New England, or Long Island, or north Alabama (Screw Pizza—Eat Fish!) as you could get without falling off the edge of the earth, and he would have their parents to boot.

"Come on," said the leader, who would soon become simply Pell, "help us with this baby island." Carl went for the black Swiss army knife he'd removed from his father's bag. He joined the gang. Simple as that.

Marsh oysters unhinged on hot sheet metal had not up to now been known to Devereux, but as the day wore on toward twilight, the sun settling itself above the peak of the A-frame, then vanishing behind the loblolly pines to the west of the brackish creek, he learned a lesson of succulence he had forgotten since the blue crabs of Jack Vilna's cruel Cape Hatteras. A dollop of Barbados pepper sauce (the color of squash) should first be applied to the oyster's warm shell-broth, the creature itself having been cut loose from its mother-of-pearl with a paring knife provided by the hostess; then lift the stunned glob of ugliness to the lips, the shell held suspended between thumb and forefinger; tilt the shell, tilt your own head, and the thing will slide home for the teeth-snap—a small, peppery notion of perfection. Follow with mullet fingers fried in butter in a skillet laid to the sheet metal, and the rest is listening.

"Marn and I," said Pierre, "long ago found ourselves in a hotel in the tropics, in a country where we didn't speak the language as well as we thought." His face glowed red in the waning light. "Around midnight, both of us woke to the sounds of a horrific fight in the next room. A man's voice—violent and growling. A woman's—hysterical, begging, shrill. A SLAP! A moan. The woman cries out. SLAP!"

Tessa, in shadow, recoiled from his sound effects.

"The other side of the wall above our heads is slammed so hard with a fist that plaster dust flies into the darkness and almost blinds us. Now, from the man a long string of guttural obscenities. Her reply is the word, we think, for blood. SLAP-SLAP. Punch and Judy, for real. A lamp smashes to the tiles. Silence. Is there weeping? 'I'm going,' I say to Marn. 'He'll kill you,' she says." Pierre's hands were now waving in the air, and the next blow he imitated by striking a palm against his own cheek. BAP! "I'm up on my legs now, saying, 'Well, shit, he's killing *her,* Marn old girl, can't have that.' The poor woman next door whimpers, which makes the thug hiss and wallop the wall again. I slip into my trousers before Marn can remind me again it would be better for the desk clerk (or the police) to make this nocturnal visit. I'm in the hallway—SLAP! SLAP! SLAP!— and my knock is louder even than the slaps . . . most untropical." His pause was masterful, if studied—the tiny Vesuvio about to confront an all-too-real brute. Tessa's lips were parted, her face pale. Devereux believed the punch line would involve some cosmic dropkick that would render the brute into smoke.

"The man who answers the door is as handsome and as cool as Rudolph Valentino, though his face and neck are covered with angry red welts. He raises one thick eyebrow at me, his robed body blocks any view into the room, and I can hear nothing but my own panting. I say, as best I can, 'What is happening? . . . the noises?' He frowns, crosses his arms, lifts one olive forefinger to his nose, takes a deep breath, widens his eyes, and says, 'Ohhh . . . Aah!' then slaps himself along the side of his head, and his slicked hair bursts into tufts. I nod solemnly, cocked for action. Again, the olive forefinger rises between us and circles in the night air, circles as if he's telling me I'm balmy, maggot-brained . . . but the circling forefinger is accompanied by the distinct sound of bzzzzzz coming from between his pearly teeth." Pierre stopped.

"Mosquitoes!" he cried.

Relieved laughter from Tessa, with perhaps a dubious edge to it. She looked at Devereux, her eyes deepening their blueness, and he smiled by way of saying, "A harmless little parable about walls and the imagination, eh? We are among strangers, but their hearts seem as good as their food, and nightfall is coming . . . together we'll know this island night."

If she received this message, she showed it only in the way she turned to Marni and said, "Could you show me the bathroom, please?" Marni led her into the dome after a cheerful word to the ducks, who remained by the stoop disappointed and bobbing.

"I wonder where Carl has got to," Devereux said to Pierre. "We should think of going before the sun sets."

Pierre busied himself with cleaning up the debris of their meal. "He's with the twins," he said, his hands releasing a mess of empty oyster shells into the basket. "They could be among the penis bones in the yurt, they could be at acrobatics in the A-frame, they could be making bologna sandwiches in the dome, they could be out spotting little blue herons or a white ibis." Everything this man said seemed as plainly true as surf or the chatter of palmetto fronds, even if a lot of it must be blarney and hocus-pocus. "Your son loves you," he said, his hands now occupied with the pepper sauce, the skillet, some paper plates, "and you might let him bump into more of the world's mosquitoes."

Devereux made a *huh* sound at the back of his throat. "He's had his share of misapprehensions, if that's what you mean. I'd say he's seen and heard a shitload."

Pierre shook the pepper sauce bottle until its contents swirled into a primeval yellow soup with flecks of wicked red and black. "I believe it," he said, "but there's more. A chap's got to keep moving out to sea, even if one parent or another is most often on the shore crying, 'Come back, you dolt.' "

"What are you saying, Mr. Vesuvio?"

"I've asked him to stay here, add a new circle to his life, teach the urchins his own circles, study the island, study us." He smiled. "Stay away from the pizza circus a bit longer. I might even arrange some wages for him. I understand you're no rich man."

"Aye!" Devereux affirmed, suddenly weary from sun, vast perspectives, love, and three-fingers of truth. "What does Carl say about this?" he asked.

"Jeepers," said Pierre, turning for the dome, "I don't know. I swerved the jeep to avoid a deer, Carl bashed his ear, and he never did tell me. Why don't you walk around to the creek and see if you can spot the ibis. I'll send Carl out to you directly." He waved the sauce and was gone.

Followed by the complaining ducks, Devereux did as he had been told. The creek marked the edge of a saltwater marsh, its low, still cord-grass just visible beyond a line of trees on the other side of the gray-green water. He saw no bird life except for the babbling domesticity of Madge and Milly, who stood beside him as if to wish bon voyage.

Here, facing west to the mainland and the setting sun, Devereux underwent a memory long-stored in the root cellar of his mind, a cellar that may well have been invaded by the mosquitoes story, although he would never be certain about such cause and effect in a person's biography. Never had been. In any case, instead of the white ibis, he saw—suspended in the pure night gloom of a guest suite in his own parents' house—an ancient bird's-eye-maple bed, its pillows and mussed bedding illuminated by the white ray of a high intensity lamp. Reclined on the bed, one in blue, the other in pink, were Devereux and his first wife, Tracy, both of them drunk on confession—trading confessions of a decade of adultery, trading these confessions with all the fascinated horror of war exploits—the one in blue also drunk on tequila, and almost gleeful in his desire for the whole truth and nothing but the truth, given and taken. Unknown to them, their voices rose above the invisible air-conditioner hum and carried through the doorway and wall to the next room, where Carl—age twelve—heard every damn word of the litany as if it were spoken by actors trained to reach the back of the theater of their crimes.

Another parental bedroom, this one belonging to his own absent parents, this one sunlit, full of art and electronic gadgetry: a man and a boy sitting close together at the foot of the huge, quilted bed. They were both staring out the windows at a gray-green fig tree. Carl said, "Pop, all I want to know is does everyone do this? What you and Mom were saying." The boy was big-for-his-age, galumphish, his bare feet as thick as steam irons. Oh yes, hung over Devereux noticed such things. "No," he said, and his son thanked him. It was with his mother that he had gone tearfully, wretchedly limp.

One of the ducks skimmed its tangerine bill in the creekside mud, while the other looked up at Devereux with an imperious eye, which struck Carl as funny as he avoided the chartreuse palmetto fans on his way to the creek. The duck seemed to have his dad's number. Perhaps Marni had trained her to cast a cold eye on all men.

"Dee-Vo!" Carl called out to his father's slumped back. "Guess what?"

Devereux turned, his sunglasses were gone, and his face looked almost beardless, beautifully naked against the sun's last flinging of burnt orange light. Yet the old man's eyes were alive with tears. Whoa now. But before Carl could change his tune, he was seized in the rough vise of Devereux's embrace—butter and fish and peppers and Tessa's darn hand lotion—and they almost toppled onto the stern duck before Carl got them balanced, returned the embrace, then stood away to hear his father say, "What? You've discovered that life is incomprehensible?" Smiling, he wiped a forefinger across the white patch under each eye. "Amend that. Life's a renovated sneaker. New innersoles, a little tape. Whatever elixirs you can put in your bucket for the soaking."

"I'll take your word," said Carl, wiggling his toes in the

shell grit picked up so readily by his gappy sneakers. "What's the matter?"

"Not a damn thing," he said, then hissed at the duck nipping his cuff. He blinked several times. "I'm sorry about the past, believe it. I am so fucking sorry."

Taking Devereux's hand in his own, knowing this had something to do with old-time American fuckery, knowing quite a bit more in fact, Carl said, "Don't sweat it, man. Fix your sneaks and get on with it." He took a breath, squeezed the hand in his own. "Why don't you marry Tessa?"

Devereux laughed aloud, a great bellow, there at the edge of the marshlands. "I'm going to, you wise little bugger, I'm going to as soon as I can . . . if I can get her off this island."

Carl let loose of his father and smacked his fist against his palm, startling the ducks into a patch of fern. "All right!" he shouted. "When?"

"It depends on your plans."

Here we go, Carl thought. "I'd like to stay here for a couple of months. I love this island, and I like these bonkers people. Pierre says—"

"Do it," Devereux said.

"What?"

"Do it. Bonkers-smonkers. You don't see Natalie around here, do you?"

Ouch.

"Shit, Dev, does a pileated woodpecker sing in the sauna?"

Ignoring this, Devereux barged ahead, reimagining their lives. "Tessa and I, we'll get married Labor Day, before you go back up to school." He looked at the last fiery arc of sun visible through the tree line. "Stay here," he said, "learn the differences between an ibis, an alligator, and a feral horse. Tutor those twins. Read them the story of Pip. And listen to Pierre's stories. It seems to be his business, his only tangible business."

"He's retired from the circus," said Carl.

"And I'm Captain Nemo." Devereux was now in shadow.

"One small matter," Carl said, and immediately sensed

Devereux's frown. "It's not money, I have plenty, I hate money. It's my stuff, my duffel bag in your car."

The shadow shrugged. "Tomorrow, after the ferry docks in St. Marys, we'll give it to Bevan Smith. He can send it back out here on the late-morning ferry, and you can find a way to pick it up. Anything else?"

Carl did not have to think. "I love you," he said to his father's indistinct face, offering up the declaration *first*, for the first time in his life. "Thanks for the trip," he said, "the two trips . . . shoot, all the trips."

With another great hug, Devereux confirmed the emotions, and the two of them turned back to the glowing windows of Vesuvio Center, the ducks gabbling like earnest fowl in their wake. That night, Carl Hoopes would sleep on the warrior's armor padding of a futon surrounded by feathers, bones, flute music, the gang of Pell and Mell, and their completed island.

Beach Coda. A northeast wind had cleared the night sky of the daytime city of clouds, and even the more modest stars were visibly engaged in their business of the best presentation of old light to anyone who cared to look to the heavens. A gibbous moon hung above the westward horizon, its interest in tides not so obvious to the naked eye. Yet the phosphorescent surf was rolling ever higher on Cumberland's Nightingale Beach a half-mile south of Sea Camp. The couple walking through the narrowing space between surf and dune had made their meandering way this far without needing to define the qualities of the beach that had drawn them here in the first place. Some might insist on the sighting of a mother loggerhead, caught by a flashlight in full, barnacled regalia; many others could favor an encounter with a perfect starfish, its arms aglitter from its sand bed in the wet aftermath of the surf's subsidence; others are only excited by the conjuring of a great and stunning storm; and a few, like these two, craved only a walk through the vagaries of moon- and starlight, content with surf sound, empty space, and the absence of accident, pain, and human signs.

This may explain why, when headlights showed up from the south and came on toward them over the sand like round reflectors of civilization, both Tessa and Devereux headed into the dunes—without consulting each other—to conceal themselves from the rude lights. But no. Perhaps the lights caught the dull gleam of a red boot, or simply the flickering of human legs in haste, because the vehicle sped up as best it could in the sand, and before they could pass through the first clumpings of sea oats, they were pinned by the beam of a powerful flashlight, an emergency brake was pulled, and an amiable but stern voice said, "That's pretty naughty, Ms. Dixon."

Bevan Smith.

While his jeep engine idled fitfully, he moved the light beam away from them and played it over the crest of the dune. "These oats," he said, "and the viny things, make dune buildup possible. They're sand trappers, you know, and you folks are fouling up the system by tramping around. So come on down."

They did so, with care, and stood abashed by the jeep. The dashboard lights of the open vehicle made the ranger seem larger, as if he were driving a toy.

"I know Ms. Dixon holds this island sacred," he said, "and I thought I told you, Mr. Hops, the few rules we have."

"Hoopes," said Devereux. "We made a mistake."

"Your first mistake was to miss the last ferry. You're not registered to camp."

"He'll be in my tepee," Tessa said. "You can't object to that."

"I object to not knowing where individuals are. Your son, for example."

"He's staying with Pierre and Marni Vesuvio," Devereux said. "For the summer. You'll always know where he is."

Smith lifted the bill of his cap and seemed to relax. "Vesuvios, you say. That's quite good luck for your kid. I think old Pierre has been reincarnated seven times on Cumberland alone." He chuckled. "You have to watch him, though. He'll marry a tree and sit in it for a week. I hope your boy is prepared."

"You bet he is," said Tessa. "Unlike his dad."

"Well," said Bevan Smith, "I've got my rounds. Care for a ride to Sea Camp?"

They would.

Meanwhile, the photographer, Carter Donner, was at work in the lamplit privacy of his scarlet igloo—an object that glowed from without like an overgrown blister on the floor of the live oak forest. From his ditty bag, Donner removed a fifty-millimeter lens that he now screwed into his camera's body as replacement for the telephoto. He added a dedicated flash attachment with bounce and wide-diffuser, then caused it to snick once, brilliantly. He turned his pressure lamp down until the mantle was only a faint nubbin of light. Donner felt on the cusp of triumph: he would within minutes possess the fifth and final panel of a sequence he had already entitled "Cumberland Ardor," for reasons deeply embedded in the lies of his back-brain. But art must be served. Would be. The bounced, diffused light would for one-five-hundredth of a second illuminate the tepee's empty, rumpled floor-circle of pleasure, would reveal the cooling heat-shapes of entangled bodies. "Scumbag," huh? He duck-walked through the round portal of his igloo, the camera a solid instrument of revelation against his breastbone, and in the blackness he approached the tepee.

His would be a simple arrest.

Along the path from the beach, following the insistent beam of a government-issue flashlight as long as a nightstick, came Bevan Smith followed by Tessa and Devereux. The ranger, in recognition of the realities of nocturnal life within the boundaries of a National Seashore, carried on his right hip a holstered revolver, an atomizer of military CS gas, a pair of handcuffs, and a short-range walkie-talkie—tools of the trade, which Devereux found incompatible with both the man and with the promised peace and tranquillity of the island, whose night whispered with a wind song that carried to them the sweet susurrus of the distant surf and the more immediate creaking of the live oak branches reaching out above them. He held Tessa's hand, its fingers against his own as supple as willow twigs.

"Where are these famous gnats?" he asked Bevan Smith's wide back. Tessa squeezed Devereux's hand, perhaps in protest of the frivolous question. Smith cleared his throat, but before he could speak his answer, the tepee—in its site fifty feet down the path—flared an orange brighter for an instant than the sun. The afterimages lingered on Devereux's retinas like twin, receding images of molten cones of lava. Simultaneously, Tessa jerked down on his arm, gasped, and reached out for the stuff of the ranger's uniform shirt, as if he might not have seen her shelter become pure energy, as if he were not already striding for the tepee, his flashlight beam exposing the kneeling haunches and headless torso of the man half-thrust into the unzipped fly of the tepee.

Rigid, her arm still extended, Tessa said, "I will not go down again, I will not go down."

Halfway to the tepee, Smith called out in the voice of certain authority, "Park Service. Please don't move."

Devereux released his hand from Tessa's grip, embraced her shoulders, forced down the arm, and said, "It's all right, it's nothing, pretend he's a raccoon, a curious fiddler crab," and he misquoted Bevan Smith, "You can't know the island until you know its night."

Smith, now bent over his quarry, seized him by the belt, lifted, and he came unstuck from the tepee, bent over and limp, his camera dangling from his neck into the dirt like a sign proclaiming his misery—all of this in the flickery, comic illumination of the flashlight in Smith's right hand.

"It's the jerkoff with the camera," Devereux said, "from the beach."

"Camera!" cried Tessa, her fear replaced in her taut body by anger. "You knew? You knew about him?"

From the tepee carried the voice of Smith, "Lie prone, spread your legs, put your hands behind your back. Now." Cooperation came swiftly, although Smith had to kick the man's legs apart before he could switch the flashlight from one hand to the other, free the cuffs from his gun belt, lean over, and one-handedly truss up the wrists of his unprotesting captive, whose camera must surely be causing him difficulty breathing—the camera's lens, Devereux hoped, ground into the sand-and-shell grit in a way that would hopelessly scratch and pit its peeping convexity. What could he ever have wanted with the stolen image of an empty tepee?

Tessa elbowed Devereux out of the embrace as if he were the guilty party. In the darkness he longed for a glimpse of her telltale eyes, and thought—with superb irrelevance—Tomorrow I'll follow this so-called wild woman all the way across the pineyness of Georgia and Alabama. May her God protect us from inland woe.

"Say something, you close-mouthed, Yankee goof," she said without a trace of humor. "A simple answer. Now's your chance."

Bewildered, Devereux watched as the campsite tableau in front of them evolved from a man-down-and-splayed to man-up-and-in-custody, his elbow gripped by Smith's large hand. The flashlight beam shone upward, eerily exposing the thief's bearded chin, its bushiness the color of rust. His face was an underlit, deep-socketed mask of satisfaction. Not smug, just jolly well content, and pliantly willing to be guided along the patch that would take him past his supposed subjects and to the government jeep parked on the dreamy beach.

In the few seconds he had left before the pass-by, Devereux discovered what to say. "You're right, Tessa, I'm not studying silence anymore. On the beach this afternoon, while you were passed out in the dinghy, I bopped this guy for not minding his own business."

"Okay, thank you," she drawled. "See how easy? It's

what I don't know I fear, even if it's something rinky-dink. So much glop in this gloryland."

"Even on Cumberland."

Now came Bevan Smith, keeper of the island, his leather equipment sounding protective and efficient in the night forest. His light beam danced at their feet, then canted upward, briefly exposing the faces of Devereux and Tessa to the eyes of the unrepentant prisoner.

"I have no idea," Smith said, "what this oddball had in mind, Ms. Dixon, but unless this is your camera around his neck, he didn't take anything."

"Maybe it is," said Tessa. "Let me see it."

The prisoner drew back in the face of what he, Devereux, and Tessa knew to be untrue. "The sucker's mine, ma'am," he said in a low, uptown voice.

Looming Bevan Smith took him by the arm like you would a wayward child. "Button your lip, sir," Smith said. "I haven't dealt with your rights." He let go the man's arm, lifted the camera off his body by its strap, and handed it to Tessa. She scrutinized it in the direct beam of the flashlight as if she might be in the market for a single lens reflex camera with flash attachment made in Japan. Blemishless. And then, rather expertly, she slid the latch that popped the back open like a trapdoor. Blessed by the prisoner's sigh, she hooked a thin forefinger under the exposed strip of black film running from yellow spool to take-up spool and pulled until several feet of film looped outward from the body.

"Whoops," she said, handing the hurt property back to Smith. "Not mine." Her smile was a wonder of polite victory.

Bevan Smith rehung the camera on his prisoner, whose aplomb could not hold up under the indignity of such a queered mechanism. He slumped.

And so, after bidding the ranger a good night, promising to see him tomorrow at the midmorning ferry, when no doubt the photographer would be led aboard in irons, Devereux and Tessa repaired to the tepee where, in the bashful

glow of her shaded flashlight, they reaffirmed their owner-
ship of the space by means of the sober language of love. The
island—its complexity of forest, marsh, dune, and sea-struck
beach—wished them well. No gnat, no snake, no tick set
upon them. In Vesuvio Center, peaceful upon his futon, Carl
Hoopes dreamed of a mother loggerhead in the moonlight.
No one on the Atlantic Coast that night, from Calais to Key
West, knew what would happen tomorrow.